SAGITTARIUS

The Urban Oracle Series

Book One

SIERRA ZOUNES

Also by Sierra Zounes

Teacher Haikus for the Educator's Nonexistent Free Time

SAGITTARIUS

To my husband,
who doesn't believe in astrology,
but believes in me.

November 27th, 11:59pm

No one was around when the ocean turned black.

Moments prior, the glossy surface oscillated with repeating waves of witching-hour blue and deep green, pinpricks of light along the surface as stars decorated the sky above on a moonless night. The wind whispered through the dark, greeting the crashing waves like old friends.

But then all movement suddenly ceased. All sounds cut off with a violent silence: a frozen painting of nature gone still.

And the Pit appeared, a gaping maw swallowing the last bits of starlight. Water that had always flowed in horizontal waves now cascaded into an impossibly steep, circular waterfall, the salted sea water crashing down into a bottomless well that continued deep, deep into the earth. Fish and other nearby creatures fought desperately against this new current, dragging them backward and down into an unfamiliar abyss. The larger, stronger animals were successful in their escape. Others, less so.

Above the din of the rushing water, a collective roar sounded from the Pit, echoing from beneath the surface of the sea.

Dark, undulating masses appeared, each as unusual and distinct as the last. One, two, three shot from the tear in the ocean, careening into the sky, slick and black as the sea below them as they tore away into the night. The next beasts to appear were more cautious. Ancient talons and scaled hands gripped the edges of the well as they pulled themselves up and over, slipping back under the water on the other side and moving away, out of sight.

The last few merely lifted the tops of their heads outside the Pit, glowing eyes evaluating this new world. Some found it lacking, choosing not to explore it and preferring to sink back down into their home. The rest followed their brethren, escaping, skimming the surface of the water like a stone tossed across a pond.

The disturbance ended more slowly than it had begun, the hole *diminishing until it closed over entirely. Much like eyes adjusting to darkness, the ocean began to remember who it was. The unnatural blackness eventually regained its cobalt hue, the waves recommencing their practiced dance.*

But the usual animals of the sea did not return for many days. They were aware of a new predator now lurking here, hungry and desirous and wanting.

In search of prey.

chapter ONE

"I don't know what else to tell you, but your grandfather wants to be left alone," Claire said resolutely before resting back in the chair. Her elbow was braced against the top of the torn velvet backing while her fingers drummed the top of the hexagonal table. The woman across from her leaned forward, supporting herself on her forearms. Claire did her best to meet the woman's glower with candid indifference beneath her freckles.

"My grandfather loved me, so excuse me if I don't believe you," the woman spat petulantly.

Stifling a sigh, Claire looked to her right, where a translucent elderly man hovered by the window, the late afternoon sunlight limning his semi-transparent form. If she hadn't been able to see the wooden window ledge through his lower abdomen, she may have been able to convince herself he was just another client.

In a way, he was.

They made eye contact, and Claire shrugged as if to

say, *Hey, I tried.*

"What's he saying now?"

The woman extended a hand across the table over the glass orb, snapping her fingers inches from Claire's face. The skin that hung from her triceps wobbled like layers of unsteady gelatin, and Claire wondered if she could charge the woman extra if her sagging batwings knocked over the useless orb perched in the center of her table.

Claire closed her eyes and counted to three in several languages before slowly turning her head back to the client. It was a tactic she discovered in her late teens: whenever the weight of the living—or dead—threatened to drag her down from the high road, she counted in her head in a language of her choosing. It helped her keep her composure in moments when she felt her stress levels rising; it was a good thing she knew so many languages.

It was either this mental counting game or a couple shots of Jim Beam, if readily available.

So far today, she'd counted in the minimal Russian she learned from her mother, Italian from her late father, and Spanish, which she inevitably picked up living a mere twenty miles north of the Mexican border.

…Ocho, nueve, diez. Let's fucking go.

She opened her eyes. The woman was pockmarked and too tan. Frown lines framed her arrogant expression, the cracks beside her eyes a mimicry of the same. She didn't need to be a Seer to know that the woman likely had some unfortunate health news coming in her near future. Claire half expected to see the heads of several shining plum-colored worms to wriggle their heads between the gaps of her

yellowing teeth.

"Tell Lani that she's always been a pain in my ass, and I should have known it'd be the same whether I was alive or dead," the spirit grumbled.

He strode over to his granddaughter, his steps soundless, and glared down at her hunched, frustrated form. Claire repressed a small shiver—the echoey vibrato of the dead was like a sudden surge of tinnitus—but she smoothed the marble of her face. *You're a professional. Act like it.* She forced her voice to be level.

"He says you're the same as you've always been, Ms. Olsen."

The woman sucked in her checkered cheeks. "What's that supposed to mean?"

"It means that our time is up," Claire said. "If your name wasn't in the will when he died, then there is not much else I can do for you."

Claire shoved her chair back and stood up, cracking her knuckles and blowing out the candles that littered the deep purple tablecloth. She hated the color; it reminded her of the artificial cough syrup she'd had to force down as a child. Granted, it was better than the mucous-green tincture of herbs her mother would concoct in their trailer. "Nature should be our pharmacy," her mother would argue when Claire's father brought the plastic medicine bottles home from the grocery store. He would nod his assent to placate her even as he spooned out a capful of saccharine liquid for Claire to drink.

And the putrid purple medicine worked, just like the garish purple of the cloth and the beads and the crystal ball worked to uphold the mystical expectations of her clientele. Satisfied clients meant another dent in the rent, albeit small, and that's what mattered to her.

Still, some people were displeased no matter what.

Ms. Olsen remained seated, her fleshy lower half spilling over the edges of her chair. Her paint-chipped nails dug into her arms, her jaw set.

"You're a scam artist, is what you are. I'm thinking you weren't speaking to Granddad at all this whole time, were you?"

The woman pried one of her hands off her arm, leaving small crescent indents in her doughy skin, and gestured around the room. "Is all this some sort of show to you? Taking advantage of the grieving and desperate?" Claire's stomach tightened, heat spreading up her chest and turning her face the same hue as her slightly frizzled red hair.

Yes, the way she chose to decorate her office was partly for show. The wooden floors were dark, the accents of the walls ornate to invoke feelings of the mystique and unknown. Along the walls, zodiac charts painted her in the role of an astrological explorer, sifting through the stars for answers from beyond the veil. Books she'd never read were stacked with purposeful abandon, allowing visitors to gape in awe at the ancient texts holding forgotten knowledge of the occult. In truth, she'd snatched them for free at garage sales in and around the city.

Despite her décor, she was no scam artist, and she resented the woman's accusation.

Un, deux, trois, Claire counted, tapping her fingers on her jeans, trying to hold back the tidal wave of her mounting anger. Claire stalked forward, each step punctuating the start of each jab against the sullen woman. "*You* chose to enter my establishment. *You* chose to pay my fee. *You* sat there while I contacted your grandfather. *I* did my job; if you feel that you were scammed, you're every bit of an idiot as your grandfather says you are."

He'd called her an ass, but that was neither here nor there. Both could be correct at the same time.

The woman shrank back into her chair, and satisfied with her reaction, Claire walked over to a pile of newspapers stacked precariously by the bookshelves, grabbing the topmost one. She spun on her heel, towering over the other woman, and threw one in her lap.

"There; you can read your fortune on page three. Hope you got your money's worth; tell your friends," she sneered. *So much for keeping my cool.*

Claire held the door open as the woman left, muttering about the waste of time and money. She wasn't worried about a poor review; most people's anger fizzled out by the time they returned home, having found something new to complain about by then.

She stayed in the doorway for a moment, taking in the San Diego autumn sunshine. Commuter cars and absurd pedicabs filtered down the one-way street as pedestrians jaywalked between traffic. A homeless man pushed a cart filled with stained blankets and torn cardboard signage. "MAY GOD BLESS YOU" was scrawled across it in barely legible writing. As he passed, a whiff of soiled clothing briefly permeated her storefront, blown away the next moment by truck exhaust.

Watching a couple of teens weave precariously through traffic on e-bikes as expensive as the phones they were simultaneously checking, Claire was a little surprised that she didn't have more ghostly clientele from people smashed to death by disobeying basic traffic laws. She supposed when everyone was constantly living in chaos, it was just a normal, deadbeat Tuesday.

Clicking the switch on the neon "CLOSED" sign, she locked the front door and headed to the back of her office. The old man, "Granddad," still stood by the table, taking in his surroundings. With a wrinkled hand, he tried to smooth the cloth on her table, only to have his palm drop through the surface. He lifted his hand close to his face, his pointed nose nearly touching his skin. Pursing his lips into a thin line, the man looked as though his hand had somehow betrayed him, and he was deciding how best to chastise it.

Now that they were alone, Claire felt a sliver of unease crawl under her skin. The cold emanating from the dead was always stronger when she was on her own, and now that the heat of her annoyance was dissipating, her office had turned into an icy northern moor. She momentarily imagined a heavy mist caressing her jeans, coils of fog trying to latch onto her skin and soak her to the bone.

Eins, zwei, drei . . .

Claire pretended not to see the man, turning to head up to her loft above the store.

He, however, turned his attention to her. "Hey lady, what am I supposed to do now?"

He trailed after Claire, a Boston accent tinging his line of inquiry. He straightened his back, his shoulders somehow broadening, and Claire wondered what he'd done for work in his life. Flashes of the man making house calls—collections for some Northeastern mafia syndicate—floated in her mind's eye. Maybe that's why his granddaughter was so determined to be a part of his final wishes; anything to protect her from getting her knees capped by his constituents.

If that was the case, she couldn't blame the woman; Claire would have wanted the same protection, some sort of safety net. Instead, she'd had a mother selling crystals out of a trailer in Arizona and a father rotting away somewhere in the Pacific. She wasn't exactly a trust fund baby.

Claire was her own safety net, tattered though her net may be. Claire ignored the elderly man's question, picking up a paper can of salt from a nearby shelf and reapplying the line at the bottom of the stairs. She stepped over the line before turning back to the apparition.

Alive, he might have been imposing, his face enlivened by the charisma and power he'd used to get ahead in the workplace—*or for his Godfather*, Claire thought humorlessly. In death, however, she found that even those eyes that had shone the brightest were dulled in passing.

She pressed her lips tightly together as she took him in, doing her best to avoid staring at the trail of blood that dried at the edge of his wrinkle-lined mouth. She wondered how he died. Organ failure? Brain aneurysm? Enemy poison? She knew better than to ask.

"I release you from your visitation. Go home." She waved a hand—bitten fingernails and cuticles picked dry—as she turned to go back up the stairs, but the man continued speaking.

"I don't know where I am! One minute, I'm with my wife at Somerville Hospice. The next, I'm here listening to my granddaughter squabble about money."

Ah, lord. Claire rubbed her eyes, the headache she'd been repressing all day finally fighting its way to the surface. She thought about the half-bottle of whiskey left out on the counter upstairs, and the pressure at the front of her head tightened as though trying to pull her toward it.

Claire fought against the tension and responded, reciting the script she'd inadvertently created over the years. "Look, I'm sorry. When I initiate a calling, it pulls you to this room but cuts ties with where you were. We're in California. The Gaslamp of San Diego, if you want to be specific."

The man's eyes widened, and his eyes flickered to the storefront window. Outside, a constant stream of distracted pedestrians littered the sidewalk. The one-way streets that confused both tourists and locals were filled with red brake lights and the occasional car horn that did nothing to disperse the traffic of the city. With the windows and doors shut, the smells of Little Italy with undertones of cheap beer from nearby clubs were muted but ever-present, alongside the cacophony of the Civic theater crowd and House of Blues enthusiasts.

To Claire, the city was the inconsequential backdrop to her daily life.

To the specter in the room, the Gaslamp was a sign he was far, far from home.

The man's accent thickened as his panic grew. "How the hell am I supposed to get back to Massachusetts?"

She gave a shrug of her shoulders that read more

apathetic than truly apologetic; she pushed down her guilt with practiced precision.

"I just make calls; I don't do return service. Sorry." *Can't*, she corrected herself irritably.

She turned to retreat up the stairs, and as she did so, the man lunged forward, reaching out to grab her—to do what, she didn't know, and didn't care to find out. Whatever he'd learned in his hypothetical mafia training, she supposed. But his fingertips stopped short mid-air, his hand recoiling as though burned. He hissed, backing away from the line of salt that blocked his way. He clutched his hand to his chest, bits of his fingers now but a mist of deconstructed spiritual mass, temporarily dispersed but already re-forming in a swirling fog around his palm.

Claire had discovered salt's protective qualities against spirits from a client of her mother's shortly after the dead began to appear. The woman, draped in heavy floral veils and turquoise jewelry, had mentioned offhand that salt made a ward against the dead. Claire doubted she was right, but she'd gotten so desperate for some kind of protection from constant spiritual interruptions, she'd tried everything. Sage did nothing, nor did water left out under a full moon, hastily muttered spells she felt silly reciting, or obsidian beads. When the salt worked, providing a true respite, a wall she could hide behind, however temporarily, Claire was overwhelmed with relief and gratitude for the woman she'd initially judged for a crackpot.

Claire's mother, Deb, would have disapproved of both her judgment and desire for protection against the dead. *"I've raised Claire to be accepting of all people, living or otherwise,"* Deb had said in her feigned mystical voice.

Claire didn't care; it wasn't as though her mother could understand what it was like. She didn't truly have the gift of Sight, as Claire had. She didn't know what it was to always be watched, groped at by ghosts longing to feel the pliable bodies of the living, deafened by the wails of confusion and depravity of the deceased—it was a constant, eternal curse that climbed into bed alongside her at night and shook her awake her each day. It was too much for an adult to bear, let alone a child. The salt at least gave her a safe space now and then

Claire did her best to ignore the man's yells and insults as she made her way to her apartment.

She locked the door behind her, the soundproofing she'd done years ago suffocating the man's cries. Releasing a sigh, she replenished the salt lines at the entryway, door, and window. It wasn't a perfect system; it kept the apparitions out of her little apartment but did nothing to stop them from sitting outside her window from time to time. They'd rap their knuckles on the glass, sometimes crying for help, sometimes demanding a response. Some merely floated, staring, as if years of death had sapped away the memory of speech. It was why she kept the curtains closed most of the time.

She missed the days of sitting in the Arizonian sun— those years before the ancestral gene took hold and the visions began—and could bask in the chirping and whistling and chittering of living nature. Nowadays, she rarely went outside.

She had begun to look like the ghosts she was avoiding.

Her stomach gave way to a nauseating groan and, headache growing, she opened the bathroom cabinet to pull out a small handful of aspirin. Filling a mug with tap water, she downed the pills, then paused to consider drinking the rest. Instead, she poured it out in the sink, opting for the bottle of cheap amber liquid on the scuffed counter and a slice of stale bread from an opened bag. *Girl dinner*, she thought to herself. She let out a raspy chuckle, then rubbed her temples to dull the pain.

Nursing both her headache and drink, Claire surveyed the room with mild bemusement. Piles of half-scrawled sketches and dulled pencils laid around the room. She leaned against the counter, her elbow wrinkling a sketch of a young woman attempting to wrangle and walk several dogs outside her apartment. Claire glanced down at the image and snorted at the look of panic she'd captured as the woman was yanked off her feet by the excited pit bulls and Australian shepherds, spilling her coffee across the sidewalk.

Wonder how much I'd get drawing caricatures at the pier, Claire thought halfheartedly, kicking away abandoned drawings on the ground as she walked to the couch. There was a time in her life when making money from her artwork could have been a legitimate—albeit untraditional—option.

Too bad she had to go and screw it up.

She tried not to think about it.

As she readied herself for a few hours of sitting on the couch in a self-inflicted stupor, Claire heard tapping on the window and a nasal voice called into her apartment.

"Oi! Doll face, you done yet?" it called.

Claire tried to roll her eyes, but the movement hurt

her head, the pain a knitting needle working its way through the gray matter of her brain like a failed lobotomy. Instead, she opted to lay down on the couch, the pile of dirty clothes and sheets of paper acting as a cushion against the broken springs beneath. She wrinkled her nose and made a mental note to do laundry . . . at some point. Claire closed her eyes, an arm slung across her head, while the fingertips of her other arm trailed along the oriental carpet.

"Go away, Henry, I'm busy," she called back a moment later.

"Busy doing what? Lazing about while I'm stuck out here with the rest of these jamokes? Let me in before I catch a cold."

"You're dead, Henry; you can't get sick."

"You can't know that for certain."

Claire groaned and rolled onto her stomach, her face pressed into a wrinkled shirt. It smelled like the leftover pasta she'd microwaved last week. With a pang, Claire realized that was the last time she'd actually made a real meal for a herself.

Claire grunted, "Go away; my work hours are over. Go bother someone else."

There was a pause before Henry replied. "There is no one else, doll."

Her heart squeezed for a moment, empathy she couldn't push away outpacing the painful fog in her head. He was wrong; she knew that. There were plenty of mediums he could speak to throughout the county. Despite many of them being swindlers reminiscent of her mother's old crystal shop in Sedona, there were still more than enough with whom Henry could converse. Even so, his words pulled a chord that was louder than the symphony of fatigue in her mind. He always knew how to get a reaction from her.

Annoying little turd.

Letting out a noise of frustrated assent, she stood up and pulled open the curtains, revealing a 17-year-old boy in a school uniform, one hand in his jacket pocket, while the other hung down by his side. He was short for his age, his face narrow, with eyes much older than the rest of him. He sneered as she opened the window, victorious, but beneath his arrogance, she felt his relief.

Surveying the alley behind him, Claire spotted a young woman drifting along nearby, her toes barely trailing on the ground. Keeping her eyes on the other apparition, she drew a finger through the line of salt, and Henry clambered through the window and she reapplied it behind him. Before anyone else could see what was happening, she drew the curtains shut again and headed back to the couch to pour another drink.

"You know, for someone who enjoys her giggle-juice, you sure aren't fun to be around," Henry said, perching himself on the counter. He swung his legs back and forth, his heels moving in and out of the cabinets below his feet.

"For someone who should be six feet under, you sure talk an awful lot," Claire retorted. He stuck his tongue out at her, and Claire quickly looked away. It was the only physical clue as to how he'd died. Henry's tongue was swollen and dark, mottled and decayed behind his teeth. She was certain if she looked into his open mouth, she would see his throat nearly closed. Perhaps all teenagers from the early twentieth century sounded naturally nasally and strange, but she guessed that his cause of death may have contributed to his tight and whistling voice, which she heard all too often.

"Alright, Henry, what are you doing here?"

She took a long draft, nearly emptying the glass, and pulled a dusty patchwork quilt over her shoulders as Henry's presence dropped the temperature in the room. Ever since they met her first week in the Gaslamp, Henry had been a continual presence. Perhaps it was his age or the way his pride kept him from begging for her help, but she had felt more at ease with him than any of the other deceased she'd encountered.

Or maybe he annoyed her to the point where she could forget he was dead. Either way.

He examined his nails as if bored, but she knew it was a front. Henry never did anything that would bore him; he valued his afterlife too much to let it waste away with useless daily drivel. This was personal.

Henry kept his eyes on his hands, picking at his thumbnail as he responded. "Figured you might want some company today."

"And pray tell me why I'd want you around."

"Because it's November 28th."

Claire's breath hitched. *Of course, this shit again.* She took a sip to cover her reaction.

"The guy ditched me the moment things got difficult," she said, "I'm not going to pay tribute to an asshole who abandoned his family. Sorry, not sorry." She looked down at the chipped mug cradled in her hands.

Henry crossed his arms. "I'm just saying, instead of spending the night in your own personal speakeasy, you might want to consider *doing* something for a change."

She drained and refilled the mug, nearly finishing the bottle. Claire made a mental note to restock. "Huh," was all she said. She examined the dark stains in her ceramic cup, her mind elsewhere.

On this date five years prior, the SDPD had located a male, around forty years of age, who had drowned in a boating accident. His body was too destroyed by watery decay and bites from wildlife to be completely identifiable, until the coastguard found his ID tucked away in one of the boat's compartments. Claire could still recall the phone call she received from one of the officers who found her father, though she did her best not to relive the moment.

She imagined her father's corpse, with strips of his skin hanging like decomposing flags of human jerky, a milky film coating his lifeless eyes, floating between uncaring waves. *Better than he deserves*, she thought viciously, but a small part of her recoiled at her thoughts. He was her father, after all, biologically, in any case. He'd left Claire and her mother the day she turned twelve, the day after the family "gift" appeared. She was never sure why he'd left. Her mother refused to talk about it, claiming it affected her aura and the crystals would absorb the bad juju, but Claire had a faint idea.

One psychic—albeit fake—in the family was one thing.

A haunted daughter was another.

As she'd grown, so had the bitterness that had calcified in her bones. She had denounced him, thinking of Julian as a stranger who happened to be around for a small fraction of her life. After years of sobbing quietly into her pillow each night wishing he'd return, she'd decided that being angry was easier to work with than the pain of abandonment. That, and a couple of shots a night was a good start.

"You still with me, doll face?"

Claire shook her head, returning to the present—her dingy, broke present.

"And what do you reckon I do?" she said, looking up at him. "Chuck some orchids into the ocean and cry in front of a bunch of tourists?"

Henry rolled his eyes. She couldn't think of anything more appropriate to mark the occasion than drinking in the dark. Her head pulsed painfully, and she drank the last dregs of amber from her mug before pouring more.

"Maybe you should honor his death in some way. He was your father, after all," he said gently.

"He stopped being my father the day he left," Claire spat, a knee-jerk response that caused droplets of whiskey to dribble out of her mouth. Henry didn't say anything, only watched her as she cozied further into the pile of laundry, crushing a handful of her sketches in the process. She meant what she'd said, for the most part.

Despite the betrayal of his departure, she still thought fondly of the days he'd read to her at night, making funny voices and acting out the scenes while she giggled sleepily. Eventually, she'd fall asleep, dreaming of his wild tales. She'd even enjoyed his ghost stories until she became one.

No, don't think about it.

Another sip.

More fog.

Henry shrugged and leapt off the counter, walking around the room with his hands in his pockets. "I'm not saying to spend a whole lotta dough or make it hotsy-totsy; I'm just saying maybe it would be nice to visit and say a few words."

"You know I actively recoil when you use words like 'hotsy-totsy.'"

Henry gave a crooked grin. "You can take a cat out of the twenties, but not the twenties out of the cat."

"I hate that, too," Claire grumbled.

He laughed, a carrying, wheezing noise, like a dying train whistle.

"Well, if you're certain you just want to sit alone and wallow, I'm going to blow. Or 'leave,' if that makes you feel any better."

"It does make me want to stab out my ears less, thanks."

Henry strode to the window and waited for Claire to let him out. She was reasonably sure he'd rather remain in her apartment than go back on the streets with the rest of the deceased, but she'd made it clear years prior that she refused to sleep with any ghosts present in her one-bedroom apartment. He'd respected her wishes, albeit begrudgingly.

She pulled back the curtains and sucked in a startled breath. The floating woman from across the alley had moved. Her nose was now nearly touching the glass. The woman's eyes were wide and pale, possibly blue in life, and bore into Claire's surprised gaze. The apparition's mouth opened and closed, gaping like a fish. One of her slender hands—young, smooth, and unwrinkled—clutched her lower abdomen, the other pressed to the window.

"Please," she croaked. Her voice scratched against Claire's eardrums like static on a radio. "Can I see my baby? Where is she?" Claire's eyes trailed down the woman's body, taking in the paper-thin hospital dressing and the trail of something dark and wet dripping down her leg.

Claire could feel the first stages of a panic attack begin to form, a nest of cicadas in her head vibrating in a building crescendo. Claire looked at the line of salt on the chipped windowsill, untouched and in place. Logic told her this would keep the woman out.

The cicadas sang, "*But what if . . . ?*"

"I'm sorry, but your daughter's not here. Please go. I can't help you," Claire whispered, her voice breaking on the word "help." She couldn't help her; she couldn't help any of the deceased who came calling and begging. They always came to her looking for answers she couldn't give.

Henry's whistling voice pierced through the loudening vibrations. "Oi, lady! Your kid isn't here. Make like a tree and scram, will you?"

The woman's eyes flickered to Henry, registering him for the first time. "Do you know where she is? The doctors took her away before I could see her. I need to see her." Her voice dripped with motherly love and distress, and the hand on her stomach clenched in a fist, pulling the dress up slightly, revealing more of her pale legs.

Henry wasn't having it. He turned to Claire, and she pushed herself past the chaos in her head to listen. "The broad isn't going to skedaddle willingly, so it's your turn to try."

Claire ran a hand through her hair, trying to clear her mind. The panicked buzzing dulled to a low murmur, but her headache threatened to return. "Yeah, I know," she sighed. "Give me a sec."

Claire grabbed the salt tin and poured a small handful into her palm. It reminded her of white sand beaches she'd only seen in pictures, an oasis of safety. She wondered if the deceased on an island were more at peace than those in the city. *It shouldn't matter; they're still dead*, Claire thought bitterly as she unlatched the window, careful not to disturb the line on the sill. As the window inched open, the mother shifted down, her body blurring with the motion. Her face reformed at the opening, her eyes peering into the apartment. She darted her desperate gaze left and right, looking for her lost child within.

"I'm sorry," Claire muttered, then tossed the salt grains into her face. The woman let out an unearthly wail of shock and pain, briefly raising the panicked buzzing of Claire's mental cicada symphony. Her face exploded in a burst of ethereal ectoplasmic mist, and her body twisted and turned, pushing away from the fire escape. The woman's body tumbled down through the metal steps, contorting wildly until she collapsed to the asphalt below, out of sight. There was a brief moment of silence as Claire tried to determine whether she was in the eye of a storm or if the turbulence had passed.

Henry determined that it was the latter. Straightening up, one hand smoothing his hair, he said, "You know, I'd be happy to stay around and keep you company, doll face. Might be good to have a man around to keep you safe."

Claire crossed her arms, allowing the pressure of her own embrace to calm her racing heart. "I don't need a *child* eleven years my junior to 'keep me safe,' especially when you did nothing but agitate the poor woman."

Henry smirked. "I was born before your great-grandparents, doll. Don't sass your elders."

Claire didn't respond, only made a line in the salt and gestured for Henry to leave. He gave her a final, jovial wave before going over the sill and down the alley. She slammed the window closed behind him.

Finally steadying her breathing, Claire reapplied the salt and locked the window tight. She felt the cold disperse once she shut the curtains, blocking the sunlight. Despite Henry's irritating slang and wheezing voice, she realized after he left that he was right; she didn't want to be alone. Without his presence to offer distraction, the reminder of her father's death floated precariously back to the forefront of her mind. Her stomach churned. The acid from the aspirin, the momentary shock, and the fog from the alcohol worked together to create a wave of sickness.

Claire grabbed the partially eaten bread, crunching into the stale surface. It tasted musty, like the bread itself only had a vague memory of what it was. As she ate, she pushed the ghostly woman's pleas from her mind. *At least she wanted to be with her daughter,* Claire acquiesced. She didn't care to admit it—out loud or privately—but she'd missed her father terribly. Deep down, when she had looked up his name upon moving to the West Coast, she had stupidly allowed herself the hope of perhaps reconciling and finding him as an adult, rekindling what they'd had as father and daughter.

But hope had only gotten her a nearly empty bottle of "giggle-juice" and a hollow apartment. She sat staring aimlessly at the thinly papered wall. Perhaps an hour went by, or maybe it was only several minutes, but as each second ticked onward, an idea formed in her mind: something small, just a little, insignificant tribute to her father. Maybe it would at least help her get rid of the guilt and sadness inside her chest.

Claire stood up unsteadily, snatching her bag from the table. She glanced inside to ensure the essentials were packed: phone, wallet, keys, salt. Picking up the bottle with the last bit of whiskey, she placed that in the bag, too. Another essential.

She pressed her ear against the door that led back down into the storefront, listening for the man from her last appointment. Briefly, she considered the woman at her window; *would she still be outside?* Immediately, she brushed away the thought; it took time for the spirits to reform after her salt barrages, and most of the time, they knew to stay further away, wary of another attack.

Satisfied by the silence, Claire lifted a pair of thick headphones from a hook on the wall and placed them over her ears, plugging in her phone and pressing play.

A loud '80s ballad blared out of the speakers, blocking out all other sound. She knew the vibe she gave off: hipster 28-year-old, too cool for wireless headphones or whatever the newest tech was nowadays. Long ago, Claire stopped caring about the opinions of others; she'd wear obnoxiously large and brightly colored furry earmuffs if it meant she wouldn't have to hear more wailing. Taking a deep breath, Claire turned the volume up even louder, steadied herself, and left for the pier.

chapter TWO

Claire knew walking alone through the city at the cusp of nightfall wasn't the safest choice. On top of that, wearing headphones blasting music made it sure that she'd be an easy target for a mugging. Or worse. Despite the danger, she couldn't handle the onslaught of spirit voices that she knew would eventually bombard her without it. If she could have gotten away with it, she would have journeyed both deaf and blind to avoid seeing all the ghosts, spirits, and apparitions that plagued the city streets. The headphones would have to do.

She set off, glancing back to ensure her storefront was completely locked. The "Madame Clarissa the Medium" sign hung in thin, gothic lettering above the door, lightly aglow from the "CLOSED" sign beneath it. She cringed at the name; adding "Madame" made her sound like a middle-aged, shawl-wearing woman with curling gray hair and large, owl spectacles rather than the broke millennial she was. Claire had added the word in a weak attempt to draw in clientele but could not live up to their expectations. Most clients were taken aback to walk into her shop and find someone who barely remembered the 90s and dressed as though it was still the early 2010s. Nevertheless, once they were there, they were usually too embarrassed or desperate to leave once they set foot across the threshold, so Claire had kept the name.

She crossed streets and edged along crowded sidewalks, carefully avoiding living and translucent passersby. She spied a man in a navy blue suit waiting to cross at a light, ignorant to the older gentleman with a crushed shoulder yelling in his ear about the deal *"you're going to screw up, idiot, if you keep sleeping with his fucking wife!"* The living man chuckled at something on his phone—perhaps a text from his mistress—before walking across the street, the ghost following him.

In the archway of one of the closed nightclubs, a many-layered woman, both clothes and skin, sat huddled at the entryway. She reached out with gloved hands, begging for change, only to have passersby walk through her extended arms. Occasionally, a pedestrian would pass through her hands and shiver, only to immediately forget the sensation and move onward. Even if the beggar had been alive, Claire felt people were too absorbed in their lives to take note of the haggard-looking redhead.

Most people's attention spans usually began and ended with their thoughts.

By stark and unfortunate contrast, the deceased felt Claire's unintended siren's call emanating from beneath her thinning jacket and torn jeans. They noticed everything. They'd be drifting among the breathing masses, perhaps trying fruitlessly to engage in conversation or wailing in their misery, then as sudden as a wasp bite, they'd feel her slinking past. In a flash, they'd move like moths to an open flame, a line of haunted goslings trailing behind their reluctant mother goose.

As such, Claire ducked down alleyways and turned onto roads that hosted minimal entities, alive or otherwise. Primarily, she preferred the loopers if she had a choice.

Loopers were spirits who replayed their deaths on repeat—a torturous game of ring around the rosy in which they continued to circle and circle and circle, never ending, never "falling down." Stuck in their repetitive hell of dying and reviving, they never took note of her presence, too overwhelmed were they with their own troubles.

More often than not, they were people whom death surprised on a whim—a fickle reaper. Claire wondered if these people felt pain each time they died, but did not dwell on the thought. If it stopped them from noticing and bothering her, then so be it. She locked away the guilt at her iciness with the rest of her culpability, telling herself she'd be different if she could actually help them instead of just bearing witness.

It was a looper she'd encountered the very first night she saw the echoes of the departed. Compared to the other spirits with violent deaths she would encounter as she aged, this one had been relatively tame: an old woman who died in her sleep. However, Claire had been alone at the time; her father was working, and her mother was sleeping off the migraines Claire would eventually inherit.

Claire had accidentally found an early birthday gift hidden under one of the couch cushions in the living room.

That was the thing about living in a rinky-dink mobile home; nothing could ever be hidden for long, neither presents nor secrets.

"Happy twelfth birthday, our blossoming pre-teen!" was printed in exaggerated looping letters on the front of a large sketchpad. Claire had been pleased and shocked; she'd wanted this notepad for her drawing with all her middle-school heart and soul. She smiled, opening the first page and running her pale fingers across the thick cream-colored surface. Unlike the nearly translucent lined paper she doodled on in her school composition notebooks, this paper was textured and luxurious. Emotion swelled in Claire's chest; it wasn't often her parents could afford the gifts she had explicitly pointed out, but it seemed her father had some extra money from his recent contracting gig. Or perhaps her mother sold a few more crystals to some tourists looking for a sign to delve into their spirituality, a sign her mother was always happy to provide.

She hadn't meant to find the gift early and thought she'd make amends by putting the pad to use to make up for it. It was the moment Claire decided to outline a quick "thank you" sketch, when the graphite of her number two pencil chipped as it made contact with the paper, that the woman emerged from the kitchen pantry.

She wore a thin robe that may have been fuzzy at one point, but the patches were worn thin and rough from noticeable wear and tear. A nest of white hair pulled into a messy bun sat on her bowed head, her withered, arthritic hands pulling the robes across her chest. She shuffled silently along in pink slippers.

"Good night, Frank. I'll be up early to make some banana bread for the church potluck tomorrow," she said in a quiet, cracking voice.

Claire had frozen, her pencil still touching the paper, a smudged gray dot on the pad's center. She kept her head down, but her eyes latched onto the woman. She watched as the old woman walked to her parents' room, passing through the door and out of sight.

Claire might have thought she'd imagined it—or perhaps hoped she had—if the woman hadn't returned the next night, and the next, and the next. For a short time, she blamed herself—*I never should have opened my present early; it's karma*—but eventually, she learned that it didn't matter.

Looking back, she would have thought that night would have sparked her first panic attack, but that didn't happen until her father left.

This is so stupid. She gritted her teeth as she walked, dodging the shantytowns that crowded the stained walkways.

The jaunt was barely over a mile, and with limited funds, she opted to walk. She was too inebriated to drive, not that she had a car in the first place. A car meant maintenance fees, Californian gas prices, city garage permits, and insurance, all of which required money she didn't have.

Due to her circuitous route avoiding spirits, the 15-minute walk took nearly half an hour. At one point, a shimmering man with one eye tried to speak to her: "I know you can see me, psychic." Claire pulled a pinch of salt from her pocket and tossed it like a horse's tail, flicking away a pesky fly. The man yelped and backed away as Claire continued, her music muffling his cries.

By the time she reached the pier, the bottom of the sun had begun dipping behind the horizon, the golden light melting into the waves. She took note of the people on the concrete walkway: a tourist couple arguing about which Michelin guide-promoted restaurant to try, a homeless man sleeping precariously close to the edge of the water, a group of fishermen slinging their poles over the side hoping to catch a bite. She imagined one of the men holding his captured prize and posting the image to one of his multiple dating profiles with the caption: *Fishin' for a partner whose beauty is not just scale deep #imacatch.*

Grinning to herself, she sat down at the far edge of the pier, brushing away a used paper cup plastered with the Padres logo. Several yards away, a group of amateur photographers and inland visitors were taking poorly framed photos of the sunset. However, she found it hard to indict them; the sky was a mixture of brilliant pinks and oranges, sky-bound sherbet overlooking the city.

This wasn't the spot where her father had drowned; she knew it was somewhere deeper in the Pacific, the exact location known only to the deceased and the reaper itself. Nevertheless, these were the waters in which her father had lost his life; it was the closest she would ever get to visiting his grave.

Her feet dangled off the side of the pier, too high to touch the water, even with the lapping waves sending little spittles of salt flying toward her. It was one of the reasons she was drawn to the coast in the first place: she doubted any apparition would chance getting so close to the salt-soaked currents. Claire fantasized about living alone on a boat in the middle of the Dead Sea, the lake aptly named not for its attraction of the dead, but for their destruction. However, a trip to Asia was outside both her comfort and financial zones, so she made do with her paper can of table salt and proximity to the Pacific.

Claire flicked through her playlist, and *Styx* sang through the bulky headset. Pulling out the bottle, she lifted it as if offering a toast. She paused for a moment, considering whether or not to pour some into the sea.

Nah. She instead pressed the bottle to her lips and forced down the last dregs of whiskey. Her throat welcomed the familiar burning of the liquor as her legs swayed to the music. She hummed along tunelessly. Perhaps it was time to "sail away" to something new, though unlike the band, she'd be partnerless and alone.

The sleek, black spine of a seal broke the surface of the water briefly, then submerged back into the sea half a mile away. She smiled; animal sightings weren't always common here with the commotion of the city and screaming tourists so near. Her last interaction with a wild animal in San Diego was the raccoon who had hissed at her from inside the garbage can on the street. After yelling at it for several minutes, she gave up and allowed "Shit Bandit" to claim its precious molding apple cores and stale pasta.

While she was lost in thought, the seal reappeared, closer than she'd expected. She frowned, blinking and squinting at the dark mass, trying to focus through her building stupor. Was there a second seal? She was no marine biologist, but even she knew that seals couldn't swim so far, so fast. Or maybe they could; it'd been a long time since freshman year Biology, she thought with a tipsy inner shrug.

Claire pulled off her headphones and hung them around her neck. The song continued to play, a tinny noise of guitars and vocals wavering into the night. She looked behind her to see if anyone else had noticed the animal and saw that the pier around her had emptied considerably; now that the sun had entirely slipped beneath the horizon, people took it as a sign to leave for the evening. She turned back to the ocean, peering down into the water. Her squinting reflection looked back at her in a blur, nose scrunched into her freckles, much like the scattered stars that had begun to emerge above her.

The surface of the water shattered, and with a gasp, she was pulled off the edge of the pier and dragged beneath the surface.

D ark, salty water enveloped her, and she fought to keep her head up. Claire barely had time to register that something had grabbed her ankle. Pruney, webbed claws had erupted from the waves below and latched onto her leg, too powerful for Claire to have resisted, even if she hadn't been caught by surprise.

A sound escaped her lips, a final hitching breath, and then the muffled roar of water flooded her eardrums in a great splash. She couldn't see anything in the dark beneath; the shadows of the pier and the night sky shrouded her vision, and the salt burned her eyes as she tried to catch sight of the beast pulling her body down into the airless depths.

Death had finally come for her. She was constantly surrounded by the deceased, and now she would officially join their community. Despite the daily reminders that each and every living creature would one day meet their end, Claire had—incorrectly, it seemed—believed she had more years left. She'd thought she had time to re-establish herself, garner stability, and find some modicum of happiness and peace.

Mors est pro nobis omnibus. Death comes for us all.

Still, stubbornness won out against submissive acceptance, and Claire thrashed against the thing that pulled her down into the dark, soundless catacombs of the freezing ocean.

Jedan, dva, tri . . . one, two, three . . .

Her hands reached down to pry the grip off her leg, but she sank too fast; the resistance was too challenging to allow her body to bend. She smashed her heel into the vise-like hold using her other leg, but that, too, did little to stop her descent. Finally, she tried to scream, desperate for something—anything—to hear her pleas. The last of the oxygen rushed out of her lungs—replaced by icy water—and her voice was lost to the soundlessness of the sea. She was going to die.

Claire closed her eyes, waiting to reach the marine floor, for sharpened claws or jagged teeth to tear into her flesh. The blood would cloud the water in a crimson haze, sounding an alarm for all nearby carnivorous sea life to approach for an evening meal. Her lungs screamed in agony, desperate for air and fighting against the cold. As the seconds passed by, her body grew weak, exhausted from futile resistance.

She was feeling the dregs of her consciousness fade to wisps when an unearthly scream pierced the darkness, and the hold around her ankle disappeared. Her eyes opened, and she expected to be greeted by the unseeing void of the ocean as her final sight. Instead, sickly orange eyes stared back at her, large, round, and unsettling, inches from her own. Its face was gaunt and scaly, a light from behind her shining off slick, mucous-covered skin. The monster's lipless mouth was pulled open like a pit, revealing rows of tiny, yellowed, razor-sharp teeth. Long, throbbing gills opened and closed rhythmically along its neck, its flesh a rotting gray.

Though she was losing consciousness with every passing moment, the shock and terror of seeing this fish creature coursed through her veins and released a bolt of adrenaline. Claire lifted her feet and kicked out with her heels, striking it in the chest. She doubted she did any damage, but the surprise caused it to reel backward. It pushed itself away, allowing Claire to see the rest of its body.

It was a minor miracle she hadn't already died from the fear that sliced through her heart. The creature was large, its body twice her size. Its skin was semi-translucent; she could see its organs and muscles twitching. While the monster had long, sinewy, webbed arms, it bore no legs, merely a fish-like tail, the fins seemingly gossamer and flowing in the fray. It didn't approach her again. Instead, its massive eyes were focused on the light from behind her. Perhaps she had died after all, and it was the tunnel that would bring her to the other side. She'd go anywhere that *thing* wasn't.

It hissed, baring its needle-teeth in a wordless threat. Claire could see its pupils darting side to side, assessing the situation in which it found itself: Eat the prey. Leave the prey.

It chose the latter. The monster released another screech and spun around, swimming off into the night. Still, Claire was no closer to salvation than before. The fear had only awoken her body briefly, and her strike against the creature had depleted the rest of her energy. The time to "come sail away" had arrived at long last.

Claire closed her eyes again, feeling her body drift slowly downward, hoping (but doubting) she'd fall into the light. But the light caught her. Something gently cradled her body against its own, a surge of warmth flooding her skin. Eyes still closed, Claire curled into the sensation, toward whatever—or whomever—was holding her. Maybe it was the lack of oxygen, perhaps it was the acceptance of death, maybe it was the relief that the creature was gone, but Claire felt secure. Despite the dire circumstances, she ironically felt safe for the first time in a very long time, like a blanket had encircled and swaddled her form.

With extraordinary effort, Claire opened her eyes into narrow slits and registered a gaze of fiery blue staring down into hers.

Yes, this is definitely oxygen deprivation, she thought to herself before her eyelids dropped shut and the world turned black, taking the flaming gaze with it.

chapter THREE

I t wasn't the incessant metronomic beeping that awoke Claire.

Nor was it the quiet mutterings of doctors exchanging notes or the whimpers of patients painfully adjusting themselves on the creaking hospital beds. Televisions played reality TV on low volume, and glass bottles clinked together as they were gathered by nurses, phlebotomists, and physicians' assistants working overtime. What awoke her was the begging.

Though she was only just regaining consciousness, her mind sluggish and dazed, she immediately recognized the chill pawing at her arms, caressing her face, and encircling her resting place. And there was the crying …

"How do I get home?"

"I need to get to my son!"

"Why can't anybody hear me?"

"I can't breathe!"

Don't look, don't move, Claire thought to herself. She

struggled to remember why she was in the hospital. Sifting through the haze, she recalled snippets of the last few hours: the pier, the water, the undulating, the gaze of flaming blue, the transparent skin of a predator—

Her eyes flew open, unable to stay in the dark any longer, not with the memory of the animal—the *monster*—flooding her vision.

She lay in a thinly padded bed, her clothes replaced with an unmalleable hospital gown the color of a robin's egg. An IV pierced her left arm, a thin, clear tube trailing from a bag of clear liquid hanging on a pole by the rest of the beeping, glowing machinery. On a chair by the bed, she saw a plastic bag that held her clothes, dark and soggy from her violent tryst in the ocean. Taking all of this in was secondary to what really grabbed her attention: the crowd of people standing, kneeling, and floating around the room.

A man missing a part of his torso leaned against the curtain frame.

An elderly woman knelt beside the bed, her chest distorted as though smashed with a mallet.

A figure whose features were too mangled to determine age or gender rested on the chair next to her clothes.

A child and their older sibling—both boys—huddled next to each other, both bleeding from wounds in the back of their skulls. Claire inhaled sharply when she saw the brothers. Visions of deceased adults were one thing; she never could get past the apparitions of children, taken too early, too soon. Still others were filing in, moths to her flame. Some entered through the break in the curtain; others floated straight through the fabric or over the tops of the rods.

Too many … it's too many …

Claire began to hyperventilate, wheezing gasps tearing from her chest. Through the buzzing in her head, she could hear the ghosts speaking at her in a chorus of vibrating voices: some as though speaking through a radio, others as if inside her skull. She grasped at her neck, trying to grab her headphones, only to realize they were missing, along with the rest of her effects. The reality of the situation came crashing down on her: no headphones, salt, or escape.

She might as well have still been at the bottom of the ocean.

Claire opened her mouth to scream, unsure if commands or a stream of wordless shrieks would erupt from her lungs. The monitor beside her bed let out a high-pitched cry. Her heart thudded in time with the machine, the quick tempo *rat-a-tat* of a snare drum. Her eyes lifted to the screen, and she saw her reflection staring back at her.

She looked awful, her hair askew, her skin sickly pale beneath the freckles, lips blue and chapped, bags under her eyes hanging like swollen plums. Just then, her expression changed as she watched herself. Replacing her grimace was a fox-sly smile, its—*her*—lips stretching much too far up toward her cheekbones. The face *winked,* and she jumped. The next moment, her regular reflection returned, panic-ridden. But the room's buzzing, crying, wailing, and begging had gone quiet. Sitting up with a groan, Claire peered around the room again. All her visitors had vanished as if they hadn't been there in the first place.

Where had they gone?

"Glad to see you're awake, Ms. Reed."

She started again, her blanket toppling off the mattress, her heart giving another painful stutter. A woman stood in the doorway, wearing teal scrubs and a weary smile. She held a clipboard in her hand and a pen in the other as she made her way to the heart monitor.

"I need to leave," Claire started, grabbing the needle in her arm. She didn't have time to think about how or why the ghosts had vanished. The break may have been welcome, but she felt uneasy about why they'd suddenly disappeared, not to mention what she'd seen in her reflection, if she had seen anything at all.

The woman firmly grabbed Claire's grasping hands and pressed her shoulders back into the mattress. "What you need is rest and monitoring. You were nearly dead for two minutes by the time you got here, and we need to make sure you don't have residual water in your lungs or brain damage."

"I was dead? . . ." Claire's heart gave another frantic lurch, as though confirming it was still, indeed, alive. The woman gave another gentle smile.

"And now you're not. You're quite lucky; the current must have pulled you to shore. Not everyone gets a second chance like that. How are you feeling?" She clicked her pen and looked at Claire expectantly. Claire cleared her throat, unsure how to respond. Now that the continuous moans of the dead had ceased, she could feel a reverberating headache growing, then fading, and growing again, like a circling lighthouse beacon. But if she was going to be allowed to leave, she needed to be okay.

"I guess I feel okay, Doctor . . . ?"

"Hydecker," the woman replied, not looking up from the clipboard. "Alright, let me listen to your lungs. Take a deep breath, hold it, and let go when I say."

Dr. Hydecker ran Claire through a series of checks for the next few minutes.

"Tip-top shape, Ms. Reed, for someone recently returned to the land of the living. I'd still like you to stay for the evening for observation, just in case."

Claire shook her head, then quickly stopped, as it worsened the pain in her temples. "No, really, I'm fine. I'd really just rather recuperate in my home."

"It's nearly 11 at night; it would be reckless to leave at this hour. Is there someone at home waiting for you? Children you need to take care of?" Claire considered lying, but instead said no, the truth coming out more easily than lies.

"Staying the night won't do any harm. Always better to be safe than sorry. Please let me know if you need anything. The call button is on the side table if you need to ring." Dr. Hydecker pulled out a small paper cup with three brown pills and a granola bar. "These are for the headache. Eat the bar, then the pills. The water is over here."

With a final knowing grin, the doctor left. Resigned, Claire bit into the bar—slowly at first, then with increased fervor as she realized how starved she'd been—and took all three pills in one dry swallow before settling down into sterile-scented pillows.

Dr. Hydecker was right; she was too weak to leave. Claire had yet to ask which hospital she occupied; for all she knew, she could be miles away from her apartment. And the bed—though thin—was still soft and dry and smelled cleaner than her apartment on a good day.

The last time she had been in a hospital overnight was when she needed to get her appendix removed. She was only ten, and to her juvenile knowledge, hospitals were only for old people and doctors, and she was certainly neither of those things. However, as the pain in her lower left abdomen grew, her father had carried her into the family's truck and driven her to the nearest emergency room, despite her mother's protests about trying some natural solutions instead. He had stayed by her side all night, improvising little tales of heroic princesses saving knights in distress—she'd always demanded to be warrior savior in his stories, and he'd acquiesced. Claire wished he would tell her another story now.

Doing her best not to think about how much this hospital stay would cost her, she closed her eyes and drifted into a troubled slumber.

C laire dreamt of watery depths and needle-teeth. Gasping for air, she jolted awake, her room softly illuminated by the LED lights that bled underneath the curtains. She threw her arm to the side table, forgetting momentarily that she wasn't at home and would not have her iron rod at her disposal. No salt, either.

She glanced at a clock on the wall: *4:45 am.*

This was too dangerous, too overwhelming. She could still feel herself caught within her dreams, the darkness suffocating her lungs and the vise-like grip on her ankle. Her headache had returned, worse than before. How long had it been since her last drink?

The safety she had felt from the light with the blue-flamed eyes had long passed. The residual panic, the pain in her temples, and the unfamiliar setting convinced her that it would only be a matter of time before the next set of apparitions arrived, demanding help she couldn't give. She needed to leave, doctor's orders be damned.

Claire cursed under her breath as she slowly pulled the needle out of her arm, a trickle of red dripping and staining her sheets. She carefully dressed in her damp clothes, trying to avoid the cords from the monitors, preemptively gritting her teeth at the chafing she'd experience during the trek back to her apartment. She noted that while her wallet had—incredibly—stayed stuck inside her jeans pocket, her phone, headphones, and salt were gone.

She'd need to make it home quickly.

She took a deep breath, held it, then tore off the heart monitor. As it began to trill an elongated beep as her heart rate seemingly and suddenly fell to zero, Claire burst from the room and sped down the hallway, dodging into an unoccupied curtained room as a string of doctors jostled their way to her now empty compartment. She froze, waited for the frenzy of footsteps to pass, and then exited, finding the stairway down to the front lobby and slipping away. As she passed the other hospital beds, she could see out of the corner of her eyes the heads of the dead slowly peeking between the curtains, sensing her presence like rabid dogs. Pushing through the burning exhaustion that tore through her legs, Claire dodged a skeletal hand that extended through one of the doors. She yanked open the door at the end of the hall and escaped down the stairs.

Her legs were unsteady beneath her as she took the stairs two by two, fleeing through the automatic glass doors. As she entered the parking lot, she read the glowing red and white signage above the door: UC San Diego Health Emergency Services. Only five miles away from the Gaslamp. Not terrible. Not great.

She moved without thinking and began her trek back to the apartment, her body aching. Though it'd been over a year since she'd been in the area, she recalled a bus station nearby that would hopefully be running soon. She was confident she could make the full five-mile walk back on her own if necessary, but even she couldn't ignore the weakness from having clinically fucking *died*, and the last thing she wanted was to make a wrong turn, extending her trip longer than necessary.

And without her headphones, the whispering assaults would be overpowering along the sidewalks and streets.

The bus stop was empty when she arrived. A single cobwebbed light illuminated the partially encased bench. The canopy was covered in filmy plastic, parts of it jagged and broken from careless riders or bored teens. Relieved, she collapsed onto the plastic seating, rubbing her shoulders to remove the tension that had built and begun to calcify. It had been months since she'd spent so much time outside her loft, and her legs seemed to be going into shock. Knots twisted in her lower back, her jaw clenched, her teeth chattering against the chill November air.

But now she was heading in the right direction, and soon, she'd be in her own bed, though the nightmare of the day would live on in future nightmares of her mind.

As if she needed more terror in her life.

"Is this seat taken?"

Claire bolted upright, her body leaping to the far side of the bench away from the voice. She winced as her lower back cramped from the sudden motion. She squinted in the winking, artificial light to see who had joined her.

It was a young woman, her body enveloped in a thick, dark overcoat that rose to her chin, complemented by a scarf wrapped around her neck and mouth, muffling her voice. Her arms were crossed in front of her chest, from innate shyness or the cold, Claire couldn't tell. Claire snapped her mouth shut, trying to gather her bearings. Her feet had automatically planted on the cracked concrete, ready to run.

It turned out the woman didn't require an answer. Without waiting for Claire to respond, the woman sat down, relaxing her arms into a crossed position in her lap. She gave Claire a bright smile, her teeth perfect ivory pebbles in neat rows. She gestured around the station.

"Thank you very much. It's quite the storm out now, isn't it? I really do need to invest in a car at some point."

Calming slightly, Claire turned her body to face the cheery woman fully. She agreed that the early morning air was quite cool, especially for a Californian fall; it'd been years since she had to endure an icy Arizona winter, and living in San Diego had ruined her resistance to anything below 72 degrees. However, she'd pause before she'd call it a "storm."

"I suppose?" Claire said. "I mean, normally there'd be water falling from the sky in a storm." Claire narrowed her eyes at the woman who, to her credit, didn't seem to mind

Claire's suspicious gaze. If anything, she seemed to be having a conversation all on her own.

"Why, yes! I'm from Ohio, best known for hunks of black rocks. How boring is that?" She let out a laugh that fell heavily in the night air.

Claire shrugged, resting her back on the bench, resigning herself to conversation. "I've never been, so I wouldn't know."

The woman tightened her coat and looked back at her, raising an eyebrow.

"I'm sorry, but I really shouldn't say."

Claire gaped a moment. "Shouldn't say what?" Claire replied, puzzled.

The woman was beginning to look uneasy, and Claire chanced a look around the empty streets. What was she … Claire froze. She hadn't been truly paying attention.

The woman stood up and slowly began to back away. "Actually, you know, I have someone waiting for me. It's only a short walk; I might as well get a move on. It was nice to meet you." The woman trembled.

Claire stood up and took a step forward, her hands lifted in an attempt to pacify the frightened woman, knowing it was fruitless.

"Hey, are you alright? Do you need help?"

The woman spun on her heels, trying to run away, but an invisible hand wrenched the collar of her coat back. A shriek attempted to escape the woman's lips, but the sound was only a gag, as though her mouth was suddenly and violently restrained. She twisted and turned frantically, her hands clawing at an invisible arm that pressed against her face, dragging her to the ground.

Claire watched in horror as she realized too late what was happening, too focused on getting home. She squatted down on her heels, forcing her eyes shut, her palms covering her ears.

Come sail away, come sail away . . .

She repeated the lyrics in her head, trying to block out the loop she'd stumbled across. She should have caught on much sooner. This young woman from Ohio, looking for passage during a storm, had met her untimely end in this place. Claire was unlucky enough to experience it with her. This was one of the many reasons she only left her loft when necessary.

A loud horn rattled her from her thoughts. A blue bus had appeared, its door already open, while her eyes were squeezed shut. The stubble-faced driver appraised her, deciding whether she was worth the trouble to allow on his transport.

"Ya getting on, or do ya just wanna sit there like an armadillo?" he squawked, smacking his gum.

Claire glanced back to where the woman in the loop struggled for her life, but found the area empty. She turned and ascended the groaning metal steps and sat in the empty seat closest to the exit. The driver rolled his eyes before closing the doors with a tattooed hand, grumbling about the "weirdos being out early this morning." He shifted into gear and said, "If you get sick in my bus, you're cleaning it and clearing out. Got that?"

Claire didn't bother responding; if she looked as bad as she felt, she couldn't blame the man. As the bus jostled and hummed along the slowly busying city streets, Claire noted the travelers seated throughout the car: an old woman crocheting a purple scarf, a man in an ill-fitting suit tapping on his cell phone, and a couple sitting silently together, the young woman resting her head on his shoulder as he read.

Deciding that they were all truly alive—or as alive as anyone was nowadays—Claire let her gaze drift to the buildings moving past her tinted windows. Most were large, boxy commercial buildings, hives for worker bees toiling for an unknown capitalistic queen bee, receiving a small modicum of honey in return for their twelve hours of daily labor. Here and there, some storefronts seemed out of place in the beige colors of city life, with colorful neon signage drawing in passersby who wanted to escape their nine-to-fives.

On the city's periphery, they passed juxtapositions of destitute areas and heavily remodeled houses bookended with carefully selected palm trees. Claire had often dreamed of living in one of those perfectly staged houses, new-age millennial gray, the porches surrounded by gravel-and-succulent zero-scape yards.

As it was, she'd be lucky if she didn't get evicted within the next year from the ratty loft above her shop. Running seances out of a hole-in-the-wall storefront near other so-called mediums wasn't the money maker she'd hoped it would be after her suspension from the SDPD. And even then, listening to victims and sketching criminals barely paid the bills in the first place.

The sun rose in the morning sky, gently suffusing light through the thin cloud cover. A single ray broke through and grazed the faces of the passengers. Claire looked over at the elderly woman, whose hands still worked the yarn. She and Claire exchanged a brief smile before returning to their projects, the woman's reflection in the window behind her mirroring her arthritic hands and weather-worn face.

And then the woman's reflection in the window spoke.

"Leaving the hospital so soon? Not a move We'd make. Death would checkmate you in a heartbeat. And it'd be your last one, too."

Claire blinked. The crochet needles continued to click and weave in the woman's hands, but Claire fixated on the tinted reflection. Same wrinkled eyes, same hooked nose, same yellow blouse. Yet, it was not the kind-faced elderly woman. At least, not entirely. The reflection stretched the corners of its lips upward, reminding Claire of her own warped reflection in the hospital room. Its pupils were large and dark, overtaking the woman's irises completely.

It was only for a moment, and then, like a candle melting under flame, her reflection remodeled back to its rightful place, an echo of the knitting woman.

Claire looked to her right at the man tapping away on his phone. *Did he see this? Did he hear?* No, he didn't. But his reflection did.

"We're not used to being ignored, Clarissa Reed," the man's reflection said.

His face remained fixated on his screen, but his image in the window snapped to attention and wriggled its fingers teasingly at her with the same, taffy-stretched smile and olive-pit eyes as the old woman's windowed reflection.

"Nope! I'm done." Claire stood up and pulled the red

wire trailing along the bus's top. The tires screeched to a halt as the driver applied the brakes and pulled over to the side. Without waiting for the doors to open, Claire shoved the door open, nearly falling onto the sidewalk.

"What the hell, lady?" The driver yelled after her, his curses and insults melting against the sounds of the morning traffic. Claire blocked out his yells, the ache in her knees, and the soreness in her spine. She had to get back to her apartment at once. There was something new out here.

And it demanded her attention.

chapter FOUR

She met few obstacles in the final stretch back to her storefront. Despite the cries from various apparitions, and a few insults from drivers as she jaywalked across the one-way streets, Claire found herself back in her loft.

More specifically, she found herself heaving on the bathroom floor, emptying bile into the toilet. Her throat burned painfully with each burst, the layers of her esophagus stripping away like epidermal paper mâché. She rested her forehead on the cool porcelain seat, too fatigued and woozy to consider the many days—months—it had been since she had last scrubbed any part of the bathroom, not that she'd ever had any living visitors. She had no desire to impress the deceased.

Her thoughts drifted like waves frothing at the pier— no, not the pier; never the pier, or the beach, the ocean, any sort of body of water, just in case that *thing* could travel from sea to creek. Her thoughts drifted like the dead woman in the alleyway, aloof and dismal and—

Stop it, just stop.

Moaning, Claire crawled back to the couch, cushions still indented from when she last reclined there, bickering with Henry. Her mouth acrid and smelling of sick, she fished out a crumpled plastic water bottle from underneath the coffee table and swallowed the last dregs of water before laying back down.

She never should have gone out. What was she thinking, taking the advice of a teenage ghost? She knew better than to listen to anything any of *them* had to say. Stick to the paid seances, answer the questions of the living, retire to her booze-addled homelife, and repeat. That was what had been working over the last year since she left the force—*been fired*, she inadvertently corrected herself.

No matter what, though, no more trips to the beach.

Claire checked the clock, glowing green on the microwave: *6:30 a.m.* "Madame Clarissa" wouldn't be opening her doors for at least another three and a half hours. She considered making breakfast—the eggs were only a week past their sell-by date—and maybe brew a robust cup of coffee. She was exhausted. A headache speared into her skull, but she could not summon the will to leave the cushions despite their poking springs and worn stuffing.

As she considered rising from the couch, the images of demonic entities, malevolent smiling reflections, and screaming women in overcoats hooked into her mind. Yet, as exhaustion won against the nightmarish memories that plagued her thoughts, her heart could not help but flutter at the thought of blue ember locking into her own, a frisson of peace finding her.

A re you paying attention? We're not paying to watch you nap on our dime." A large man, his face reminiscent of a turnip, waved his hands about as he spoke, nearly whipping a stack of tarot cards off the table. His wife—her head like the same turnip but upside down, revealing an overly prominent forehead—nodded furtively. Claire thought if she were to bounce her head that quickly and continuously, she'd need to sit down due to sudden land-based seasickness.

Claire tried to say no but failed to stifle a yawn as the man continued to vent. Waking up well past business hours, she had considered remaining closed for the rest of the day, claiming some emergency—leaky pipes, spirit-related disturbances—but noting the large stack of unpaid bills on the counter and dresser, not to mention the impending tab from the hospital, she begrudgingly got up and ready for the day.

Sometimes, she yearned for the barter system to return; she had some junk she wouldn't mind trading to pay the rent. However, she feared accidentally inviting an unwelcome presence into her office, particularly the one with the malevolent Cheshire smile and sharp tongue. Over the last hour, she'd purposefully avoided all reflective surfaces, covering the mirrors in her apartment and going so far as to cover the useless crystal ball in an ornate handkerchief, claiming to be "recharging its energies." So far, it seemed to have done the job.

Please wake up, wake up, wake up, she chanted to herself, sitting up straighter and forcing herself to appear halfway interested. Her right eye twitched with the effort, and she could feel the couple's faith in her abilities drop even further. Clearing her throat and relaxing her hands on the chair's upholstered arms, Claire affixed a look to her face that implied "haughty but powerful."

"My apologies, sir. Some days, the cosmic energies take a heavier toll than usual on my body." The man's mustache quivered, and she saw he was trying to decide if she was mocking him. To be fair, she was; it was much more difficult to be professional when all she wanted was peace and quiet.

Claire cleared her throat. "Yes, I'm listening." Another yawn bloomed in her chest, and she ducked to hide it, pretending to be adjusting the tablecloth.

"Does everything need to be an argument with you? Leave the damn girl alone," the wife snapped. As the man shot back a response, Claire considered telling them they needed a counselor, not a medium.

The two squabbled, talking over each other in ever-increasing volume. Claire pinched herself awake; the longer they argued, the longer they'd stay and impede other paying customers.

Yet, the candles gave a soft, ethereal glow to the room, her chair was soft, and she was just so, so tired . . .

Claire's head drooped slightly.

A sudden burst of sound exploded from the street. A

crash reverberated throughout the building, the screech of metal smashing into concrete and glass shattering into shards. Claire abandoned the table and sprinted for the front door, her head dizzy from the sudden movement.

Looking through the window, she surveyed the scene outside. Large swaths of darkened smoke billowed up in plumes from a totaled car, the front end halfway through the mini-mart across the street. Other vehicles were stopped at awkward angles along the road, having swerved to a stop to avoid the crash. Onlookers flooded toward the wreck, some on their phones calling for help, others filming to share the emergency with their followers online. A few brave and reckless souls ran toward the churning smoke, hoping to pull the driver free, but when a series of flames erupted from the car, they were forced to back away.

"What the hell is going on out there?" The husband shoved Claire aside and exited the shop, his wife tailing behind.

Claire locked the door behind them and drew another line of salt along the door's edge. With accidents come deaths, and the last thing she wanted was to explain to the newly deceased that "no, you didn't survive the crash" and "no, I can't really help you unless you just want a friendly chat, and perhaps not even that."

She leaned against the doorframe, listening to the sirens growing louder, watching the flames climb higher. For a moment, she thought perhaps she should leave for somewhere safer, somewhere further from the fire.

But the thought of exiting her loft again so soon held her fast in place.

The sirens screamed close now, a banshee of the law. Flashing lights of red and blue percolated the vicinity as uniformed officials began to clear the scene. She stepped slightly to the side, just out of the eyeline of the police across the street. The last thing she needed was the judgmental stares of her old coworkers eyeing her new career choices.

A twinge of selfish regret flitted in her mind; she'd enjoyed that particular convenience store, solely due to its proximity to her apartment. She didn't envy looking for a new mini-mart while this one was renovated. Secondly—and more importantly—she hoped the driver was okay.

Her eyes followed the smoke that dissipated high above the store and spread to the tops of the nearby buildings. When she was on the force, other officers had told her stories of Californian fires, when the skies turned orange and the air rained with soot and ash; they sounded like tales from the bible, a coastal city apocalyptic wasteland. Claire doubted this was anything close to the warnings she'd heard from her peers, but it gave her a glimpse into her future on the West Coast. Maybe she'd be better off heading east.

As her eyes scaled the edges of the smoke, her gaze landed on a figure balancing on one of the nearby rooftops. Her breath caught.

The form was blurred, making it difficult to fully distinguish behind the dark haze. Pressing her palms to the window, she tried to angle for a better view.

It was a person—no, an animal—no, something else entirely. From a distance, it almost seemed like a gargoyle, some Greco-Roman design an edgy architect forced through city ordinance. The Gaslamp hardly needed a new, tourist-grabbing renovation. Perhaps it was a publicity stunt, like putting costumes on well-known statues. Surely someone would eventually post a picture to social media with several hashtags they'll never use again.

But then it was *moving*, pacing the edge of the roof.

"What the hell is that?" she muttered aloud, the tip of her nose smudging the glass. Claire gripped the door handle, considering, against her better judgement, to leave and get a closer look.

But then the figure lifted its arms, one bent while the other straightened, and a new cloud of smoke shrouded it from view. Claire shook her head; perhaps she *should* have stayed the night at the hospital. The near-death experience had done something to her head.

And then something shot out of the smoke. She would have missed it if she had blinked, but there it was: an arrow-like projectile careening through the smoke, aimed straight at the wreck.

As it found its mark, a column of fire spiraled up from the wreck, and shouts of caution and surprise rang out from the firefighters on the scene. A new group of EMTs appeared, ready to enter the fire and pull out the victims. From the window, Claire could see dark red liquid streaming like a narrow hose from the driver's seat; the paramedics were too late. The arrow had hit its mark.

Along with the river of scarlet, something else poured from the car. Claire squinted to make out the thick, gossamer ribbon that spiraled and curled up out of the wreckage. It ebbed and flowed like water yet floated like a spider web caught in a breeze. The stream coiled into the air and drifted toward the figure on the roof. Claire's gaze followed it, feeling both awe and terror fill her chest. She knew what she was witnessing.

The victim's soul was being split, a portion being stolen.

As her eyes tracked the milky web, Claire saw the dark, gaping maw of the attacker. A trickle of icy horror ran down her spine as the figure seemed to swell, the web flowing faster and more erratically into its throat. She couldn't tear her eyes away from watching a soul be devoured.

As the final remnants disappeared into its jaw, the figure shuddered. Then, it aimed a fresh arrow at the wreckage, and Claire pulled violently out of her transfixed stare.

"No!" she screamed, slamming her palm against the glass. Her voice was lost among the chaos of roaring sirens, panicked cries, and raging fire.

The figure notched the arrow, arm tensing, but it never reached its mark.

Someone else appeared on the rooftop, just a fraction shorter than the first figure, though wider, broader. From a distance, Claire could make out a cloak billowing behind the newcomer. The man held something in his hands that reflected the sun's bright glare.

The archer faced the newcomer and shifted as if ready to fight. The man twisted in the air and disappeared in a bright orange flash.

Temporarily blinded, Claire blinked repeatedly to regain her sight, but the monstrous archer was alone once more. Had the other ducked out of sight behind one of the generators? Claire shifted from side to side to get a better view, but to no avail. Despite her growing curiosity, intermingled with brimming dread, she felt no desire to open the door to get a better look.

After what she had seen, she was not leaving the sanctuary of her storefront.

The archer seemed unbothered. It stood still, an enigmatic gargoyle posed far above the street below. Claire held her breath.

Another brilliant flash of light, and the man reappeared behind the attacker, leaping onto its back, cloak expanded from the rush of movement. A blaze of fire enveloped their bodies in snake-like tendrils, containing the fight in a cage of flame and motion. They struggled against one another, blurry limbs flailing around the other. Claire watched, transfixed, unsure whether to alert one of the officers out front or to watch the strange rooftop fight unfold.

"Oi, doll face, what's with all the commotion?" Claire started and saw Henry knocking on the door, one hand still stuffed in his uniformed pocket.

When she turned her eyes back to the building rooftops, the figures had gone.

Spinning back to Henry, she placed both hands on her hips. "Don't sneak up on me like that!"

"Like what? Knocking on a door? Like a normal person?"

"You're not a normal person."

"Doll, I can't hear your insults from out here. Let me in, will you? Before the rush. You know how much the dead like fresh meat."

"Stop talking for one second and just look at—" Claire pointed to the rooftop fight and stopped short.

Both figures were gone.

Claire stood stunned, gaze tracing over each nearby building, looking for signs of the struggle. Nothing.

"Yes, doll, I see everything going on out here. More, even, since I'm *still out here*," Henry said, both hands in his pockets and a sour expression. Muttering under her breath, Claire unlocked the door and drew a line in the salt. Henry breezed in, along with the thick scent of burning rubber and exhaust. Coughing, she reapplied the salt and headed up to her apartment, but not before she glanced over her shoulder back to where the two fighting figures had disappeared.

If they'd indeed been there in the first place.

"What're you waiting for? Got somewhere better to be?"

Claire pressed a hand to her chest, allowing the clammy skin of her palm to calm her racing heart. The tips of her fingers tingled as the start of a panic attack began to expand, the cicadas returning in her head.

"No, not now. Just breathe," she whispered to herself, and as the high-pitched hum of panic faded back into submission, Claire walked back up the steps, ready for the day to be over.

.

chapter FIVE

Y ou're sounding a little loose in the head, doll."
Henry sprawled on her couch, one ankle crossed horizontally over his knee, as Claire cracked a couple of eggs into a frying pan. Bits of burnt food from past meals mixed in with her yolks, but Claire neither noticed nor cared. She swirled the eggs in the pan and took a sip from her mug. A familiar burning sensation greeted her throat like a lover's quarrel, and warmth nestled into her stomach.

She eyed the last empty bottle of liquor on her counter and tried not to think about the grocery run she'd need to take soon. "I'm not crazy, Henry. I'm just tired. It's been a long day."

"It's three in the afternoon."

"I repeat, it's been a long day." Claire turned off the stove and lifted the pan to a stained potholder on the counter. Examining a fork she had pulled out of the sink, she deemed it acceptable and leaned against the edge, digging into the pan. With a mouth full of eggs, she brandished the fork at Henry.

"And don't think I don't blame *you* for every bit of it."

Henry sat up, looking affronted. "I beg your pardon? I don't remember siccing you on any demonic orca or imaginary mirror people." He wrinkled his nose as Claire took another bite of eggs, an audible crunch between her teeth.

"I wouldn't have been out there if you hadn't reminded me about the date and guilted me with your 'dead dad' nonsense." She shoveled the last bit of eggs into her mouth and washed it down with dregs of whiskey. "And none of it was imaginary."

Henry crossed his arms. "You were accosted by a fish that shouldn't exist, spoke to reflections that shouldn't speak back, and witnessed a vigilante fight atop a building. None of which was seen by anyone but you. So, excuse me if I find this all hard to believe."

"Well, if we're going by that logic, I should assume *you* don't exist either," she added testily.

Henry walked over to the counter across from Claire, placing one forearm on the surface and angling forward.

"How much did you drink last night?"

At this, Claire turned her back on him and tossed the pan into the sink with a clatter, turning on the faucet to soak the burnt patches.

This wasn't the first time he'd mentioned her drinking. In the past, he'd made comments referencing the pile of empty bottles by the overflowing trashcan or the parade of strong-smelling glasses left strewn about the surfaces of her loft, but it had been at least a couple of years since he broached the subject. She wasn't an alcoholic, but it made her feel like she was doing something wrong.

She wasn't like the half-lucid, bile-covered barflies she'd seen herding into the bus station to sleep off whatever they'd chosen as that night's libations, only to do it again the next night. If Henry truly knew what she had to go through on a daily basis, what she had to do to keep herself together and help her forget—well, he should have known better than to bring it up.

Henry spoke, his voice softening. "Hey, I'm sorry, doll. I didn't mean it, not really. If you say you saw something, I believe you." He had walked over and draped an arm around her shoulder. Looking down, she saw he had to float several inches off the ground to reach. Death had taken him before his teenage growth spurt. The coolness of his presence seeped through her sweatshirt, barely noticeable.

"I wasn't drunk." She began scrubbing the pan, the smell of soap rising from the sink.

"I'm sure you weren't," he agreed, though she knew he didn't believe what he was saying. "Come on, you need to let those soak anyway."

Claire snorted. "Saying you need to let the dishes soak just means you're procrastinating."

He gave her a crooked grin. "You caught me. Come on." He walked back to the couch and sat elbows on his knees. "Read me something out of your book pile. You know I can't open books like I used to."

"You mean like 90-something years ago?" He grinned in response.

Claire rinsed the soap from her hands and sorted through the stack of books she'd collected over the years. As a child, she loved to read, and she was sure she still did as an adult. The stress of work, finances, and life in general took hold, and most days, she was too exhausted to flip past the cover page.

As she separated the novels, she paused. As much as she wanted to move past it, she couldn't stop thinking about the pier, the hospital, and the rooftops.

"Hey, Henry? Are you sure you haven't noticed anything different with your . . . community?" He looked up from his nails.

"You mean a bunch of possessed sea life and talking mirrors?"

Claire scowled. "Nevermind."

"I'm joking, sorry. No, I haven't noticed anything remotely like that, but if I do, I'll give you a shout, I promise."

Appeased for the time being, Claire continued to sort through her stacks of books. "I haven't read out loud in years. I should be reading you some children's picture book or something."

Henry rolled his eyes. "I'm no child."

"Yeah?" Claire said, picking up a thin, red book and dusting the cover. "Then why do I feel like I've accidentally adopted a younger brother? I left Arizona to escape my family, not to start another one."

Henry stuck out his swollen tongue, and she averted her gaze, changing the subject. "Alright, how do you feel about a little poetry?"

Henry laid back on the cushions, his hands lazily

behind his head. "Read on, doll."

Claire cleared her throat and opened to the first page. The words felt foreign, and she struggled to find the rhythm in each line. *Next time*, she thought as she turned the page, *I'm reading him the dictionary.*

She began reading.

"While I nodded, nearly napping,
suddenly, there came a tapping,
As of someone gently rapping,
rapping at my chamber door.
"'Tis some visitor," I muttered,
"tapping at my chamber door—
Only this and nothing more."

A sound rapped on her window. She gasped and glanced up from her page, but the drawn curtain hid the glass. Henry continued to stretch on the couch, his eyes closed. He reminded her of the teens she'd see loitering around the beach, listening to their air pods with zero awareness. She wished she could be that carefree.

"Did you hear that?"

"Hear what? You stuttering over the verses? Yes, unfortunately, I did," Henry responded. She threw a loose sock at him that sailed harmlessly through his torso. Looking back at the yellowing pages, she opened her mouth to start again.

Another rap sounded at the window.

"I swear, Henry, if that's you mocking my book choices, I'm never reading to you again, and you can live out the rest of your dead existence without any entertainment."

"It wasn't me!" The tapping grew louder and more fervent, not quite strong enough to break through the glass, but enough to let anyone inside know someone was outside and wanted to gain entry. Immediately.

"Henry, go check and see who it is," Claire whispered, setting the book down and grabbing the iron rod beneath her bedroom pillow. Henry looked as though he was about to object, but seeing the fear etched in her face, he acquiesced, peering behind the curtain.

"What the devil?" He muttered. Henry glanced at Claire and turned to the window, his eyes scanning their potential intruder.

"Who's out there?" Claire whispered again. Henry turned back to her, frowning.

"Some living jamoke wearing too much beige. I'd tell him to kick cans and scram, but I don't reckon he'd listen to me." *Living?* Iron rod still clenched in her hands, Claire made her way to the window.

Peeking around the curtain, she drew a sharp breath, nearly falling into a coughing spree as it went down the wrong pipe. "Jamoke" was certainly not the word she would have used to describe the man standing on her fire escape.

His shoulders, towering several inches above her head, were covered by a sand-colored overcoat, beneath which was a black-and-white suit, as though he'd been running to a meeting and got caught in the rain. The stubble on his chin lent him a look of maturity, but something about how his lips half-curled at the edges made him seem youthful. Claire didn't meet many men in her new line of work—none that weren't grieving or humoring their partners, in any case—and this man had turned the heat in her body up several—hundred—degrees.

His back was hunched to fit on the fire escape, one hand on his hip while the other forearm supported him as he leaned in toward the glass. He towered above her, and she could only see the bottom of his chin, square and clenched.

"Damn," she whispered.

He looked down, his bright, effervescent blue locking onto her green.

Shit.

She pulled back too quickly, falling on her tailbone with a loud *thump*. The curtain caught on her shoulder, and the rod above broke under her weight. It fell with a crash, the fabric covering her head. Wincing and frantic, she scrambled to her feet, still holding the iron rod. The man knocked on the window again, eyebrows raised in amusement.

Tossing the fabric aside, face blazing, she brandished the weapon in her hands, trying to muster what little intimidation she could cobble back together, which was not very much. Out of the corner of her eye, she could see Henry covering his face with his hands in second-hand embarrassment.

The man in the window straightened, placed both hands in his pockets, and stared at her as though patiently waiting for her to unlock the window.

Fat chance.

She shook the rod, gripping it tighter. Through her clenched jaw, she said, "What do you want?"

From across the room, Henry snorted. "I assume he

wants to come in. Gonna try to scare him off by hiding under the curtains again? Or would you rather be a lump under the carpet?"

"Shut up, Henry," Claire gritted her teeth.

The man outside glanced right at Henry and spoke to Claire. "We normally don't speak to our elders like that, but perhaps it's different here." His voice was low and smooth, softened pebbles coalescing at the bottom of a constant river. Henry's mouth snapped closed, and Claire took another step back. Even she forgot most of the time how old the ghostly teen truly was, but to have a stranger see the boy and pinpoint his age was beyond startling. It was impossible.

And when anyone achieves the impossible, it means something is out of place and very, very wrong.

No matter how much his eyes made her toes curl.

She lifted the rod higher. "Who are you?"

The man cocked his head. "Would you like to know who I am or what I want?" His voice was a far cry from the pitch of the dead. It was raw, confident, and strong.

Focus, Claire.

She cleared her throat. "Both. So I know what to tell the police." He held up a hand as though to silence her. The movement sent a thin stream of anger throughout her body. No one was in charge of whether or not she chose to speak, let alone some strange man on her balcony.

Even if his voice helped her headache the way the bottom of the bottle tried to do.

"There is no need to get your guards involved." Claire and Henry exchanged a bewildered glance but waited for the man to continue. "I am Michael, Guardian of The

Beyond. And I would like to enter your home." He placed both hands in his pockets again as if his answer settled the matter.

In a way, it did. It confirmed what Claire had already known.

The gorgeous man outside her apartment window was a lunatic, and under no circumstance may he be allowed in her apartment.

Slowly, she reached into her own jean pockets for her phone, only to find it empty. She groaned.

The pier. The attack. Her phone had been lost at sea. There was no way to contact for help. Pinpricks of fear tingled the tips of her fingers and spread up her arms and down her spine. She fought against a motley of panic and indecision.

There are only two exits, and one is blocked. If I scream, he'll break in before anyone can hear me and get help. He can see Henry; what else can he do?

The final thought worried her the most. Her breath shallow, she maintained a steady pace moving away from the window, ready to turn and sprint down the steps into the storefront and out into the populated streets.

"How can you see him?" She pointed toward Henry, who stared at the intruder as though he'd just told him he was his long-lost uncle. The man turned to Henry.

"I recognize every lost soul who chooses not to enter The Beyond. Much like the Caretaker who nearly took you before your time," Michael said, and bowed his head slightly. Henry sucked in his cheeks and Claire winced. Henry disliked being reminded of his choice to stay on Earth after his death. But that wasn't what gave her pause.

"Caretaker?" she asked. "Explain. Or else I'm going to scream, and my husband will come up and blast you back to this supposed 'Beyond.'" She raised the rod and squeezed her grip tighter, readying herself to strike. *But maybe don't hit his face*, a small voice in her head said, but she shoved it away.

Michael shook his head, and threads of gold in his brown hair caught the light. Claire cursed herself for noticing. His eyes trailed from the rod in her hands down to her bare feet and up again. He locked his gaze with hers. "It's nice to meet another who has some fight in them. I'm sure we'll work together well." Claire tried to ignore the spread of heat rising in her face as Michael continued. "However, I know that you have no consort. Aside from yourself and the old man, there is no one else in your home. Lies don't suit you well, but that's fine; it makes you easier to trust."

Henry muttered something about being called an "old man." Caught in her lie, Claire waited for Michael to answer her question.

Michael sighed, rubbing the back of his neck. "I am referring to the demonic entity who tried to consume you in the water had I not come to your aid. A 'thank you' is typically customary, but given the shock, I've chosen to forgive you." It was his turn to pause, his face clearly indicating that she had been rude.

The pieces of fragmented memories clicked together as she held his cerulean gaze. His eyes were melted glaciers of cobalt, so different from the murky depths where she'd first seen them. These were the crystalline pools that saved her from death, and the warmth she had felt in his presence that night returned, briefly pulling her away from the present moment.

Henry cleared his throat, and Claire shook her head, embarrassed.

"Gee, thanks," she muttered. Still, she did not move.

He knew about the monster—the demon—from the pier. Slowly lowering the rod, her shoulders aching, Claire considered her options. This man certainly wasn't a safe option; anyone who could scare off something as evil as that *thing* in the water wasn't anyone to be trifled with. Furthermore, it was never a good idea to let a strange man into her apartment that she inhabited alone—something he also seemed to know, which did nothing to quell her worries.

Michael seemed to read her thoughts, and his eyes seemed to soften, the dark ocean blue softening to a twilight sky. "I'm not here to hurt you."

"How am I supposed to believe that?" she shot back. Claire realized she was being overly defensive. The exhaustion from the last couple of days was mounting. She steadied herself. "Sorry," she muttered.

Michael held her gaze and spoke as though choosing his words carefully. "I swear upon the Twelve Hallowed Caretakers of The Beyond and the all-knowing Superior that I will not hurt you."

Something in his voice hit a chord. The way he refused to look away, with no trace of deception or malice, seemed genuine. Besides, he'd be able to break in either way, so she might as well go out on her own terms.

Claire nodded and moved to unlatch the window. Henry sped over, passing through the coffee table and stepping before the window.

"What do you think you're doing?" he demanded.

"Letting him in."

She stuck her hands through his torso, grabbing the lock.

Henry tried to grab her hands, to no effect. She hesitated.

"Look," he said, his voice cracking from restrained trepidation, "I was joking earlier about the loose change in your head, but now I'm serious. Do you want to die? You live alone; no one would find your body for weeks. And you know you'd be stuck with me, right?"

Claire rolled her eyes. "No offense, Henry, but the last time I listened to you, I ended up thirty feet underwater. Besides, pretty sure I'm stuck with you, anyway." Henry pressed his lips into a thin line, stuffing his hands back into his pockets as Claire flipped the latch and opened the window. Henry strode to the opposite side of the room and leaned against the wall, tracking Michael's every movement as he climbed in the window with preternatural grace.

"Thank you," Michael bowed his head in gratitude. He walked past her, his steps confident and steady. As he passed, she caught a wave of scent like rich woodsmoke, like the cozy fires her parents used to build when they all went camping together.

Michael walked to the middle of the room and stood in place, surveying the loft. Claire closed the window but left the latch unlocked, just in case.

Claire gestured to one of the unoccupied chairs by the bookshelf. "Take a seat. Make yourself at home." She tried to sound in control of the situation, as though the request was a command.

Michael didn't seem to notice, instead trailing his hand along one of her bookshelves, picking up and examining several of her sketches. "My home is at the gates of The Beyond. This place is nothing like it."

"Well, okay then. You don't have to be a jerk about it." Claire kicked the curtain to the side and rested on the windowsill, her tailbone still aching from where she'd fallen.

Michael held up a calloused hand. "I meant no insult." He held up one of her drawings: a man waiting by a stoplight, California burrito in one hand and phone in the other. "This is very good; I see you are skilled in observation."

"Well, observe this," Claire ignored the compliment and tapped the iron rod against the palm of her hand, "you will tell me everything: who you are, what you're doing here, what the hell is going on. Then, if you're convincing, I'll let you go." She narrowed her eyes and sat up to her tallest height, attempting to be as intimidating as possible.

She saw Henry roll his eyes. Michael, unfazed, put the sketch back on the stack of papers.

"I am Michael, Guardian of—"

"You said that already. Move faster." Michael's forehead creased in annoyance for the first time, and Claire felt a small surge of victory.

Michael continued. "I am the Guardian of The Beyond, the entryway into Purgatory, the human in-between of Life and Death. Yesterday, we had a . . . breach." He spat out the last word with venom. Something orange and yellow flashed in his eyes and then disappeared; the color of turbulent seas returned.

"What do you mean by 'breach?'" Claire asked.

"Several demons have escaped."

Claire's stomach dropped, and he continued, pacing the room in agitation, his cloak nearly brushing the carpet. "I have yet to determine the cause, but the fact remains that our border has been broken, and our Caretakers have been let loose into your corporeal realm. You had the unfortunate opportunity to meet one of them last night."

From the corner of her eye, Claire saw Henry shift uncomfortably in his seat. She couldn't blame him; the underworld he had been avoiding for nearly a century had let loose a stream of its wardens. He was no longer safely tucked away in the corporeal space where their hands couldn't reach him.

They were here.

"What do you mean by 'Caretakers'? Do these beings belong in heaven? Or hell?" Claire prodded, knowing she'd never believe it if he told her those creatures were angels from the heavens. There was only one place they could have come from, and it wasn't from above.

Michael nodded his understanding. "Ah, yes, the human beliefs of 'heaven' and 'hell.' The good are rewarded, the bad punished. Is anyone ever truly and completely good? Are you, Clarissa Reed? Henry Faulken?" He went on, not expecting an answer. Claire only partially registered the use of their full names, though Henry shifted uncomfortably. There were more important questions to be asked.

Michael continued his story, now roaming the room's edges, examining the many piles of trash and discarded clothing. Claire felt a twinge of embarrassment and immediately ridiculed herself for feeling that way. She would *not* be made to feel embarrassed about her home by some strange man with a God complex.

"The fact remains that once you move on, it is decided how long you are to stay in Purgatory based on your life here in the earthly realms. Then, depending on the House in which you were born, you spend those years with your 'Caretaker.'"

Claire frowned. "And what do these Caretakers do?"

Michael's face grew grim, and he rubbed the back of his neck again. "They take care of you, so to speak. They provide discipline or reward, depending on your life in this realm. Once you have paid your dues, you move on past The Beyond."

Claire scoffed. "There's a 'Beyond' past The Beyond?"

Michael nodded his head. "It is where the Superior dwells. Do not ask me about it; it is far above the level of my responsibility. Unfortunately, the Caretakers have grown restless after years of servitude and leapt at the chance to escape. This calls for alarm, and their feeding has only just begun." A cold chill settled in the room.

Feeding?

"Right," Claire said, standing up. "I think that explains most of what is happening, and I'm going to believe you." Claire pointed the rod at Michael, who stood unaffected by the threat. He smiled, amused by her declaration. Her stomach gave a pathetic little flip.

"You cannot choose to believe facts," he said. "They do not disappear should you decide you wish it so."

She ignored his comment. "But none of this explains why you are here."

He bowed his head. "Correct. As Head Guardian, I must return the Caretakers to our realm to fulfill their duties to the Superior."

"Yes, yes, I get that." Claire waved away his words. "What I don't get is why you are *here*. With me. In my loft."

"Right. From the sounds of it, you're getting it all sorted out on your own." Henry interjected. Now that it was clear Michael wasn't—obviously—a serial killer preying on lonely, city-dwelling women, Henry had relaxed. He moved to an open chair and sat, eyes moving from his cuticles to Michael's face.

Michael turned to address him. "There is only so much I can do by my own hand. I can capture and contain the Caretakers; however, I need a Gateway. A human Gateway. One who has had a brief journey with death." He bowed his head once more toward Claire.

She gaped at him. He couldn't be serious. With each passing moment, she felt like she was the dupe in an elaborate and insidious prank. Soon, hordes of producers and camera operators would pop out of the closet, shoving lights and lenses into her face for the nation's entertainment.

She placed one hand on her hip, the rod dangling by her side. "I'm not sure I understand this. You're some supernatural being, and yet somehow, you cannot send these 'Caretakers' back without the help of a mortal? A human like me."

"You are no simple human," Michael replied, taking a step toward her. Claire matched his step, moving backwards, her heart quickening as he stepped closer. "You are a Gateway. You call upon the dead to speak." His eyes seemed to glow brighter with each word he spoke, like candlelit flames growing larger and hotter the longer he took Claire in. "You lost your life for several minutes in the waters last night, making you especially tuned to The Beyond. You are the tool I need to restore order."

Claire bristled as Michael breathed the word "tool" and crossed her arms, the rod wedged uncomfortably beneath her armpit. She wasn't something to be "used," especially when she hadn't been consulted in the first place. And though she hated to admit it to herself, Claire felt a pang of doubt; could she be of service? Or was she a dead end? Begrudgingly, she noted a weight of disappointment in the mere possibility of not being up for the task.

No, better not risk it.

"Well, I hate to tell you, but this Gateway," she said, gesturing to herself, "is closed for business and has been for some time. I can only call the dead; I can't send them back anywhere. Why do you think Henry is still around?"

"Because you enjoy my charming wit," Henry answered. She glowered at him, and he fell silent. Michael, meanwhile, was shaking his head, his eyes still aflame.

"You are not 'closed,' just untrained and unchallenged. We can change that."

Claire decided she had had enough condescension for one conversation. Claire pushed open the window and stepped away.

"Alright," she clapped her hands together, "time's up. It was a good try, but now you need to go. Best of luck with your demon hunting; I wish you all the best. Don't come back." No one moved for a few moments. Michael's eyes leveled with Claire's, and she bit her lip, forcing herself to keep his electric gaze.

After a moment, Michael turned away, walking over to the window. He made to climb out, the bottom of his trench coat swishing as it grazed the wooden ledge. With one foot on the windowsill, he turned back to Claire, nearly eye to eye. Claire fought the shiver that trickled down her spine.

"I will be back when you change your mind, Clarissa,"

In a spurt of bravery and impulsivity, Claire shoved him, and he jumped back from the window. He landed with feline grace in the alley below and looked up at her, a smile playing on his lips. She slammed the window shut.

chapter SIX

By the time the sun rose the next day, Claire was halfway convinced that the events over the last 48 hours were part of a fever dream.

Henry hadn't been back all night. After Michael had made his departure, Henry stayed for another hour, berating her. Eventually, he grew too frustrated and shouted at her. "How you survived longer than me, I'll never know!" He escaped into the night with an irritable huff. She hadn't seen him since.

If it were up to her, Claire would have spent the next few weeks inside the safety of her loft. However, as she peered into her cabinets, Claire saw only empty cereal boxes and slowly rotting apples. It seemed life wasn't going to let her stay perpetually indoors. She considered waiting longer to leave—it took at least three weeks to starve, after all—but more importantly, at least, to her sanity, the only drink left in the apartment was tap water.

She stood in front of the door for a long minute, deciding whether or not to leave. The mini-mart was gone, and the next closest location was at least a 20-minute sojourn there and back. The rumbling of her stomach and the needle pricks of her headache made the decision for her. Be fast— an in-and-out operation.

Maybe a literal In-and-Out if she found one on the way.

Jerking open the junk drawer, Claire sifted through broken pencils and expired coupons, eventually finding a pair of bright orange earplugs. She stuffed them in her ears, thinking longingly of the bulky headphones she had lost, but these would have to do. Claire grabbed a used Ziploc bag and stuffed it with salt in her pocket. Going through her list of missing items, she recognized that she would need to replace the headphones, phone, and groceries. She couldn't help but note how light and thin her wallet felt in her hands.

Nevertheless, the couple from the previous day had left in such a hurry that they didn't bother demanding their refund, so Claire added the large bills to the wallet, a bit of stress easing away, at least until the hospital bill came due.

Claire made her way down through the storefront and into the street, greeted by the scene of the wreck. The car was gone, and the rubble had been swept away, allowing others to use the streets for their weekly commutes. The front of the small grocery was gone. The counter inside was demolished, the shelves obliterated, and the merchandise had been removed. There was no one inside, living or dead.

Claire felt hopeful; perhaps no one had died in the accident. But even as she felt the bubble of optimism rise in her chest, she saw the dark stains on the concrete, a dried pond of red too large for anyone to survive. She paused and looked for any sign of a spirit lingering from the crash, but perhaps the victim had immediately chosen to move on to Michael's supposed "Beyond." As much as she fought against it, the thought of Michael sent a thread of electricity through her body. A small part of her hoped, against her better judgement, that she'd run into him again. He might have been halfway out of his mind, but he had a soothing, confident presence she hadn't felt since she left the force last year.

Claire craned her head to see if the silhouetted figures had returned to the top of the nearby concrete building. She found them blessedly empty, aside from a few crows appraising their dominion—a murder casing the site of a murder.

She walked down the street. The neon earplugs did little to block out sound and instead seemed to invite looks of bemusement. At one of the crosswalks, a woman walking her dogs stared at her for a prolonged period. Fed up, Claire stared back, saying, "I'm bleeding out of my ears. It's the only way to keep my brain in place."

Face reddening, the woman abandoned the crosswalk and strode away, her two little dogs yapping uncontrollably at every inanimate object they passed.

By the time Claire reached the store, she was ready to head home. While she met few apparitions on the way—primarily incoherent and mentally distant deceased folk—she couldn't help but feel wary, as though the lack of ghosts meant an enormous onslaught awaited her on the journey back. She entered a corner convenience store, the bell chiming as she entered. The attendant at the counter, a pimple-ridden teenager, continued stocking the back area without looking up.

She picked up a plastic red basket and walked through the aisles, grabbing assorted non-perishables, some overly ripe fruit, and a carton of eggs. She paused at the liquor aisle, thinking back to Henry's question. *"How much did you drink last night?"*

Perhaps she didn't need to grab any. It was a waste of money, and a year and a half ago, she was functioning perfectly fine with only an occasional glass of wine on the weekend.

But it *wasn't* a year ago. It was now, and she deserved some escape.

She headed down the aisle and selected a few cheap bottles. The basket grew heavy, and she continued to search until a voice popped up beside her.

"Claire? Long time no see!"

Claire turned and made eye contact with a man slightly shorter than herself. He bore a wide, bright smile and held a protein bar and a large water bottle. Her lungs ran out of room for breath.

She clutched the basket closer to her chest. "Officer Santos, what brings you here?"

He let out a laugh, and her stomach flipped. That sound was something she'd sorely missed hearing in the precinct. It was always the last thing she'd hear whenever she left for home and, later, the first sound she heard when she woke up. "We worked together for nearly three years; what happened to calling me Carlos?"

Her cheeks turned pink. "Sorry, Carlos. How are you?"

He brushed his fingers through his hair. She watched his hand catch on a dark lock and could almost feel the memory of its softness on her fingertips.

"Tired, but you know how it is," he said. "We had a major crash a few blocks from here. Really destructive." He eyed her basket, gaze lingering on the bottles, and dropped his hand to his hip. "But how are you? Doing okay?" He lifted his eyes to hers.

It all came flooding back, and the moment turned sour. He was the reason why she was stuck doing séances for profit; he was a fucking rat who took the wrong cheese and got her caught in the trap instead. How he could smile at her now, she couldn't understand.

She narrowed her eyes. "I'm fine, thanks. Just working."

"That's good! Doing what?"

"That car wreck was right outside my place." Claire dodged the question. With a basket full of liquor and convenience store groceries, she'd rather not have to explain her living situation.

His eyes widened, and he crushed the protein bar in his hand. "You were there? Did you see what happened?"

She shook her head. "Not really. I was working when I only heard the crash, but saw the aftermath. It seemed intense."

He nodded. "It was. We're trying to gather witnesses. The driver died on impact."

Claire looked away, feigning disinterest. She began to

walk past him toward the register, but he reached out, touching her shoulder. She flinched, and he quickly pulled his hand away.

He continued. "Hey, are you sure you didn't notice anything? Nothing strange or out of place?" Frowning, Claire scrutinized his face. He still smiled—the same Carlos smile he always had—but his eyes narrowed slightly at the corners, the grip on his hip tightening. There was something abnormal about the crash. She tilted her head.

"What's wrong, Carlos? What did you find?"

It was his turn to shake his head. "Sorry, I can't say. You're not exactly on the force anymore, no special privileges and all that. If you remember anything, you'll come to the station and let me know, right?"

Claire gave a short, tight nod, and his smile grew, though his eyes remained tense. "Take care of yourself, okay, Claire?" He extended an arm and gave her a clumsy side-hug.

As he turned away, Claire decided to throw a Hail Mary. "Did you find any arrow-like projectiles on the scene?"

He stopped and spun back to face her.

Touchdown.

"What did you see?" He took a step closer, his sudden ferocity surprising. Claire took a step back. *You need to learn when just to shut up and let things go,* she chided herself.

"Nothing. I mean, I don't really know what I saw. I may have seen something fly through the wreck, but I can't know that for certain, you know?"

He reached forward to grab her shoulder again, but she stepped out of his reach this time. Sheepishly, he returned his arm to his side, thumb hooked on his belt. "Sorry. Look,

I know it might be a bit uncomfortable given our . . . history, but would you be okay coming down to the station? Not for very long, only like an hour, tops."

Leaded rage thudded deep in her chest.

"Absolutely not." She was not about to step foot back in the place that had tossed her on her ass, even if they thought they were in the right. Granted, everyone always thinks they're in the right, especially when they're not.

Shoving her way past him, she strode to the counter, dropping the basket harder than intended on the counter. The teenage clerk gave her a bitter look, putting down his cell phone, and began to scan at a vengefully slow pace.

Carlos hurried after her.

"Claire, please. We found some things in the wreck that warrant further investigation, and no one else saw anything unusual. No one except you."

"I'm not going back there. Thanks, and screw you." Her anger was getting the better of her. She tried to count to ten in her head, but none of the words were coming to her.

Een, twee, drie . . . something . . .

"Look," Carlos tried to make eye contact with her, but she kept her eyes on the cashier. The boy thumbed through a ripped laminated manual for the smushed banana's item code. "I'm sorry. Really, I am," he said, his voice lowered. "But it's my job. When you were found after hours with the evidence, I did what I had to do. I wish I hadn't had to do it, but it was my duty. It's part of the job. You know that."

"You could have trusted me. I wasn't doing anything wrong." Her voice was steady, but she could feel it about to tremble, wanting to break. *Don't you dare start crying in a fucking bodega.*

Carlos nodded. "I hear you. I wish I could have made that choice, but you know I couldn't. Otherwise, I would have been let go, too."

Claire was too aware of his logic. He had said all of this before, and deep down, she knew he wasn't wrong. But that didn't necessarily make him right.

What *she* did wasn't wrong. She tried to get justice for that little girl's brother. It just so happened that the law didn't always guarantee justice, but there were other ways to get it. Except her way got her caught.

"Look, I didn't want to say this, but I know there is more to this investigation than a basic car crash. I know you've gathered that by now. If you don't come down to the station to talk, it will be an act of obstructing our investigation."

She could feel another flare of anger. "Are you threatening me, *Officer Santos?*"

"What? No!" He stumbled a step back like she had hit him—something she would have liked to do. "Of course not. I just know that you joined the force to help people, and even if you're not working there anymore, that's still the person you are. You want to help victims and people in need. That doesn't just go away."

Claire paid for her groceries, yanking the bags from the inattentive clerk who had already picked up his phone. "Maybe it does."

She left the store and headed back to her loft, Carlos tailing close behind her. Humming tunelessly to aid the flimsy earplugs, she lugged her groceries. The added weight slowed her, but she pushed herself to move faster, sweat trickling down her hairline. Soon, Carlos caught up and managed to grab her arm.

Spinning around, her paper bag snagged on a bike rack, and the bag burst open, the contents spilling onto the street. Claire forced down a cry of both rage and despair.

"Shit, I'm sorry. I didn't mean—"

"Shut up, Carlos. Just shut up," she grumbled.

She crawled on the ground, collecting the rolling and cracked items. The eggs had upturned; more than half were broken on the concrete. Sticky yellow yolks smeared the ground, little shards of eggshells littering the vicinity.

Carlos knelt to help pick up the bottles and boxes. "Hey, look, you don't need to come down to the precinct. Can you at least talk to me? We can talk at your place; we can discuss it here. Wherever. I'm sorry I brought it up." He sighed.

Claire didn't respond.

He grabbed her hand, and she looked up, nearly nose to nose with him. His eyes were warm, mirrors of melted honey, and she could see the beginnings of a thin mustache beneath his nose. They hadn't been this close since before the incident. She wasn't sure she wanted to be this close again. So, why wasn't she moving away?

"Claire," he whispered, "I should have trusted you. I do trust you. What I need now—what our victim needs now—is for you to trust *me*. Please."

Her breath hitched, the blood pounding in her head. "Carlos—"

A thin spear spun through the air, piercing Carlos's temple and exiting the other side.

He fell to the sidewalk, his eyes still open, and spoke no more.

chapter SEVEN

All thought ebbed away.

Claire couldn't pry her eyes from Carlos's body as he lay on the sidewalk, blood pooling beneath his head. She wanted to scream, to grab him, to shake him awake. She tried to run away as much as she wanted to stay and help him. Her body refused to move, to act.

It wasn't until she felt someone slam into her side that she found she could still move her legs. Claire tumbled into the gutter, several bicyclists swerving to avoid her. Looking up, she saw Michael, large and daunting above her, his coat billowing out behind him. Her heart skipped a beat as she took in his stance, strength and power emanating from his form as his eyes scanned the skyline for attack.

A *thwip* sounded in the air, and something long and narrow pierced the dirt where her head had been. It was an arrow, thin and silver, yet it didn't seem completely tangible. Its form oscillated slightly, wavering in her vision like a ghost. The next moment, it disappeared in a puff of smoke, carried away by the wind, leaving the scent of sulfur behind.

She looked past Michael above her and saw the same creature Claire had seen the previous day. Without the plumes of smoke from the wreck, she could properly take in its form, though what she saw made little sense.

The creature was purple, the color of a bruise, like the demon from the pier, but larger and more muscular. The top half of its body was that of a human, though its bare chest was soot-colored, its skin rough and calloused and scarred. Its jaw was square, its nose was narrow, and its long, straggly hair was pulled back to reveal bright yellow eyes surrounded by pulsating veins.

Where two human legs should have been, a powerful, equine body stood, one of its front hooves pawing the ground. That couldn't be right. But none of this was right: the creature, Michael, Carlos.

Carlos.

The thought jolted her, and she looked back to the body still lying in the walkway. People started noticing, and screams echoed off the brick buildings and alleyways.

Turning back to the creature, she saw it raise an ornate bow and arrow and point it directly at her. Her adrenaline spiked, and she rolled from the walkway just as another arrow whizzed past her face. She leaped to her feet as Michael lunged in front of her. A wave of heat blasted from his form, and the arrow deflected harmlessly to the side.

"Go! Now!" Michael commanded as Claire looked between Michael, the creature, and her dead ex-lover. As she gazed at Carlos, she could see the beginnings of the gossamer wisps drifting out of the wound in his skull. It creeped into the air toward the creature.

She lifted her hands to grab the floating strands of soul, but they were carried away by the wind. Claire imagined his memories of her—their first date, first fight, first exploration of each other's bodies during a summer night that turned into a month—were sailing away with his fractured soul.

Claire stepped toward Carlos, aiming to stem the flow of his splintering soul, but Michael shouted again and grabbed her by the shoulders. His jaw was tense, his eyes burning, oscillating blue and white light embers.

"What are you doing? Get out of here!"

There was a *swoosh*, a flash of flame, and Michael disappeared. Claire stumbled into a nearby brick doorway, searching the chaos for him. When she looked back up at the creature, Claire saw that Michael had joined it there, a glowing sword of bright white and blue flame in his hands, careening down at the beast. With a guttural roar that vibrated her core, the creature lifted its front legs, kicking at Michael, who disappeared and reappeared behind it in bursts of orange light. This was the fight she had seen atop the building, reprised once more.

More shouts, more cries. Claire turned and saw a crowd had gathered around Carlos, unaware of the battle raging above them. A young man crouched by his neck to see if he was still breathing, but Claire already knew the answer.

The soul had stopped seeping from Carlos's body.

He was gone.

Claire launched herself out of the doorway and onto the street, fighting tears and terror. Cars squealed and pedestrians yelled, but she ignored them, tearing through the roadways back to her apartment. She shoved her way past a busker, the man yelling at her as she nearly upturned his hat of loose change. Her lungs heaved painfully; she hadn't run this much since high school, and the cool air burned at her throat.

A young woman with a sliced torso reached out to her at one of the crosswalks, but Claire sprinted through her outstretched arm. Another apparition, its lower half missing, army-crawled and grasped at her ankles, but she leaped over its hands and continued to sprint, her eyes stinging with cold and salty tears.

The visions of Carlos dead on the ground and the yellow-eyed beast kept her running until she made it back to the apartment. Nearly dropping the keys, she unlocked the door and tripped inside, knocking the bag of salt from its perch, the contents spilling onto the floor.

Cursing, she locked the door and pushed as much salt as possible along the window ledges and doorways. Would salt work on these demons? What had Michael called them? *Caretakers?*

The last thing she wanted was one of those creatures caring for her.

Numbly, she sprinted up the stairs and slammed the studio door shut. Leaning her back against the door, she slid to the floor, wheezing.

She had almost died for the second time in two days.

Carlos was dead.

Hugging her legs, she pressed her forehead into her knees and cried, releasing the burning, grief-filled pressure from behind her eyes.

A surge of heat filled the room. "You are safe now."

Claire lifted her head too fast, the back of her skull banging painfully against the door. Michael crouched in front of her, his suit and coat still unwrinkled. He looked utterly placid. When he blinked, she briefly registered how long his lashes were as they brushed the tops of his cheekbones.

Claire sniffed. "I guess it's safe to say salt doesn't work on you."

"No." The corner of his mouth twitched, but he gave no further explanation. Claire fought another bout of tears.

"You're wrong. I'm not safe now. No one is."

Michael shrugged. "Safety is relative. For the time being, you are not at risk of being killed."

Claire let out a choked, unamused laugh. "Well, that's a relief. Rather than being killed now, I'll just die tomorrow." Claire returned her forehead to her knees.

"You won't die tomorrow."

"You don't know that." Her voice was muffled as she spoke into her bent legs.

"Perhaps not. I do, however, know that it is unlikely. At least, it will be unlikely if you choose your next steps wisely." She felt a hand rest on her knee, warmer than it should have been, like a furnace. For a moment, she felt a kernel of comfort, then at once pushed it away. She didn't want to feel comfort. She wanted to scream, to run, to fight.

Wiping the snot running from her nose onto the back of her hand, Claire stood up and walked to the closet. Michael watched silently as she pulled out a shoebox and tossed the lid on the nearby table. Rummaging through, she pulled out a picture and thrust it at Michael. He took it and peered down. It was a snapshot of her and Carlos together, his arm slung over her shoulders, exactly as he had done nearly an hour ago.

An hour before he was killed.

"Did he not choose his steps wisely?" she croaked. "Is that why he's dead?" Claire's voice quavered as Michael investigated the picture.

Killed. Dead. Murdered. Claire shook the thoughts out of her head and snatched the picture back, placing it gingerly back in the box.

"I am sorry about your colleague," Michael said. His voice was low, softer than she would have expected.

"He was a friend," Claire corrected.

"I am sorry about your colleague and friend," Michael corrected. He walked over to the window and looked out over the city streets. "People die every day, but it is not every day that someone close to you chooses to exit into The Beyond."

"He didn't *choose* to die! Your friend killed him!" Something tensed in Michael's shoulders, but Claire didn't care. *Good; feel a fraction of the pain I'm feeling.*

"Sagittarius is no friend of mine." His voice was like steel.

This caught Claire off guard. After a beat, she moved a stack of envelopes off a nearby chair and sat down, wiping her eyes on her shoulder.

"What did you call it?" she said quietly.

Michael responded, still facing away. "Sagittarius is one of the Caretakers who chose to take leave from its duties to the Superior. It killed your friend."

"Sagittarius? You mean—hold on." Claire left the room and returned from her office with *The Coast News*. Opening to the third page, she handed it to Michael, who peered at the headline: "DAILY HOROSCOPE."

"'People are lining up for your ideas. Keep an open mind.'" Michael read, his eyebrows raised. "The Caretaker did not say this."

Claire made a noise, a mix of amusement and annoyance. "No shit. It's probably the editor's son who smokes too much weed and can't hold down an actual job. But," she pointed at the paper in his hands, "is that what you're referring to?"

Michael shook his head, placing the paper on the counter. "I speak of the true Caretakers, the genuine leaders of the Houses through which you humans entered and exited this world. Not this make-believe drivel."

Claire stared down at the horoscope page, left face-up on the table, feeling nostalgic distaste on her tongue. She was an amateur when it came to astrology, much to her mother's disappointment. Most parents would be proud of their child earning a job with the police force, even as a sketch artist, but no. Claire could still hear the staticky disapproval of her mother over the phone. *"You could be stopping crimes before they happen, Cece! Come back home, we'll do a sage bath, and let's rethink things. Venus is much too close to Mercury for you to be deciding this, especially being in the tenth house!"* By that point, Claire had hung up. Her mother had spent a fair amount of time providing astrological-based readings in her small apothecary.

"When will I find love?"

"Should I quit my job?"

Claire had grown up listening to these predictions, and even as a child, she found them false and shallow.

Returning to the present with Michael, she asked, "So, this is an entirely different thing altogether? Not astrology?"

"It's astrology in its authentic, original form, before it was diluted to meet the desires and profit of human society." Michael walked along the walls, noting her shelves, glancing at the window occasionally as though expecting something to appear.

Finally, he turned back to Claire, reaching into his coat and pulling out a small book. "Perhaps this may help clarify some of your questions." He extended the book out to Claire, but as she reached to grab it, he pulled it away, just out of her reach, his face suddenly serious. "This is one of the last of its kind. It was given to me when I was first given my place as guardian of The Beyond. Treat it with care." His eyes darted around the room, and Claire could feel his gaze jumping from pile to pile of disordered paraphernalia.

She pursed her lips. "Understood," she mumbled.

Appeased for the moment, he handed her the leather-bound manuscript. It looked ancient and priceless, the edges of the pages uneven and jagged from years of use. His fingers brushed hers, leaving a delicate ember trail along her hand. His eyes met hers briefly before he turned away.

Claire held the book carefully, reading the title inscribed on the front in elaborate lettering: "The Guardian's Tome."

Gingerly, she opened it, and the smell of ancient parchment flooded her senses, bringing back memories of old texts and journals her parents had kept in boxes, hidden in the back of their mobile home. While those may have been fifty years old at the most, this journal was much, much older. She could see why Michael was concerned about damaging the artifact; each time she turned the page, she felt like the pages would fall like dead leaves from a branch. As crucial as Michael claimed she was, Claire was sure he wouldn't be pleased with her if she were the reason the book fell apart. *Like my life*, she thought bitterly.

She gave Michael another glance before reading the first page.

The Beginnings 1:1

Some sayeth the world did doth not trickle down from the heavens; rather, it festered and expanded upward from below.

Others claim yond Creation could have only formed wherever the light could touch, and the creations themselves tunneled downward, drawn to the peace of the abyss.

Nay one entity knoweth how the Superior came to be, though one may say He was born from rumor: whispers of how He was created through the culmination of stardust from trillions of different celestial bodies; mutters yond He was formed through the blood and dirt and bone of the living in a lawless time; ruminations He was never created, only ever Was.

No matter the ideation, it was clear the world in its current form required leadership, and hence, the Caretakers did doth cometh from a place of necessity.

While the world of the living was a land of chaos, there was structure, boundaries by which to liveth. The realm of the dead was flooded with lost, directionless echoes, crowding their ignorant breathing counterparts. Those who took each breath for granted passed through hordes of screaming, wailing apparitions—their future brethren—during each moment of their waking lives.

And as every setting sun took more souls under its extinguishing light, the plight of the dead did groweth at a cataclysmic rate, an exponentially rising crisis.

For some time, the living were unaffected sentient items on a century-long conveyor belt, eventually deposited into the same corpse-ridden fate.

Yet, like toads cooked in vats of boiling water, it doth seemed as though a single beat of a heart passed, and the world was changed: cold as the bodies stacked as adjacent logs under the earth's surface; fog thick and constant, wet and depressing; the cries of the dead seeping into the subconscious of each individual trying desperately to live their temporary lives.

To be alive was to be dead, and to be dead was to travel down an eternal, nauseating spiral.

And so, the Superior, empathetic to the plight of His creations, shaped a transitionary dominion for the dead: The Beyond. There, they left their living realm and were given a place to liveth again in their transcending state.

Humankind, however, is merely children, and children are in want of guidance.

As such, the Superior brought forth the Twelve Caretakers to watch over the dead, to provide guidance, chastisement, and direction to their given faction. Humans were to be divided by birth, given to the Caretaker that presided over the celestial skies during their emergence into the world.

Fearful of the Beyond becoming a deadened wasteland as the human realm once was, the Superior decreed that the Caretakers *determine when each of their wards was ready to move past the Beyond and into the next chapter of their existence.*

It is with faith in the Superior yond that the Caretakers take their jobs as valuable as the lives in which they were bestowed, and thus, the layers of the universe continue to be maintained.

C laire stopped reading and slowly closed the book, leaning against a nearby wall. She squeezed her eyes shut, pinching the bridge of her nose, little dots of color swirling behind her lids. Ignorance was bliss; she no longer had the privilege of entertaining it.

Curiosity killed the cat, and now I'm dealing with its fucking ghost, she thought.

"Clarissa Reed," Michael said, gently taking the book out of her hands and placing it back in his pocket. Claire eyed him wearily. "Sagittarius has marked you; I am certain there will be others. You are the Gateway I need to send them back to their posts. This must be done before more blood of the innocent is shed."

Claire's mind trailed back to Carlos. Already, the memory of his laugh was being eclipsed by visions of his lifeless eyes upon the pavement.

She remembered what he said, that she cared about helping others. Was that true? Maybe it once was, before her untimely exit from the force. But now? She held seances for people trying to wheel and deal with their dead relatives and friends. Did she still care?

I'm not that far gone, am I?

Clearing her throat, she stood up, Michael's gaze following her movement. Did his eyes trail along the curve of her hip? Surely she'd imagined that.

"I am going to take a shower. If you want to make yourself useful, you can find me some food if you can manage that."

Michael furrowed his eyebrows. "I am no courier."

"And I'm no Gateway, but it looks like I'm helping you anyway. Get ready to be disappointed." Turning on her heels, she walked into the bathroom, leaving Michael in her wake.

C laire crouched, sobbing silently in the hot water for close to an hour, before making her way out of the bathroom and back into the living room. Pulling a plain gray tank top over her head and sporting a pair of ripped jeans, she tied her hair into a messy red bun as she went, uncaring that it gave the world a full view of her exhausted, raccoon eyes and the darkening bruise on her cheek. She stopped short upon seeing her kitchen counter, momentarily forgetting her fatigue.

Mounds of food littered the surface. There were bright fruits and vegetables, packets of pasta and loaves of bread, and packages of cheeses and meats. Michael stood in the same spot she'd left him, sifting through the Tome as though he'd never left.

"You got all that?"

She would have cringed at the awe and desire that

flooded her voice, but seeing an actual meal was too distracting. Claire strode over to the piles, plucking a green grape from its bunch and popping it in her mouth. The sweet liquid burst, coating her tongue, and she closed her eyes in ecstasy. She couldn't remember the last time she ate something so fresh.

Michael cleared his throat, and she looked at him. "People require food to operate at their fullest potential," Michael explained as though giving a scientific lecture or the world's most boring TED talk. "This is what you wanted, is it not?" For a moment, he sounded unsure.

Claire laughed, the smell of fresh food and excess adrenaline making her feel giddy. "You could say that. How did you pay for all of this?" She picked up a dirty knife from the sink and sliced a thick chunk of cheese, savoring it as she chewed. Dairy was not typical in her house as a child. *"Veganism allows you to be more in tune with the natural forces of the world, and nature will reward you,"* as her mother would say—but her father used to sneak her pints of ice cream from time to time.

"Our little secret, Cece," he would say with a wink, and she'd return the gesture.

"Pay?" Michael asked, placing the book back in his pocket.

"Well, yeah. Where did you get all this? This must have cost a fortune."

"My duty is payment for all of mankind."

Claire stopped chewing and stared at him incredulously. "So, you stole it."

"No. My duty is payment for—"

"Yes, I heard that. Michael, you can't just take things." He opened his mouth, likely to give yet another lecture about service and responsibility, but Claire interrupted him. "You're not in The Beyond or whatever anymore. You're on Earth. We live in a society; we have to pay for things."

Michael nodded slowly. "I understand. I will take these all back."

Claire's jaw dropped. "Umm, no. I mean, from now on." Claire sucked in her cheeks and took in the feast before her. She hadn't had this much food in years, let alone of this quality. What's done was done, anyway. She shrugged internally.

Placing a slice of salami on a buttery cracker, Claire's question spilled from her. "So, if Sagittarius is the one shooting people with arrows, who attacked me at the pier?"

"Pisces. It seems it has claimed its new territory."

The cracker turned dry in her mouth. "But people swim in the water every day. They're all going to be killed."

"Not necessarily. Our Caretakers are precise; they choose selectively. It may find new prey daily or take its prey once a month. No one can know for sure."

"No one? Are you sure? Aren't you supposed to be one of the All-Knowing?" Claire thought she saw a small smile but decided it was a trick of the light. His stubbled face was as nonplussed as ever.

"Only the Superior is all-knowing."

"And who is that? God?"

"God, Allah, Yahweh, Zeus, Superior. They are all the same."

Claire opened a bottle of distilled water and drank a long draft. "So, what's God like? I mean, the Superior," she amended.

Michael shrugged. "I don't know. No one except those who have passed through Purgatory has met the Superior. My role is to stay at the precipice, the transit point between life and death."

"Wait," Claire paused, the lip of the bottle stopping halfway to her mouth, "you're working for some all-knowing being you've never met? How do you even know the Superior is real?"

"How do you humans believe your God is real?"

Claire bit her lip. Faith hadn't been at the forefront of her mind for most of her life. Despite knowing the existence of the spiritual realm, it did little to convey revelations as to what would happen after the dead decided to move on. What little she believed in faith had left her when she was twelve.

She changed the subject. "How do we capture Sagittarius? What exactly does it want?"

"Of that, I am unsure. Its motives could be merely hunger and feeding, but as a Caretaker, I suspect it wants something more. Despite what you may think, the Caretakers are more than just predators searching for their next meal. They must feed, but they are intelligent beings. To capture Sagittarius, we need to know where it plans to go and what it plans to do."

Claire nodded as he spoke, watching as he paced the room, hands in his pockets, his head slightly hunched. For a being who held immeasurable power, he looked incredibly human. *And handsome.*

Ignoring her blush, Claire prodded, "I would have thought you'd know everything there is to know about these things, being from the same place and all."

Michael shook his head, picking up a shining red apple to examine before placing it back on the stained counter. He gave her a wry smile. "They are invaluable to the Superior, and with that, I give them the respect they deserve. Otherwise, I've done my best to have as little to do with them as possible, much to my resignation. I should have known better than to allow my prejudices to get in the way of my duty." He spoke his last words bitterly, the smile disappearing.

Temporary excitement fading away, Claire grabbed some more aspirin and downed the last sips of water from the bottle. Michael watched the movement as she swallowed and he stepped forward, reaching his hand to her face.

"What are you—" she started, but her voice broke away. His thumb traced the edge of her cheek, caressing the small bruise under her eye. His skin pressed against hers, but instead of solid flesh, she felt an intangibility in his touch, like being stroked by an open flame that did not harm her. Unconsciously, she leaned into his hand, but as soon as she bent forward, his hand was gone. She stumbled, taking a quick step forward to catch her balance.

"Is that better?" he asked. Claire frowned and reached a hand to touch her cheek, feeling the residual warmth of his thumb and noticing that the pain of the bruise had disappeared. Picking up a nearby glass, she looked into her reflection and saw her skin as pale and freckled as ever.

"How did you do that?" She asked. Her voice

cracked, and her face flushed slightly.

"One of my duties as guardian is to heal the souls of the dead as they enter The Beyond. I can only do so much for the living, but even small acts of healing are better than none," he smiled, eyes kind and warm.

Claire swallowed, looking around the room, anywhere other than his gaze. "Well, thank you."

Get a grip, Claire. One guy touches you in a year, and you fall apart? Pathetic.

She walked over to the corner of the room, grabbed her iron rod and keys, and reinserted the orange earplugs into her ears. "Okay, if we need to figure out what this Caretaker wants, we must go to an expert."

Michael nodded. "Yes. What do you believe Sagittarius desires?" he asked.

She snorted, stuffing the Ziploc bag of salt into her jeans pocket. "Me? How would I know? I might know the basics, but I'm not an expert in astrology. But I know someone who might be able to help us." Claire gestured toward the steps leading out of the loft. "We're going to give Madame Courtney a visit. And you better damn well keep your eyes open. I don't want to be attacked again today."

chapter EIGHT

T hey waited for the train, aptly dubbed *The Coaster* for its proximity to the beach. The station was empty at midday. Early commuters were still at work, clicking away at their nine-to-fives, and it wasn't late enough for them to be heading home to their delivered dinners and streaming services.

It became clear that while no one seemed to be able to see the Caretakers, Michael invariably drew attention and did little to make himself less conspicuous. His large frame, cloaked in the heavy beige duster, was easily visible and drew stares. A group of girls in tiny tank tops and yoga pants eyed Michael as Claire waited to pay for their tickets. The tallest of the girls drank from a hydro flask covered in SoCal vinyl stickers, purposely spilling a stream of water on her chest. Michael took no notice and instead complained about the lack of transit.

"Why would anyone take such slow, inflexible transport to arrive merely *near* their chosen destination?" he asked the middle-aged woman at the counter, his voice carrying along the platform and earning a few curious glances. The girl with the Hydro Flask stalked away with her friends, disappointed.

"Well, you can always walk if you don't like it." The woman extended the tickets, her eyes half-closed with apathy. Working the booth downtown required a level of "thank you" and "fuck you" energy Claire felt she could balance, and this woman seemed tenured in the art of customer service. The lady snapped a gum bubble between her teeth.

"That would be equivalent to an eight-hour journey. How is that efficient?" Michael had replied, ignoring her blatant sarcasm.

Claire quickly thanked the woman who stared pointedly at her orange earplugs and said, "I can see why you'd want to wear those, given your present company." Claire nodded in agreement and noted the little ram trinket on the woman's desk: Aries. Figured.

Claire tried to give her an apologetic glance as she pushed him toward the train. They entered the car, and she forced him to sit down in a seat before he could start purporting the benefits of instantaneous travel, something Claire had to remind him humans could not do. He immediately stood back up.

"I prefer to stand; it is easier to spot an attack from this perspective."

"No one is on this train, and no one stands unless they absolutely have to. Sit down." She grabbed the back of his duster and pulled him onto the bench beside her. Her grip was not nearly strong enough to move him, but her insistence convinced him to sit down with little argument. His hip almost touched her own, and Claire felt a small thrill through her annoyance.

"If this bothers you, you could always do your little teleportation trick and bring me along," she said.

Michael sat back upright, both palms bracing his knees. He spoke without looking at her, instead allowing his gaze to roam the cabin. "I cannot take any living creature with me. If I were to try, you would likely suffocate or be completely compressed. Your veins would be unable to take the pressure, exploding the capillaries and bursting your carotid artery, the metacarpal bones crushing under the weight—"

"Yeah, I prefer the Coaster," Claire interrupted. She peered at the map lining the wall across from her seat. It detailed the next several stops to the 101 and approximate arrival times.

"We've got a little under an hour, so make yourself comfortable."

Claire rested her head on the window, hugging one of her knees and glancing around the seating area. From what she could tell, only the living populated the train. Aside from the money she saved from not buying gas or car insurance, one benefit of taking the Coaster was the lack of the deceased. If the Coaster happened to move through an apparition that hung around the tracks, the cabin traveled too fast for the dead to register. It seemed that most people didn't die on the train—that was reserved for outside on the tracks themselves. Satisfied that the dead were nowhere near, Claire closed her eyes, trusting Michael to keep a lookout.

"Tell me about your work with the guard."

She opened her eyes. Michael had addressed her without looking at her, still sweeping the area.

"The guard? You mean the police?"

"Yes."

"We're not going to talk about that."

"Why not?"

Claire released hold of her leg, allowing her foot to plunk back to the floor.

"Because it's irrelevant, and I don't want to discuss it." She stopped for a moment, thinking back to their earlier interactions. "I don't remember ever talking to you about that."

"You spoke to Officer Santos about it before his passing." Her eyebrows shot up.

"You were listening? Were you spying on us?"

"How else am I to keep my Gateway safe?" Michael stopped looking around the cabin and settled his eyes on hers. She crossed her arms, partly because she felt her privacy had been violated. And partly because she found, to her annoyance, that she was comforted by the fact he'd been nearby.

"That's incredibly uncool of you," she forced out.

Michael frowned. "I don't see how this has anything to do with temperature."

"No, Michael, it's—nevermind." Claire rested her forehead against the window, the glass cool against her skin. The train's vibrations traveled from her hairline through her jaw. "Carlos and I worked together, and then we didn't. End of story."

She stood up and walked across the aisle, choosing

to sit alone. Michael followed and sat beside her.

"It is safer if we sit together," he said simply.

Claire gritted her teeth in response. The Coaster hummed along the tracks, the view of the ocean through the windows. The sights that may have once brought contentment now unleashed a furl of unease in Claire's chest. Where was Pisces now? Sagittarius? The others?

"How many of the Caretakers escaped?" Claire asked.

Michael paused, counting. "If I am correct, at least seven. The others chose to remain in The Beyond and continue their duties."

Claire bit her lip. "Which ones?" Michael looked away, and Claire arched her head to look at his face. A slight tinge of pink filled his face, and Claire took a guess. "You don't know, do you?"

Michael sighed and leaned back in his seat, face raised to the ceiling. "I know of Sagittarius and Pisces. I have it on good authority that Aries and Capricorn have left through the Pit as well. And then, of course, Gemini." At this, he glowered.

"How can you not know who has escaped? Didn't you check?" Claire asked. Michael ran a hand through his hair, and Claire muttered, "Sorry."

He angled his head down and smiled, his shoulders loosening. He stretched an arm over her headrest, pulling himself closer to her. She caught the nostalgic aroma of campfire again and suppressed a shiver. "Do not apologize, Clarissa. You are correct; I should know who left and who remains. I was there when the turmoil erupted at the Gate.

You must understand the chaos that reigned, the scattering of the souls, the onslaught of the Caretakers. And I could not take account of those who stayed," his voice lowered, "because I am not allowed within the walls of The Beyond."

Claire frowned. A small knot of pity tightened in her stomach as she watched this man, this guardian of the dead, fall into an uncomfortable silence.

"Why not?" She knew she was pushing it; it was clear he felt ashamed by his moment of vulnerability, but she felt the itch of curiosity and couldn't help it.

Michael, however, decided it was time for a change in subject.

"What caused you to leave the force?"

Claire narrowed her eyes and considered pursuing her question. She stopped short at how he looked anywhere but at her and sighed. "There was a piece of evidence that shouldn't have been in a locker, and I was trying to do the right thing and get rid of it."

"How would you know that?" he asked. She was pleased to see he was no longer avoiding her gaze and instead looking directly at her.

Claire drew a deep breath, readying herself, and settled into her seat. As she spoke, she almost felt the carpeted seat beneath her morph into the hard, metal chair in the interrogation room, the AC on blast drying out her throat and stinging her eyes. She never wanted to be back there.

"There was a girl who was killed in a house fire. It was a tragic accident, or it seemed like it at the time. Police later discovered that the fire was set on purpose, and evidence pointed to the older brother. It made sense; he'd gotten kicked out of the house at eighteen and hung with the wrong crowd—the works.

"A few officers I worked with found an empty gasoline canister in the rubble, so they put it with all the other evidence. The team hadn't yet dusted for prints, but they were sure they'd find the brother's fingerprints all over it.

"That's when the dead girl came to me. I could barely see her face; the skin had melted clean off, but I knew it was her. She begged me to get rid of the container. She said it was a plant and he was being framed by some people he'd double-crossed. I don't know—she seemed so desperate and genuine with her concern. She loved her brother so much." Claire shifted in her seat, arms hugging her stomach, as though holding herself tight enough would keep the guilt locked away, like the brother eventually was.

"I'm not sure what came over me. I was just the station's sketch artist then; I didn't book criminals or catch them. I just drew their faces, listened to descriptions from the living—and sometimes dead—victims. I shouldn't have done it, but she just kept asking and *asking*. The girl was just so insistent, I couldn't ignore her." Claire kept her head bowed, letting go of her stomach and rubbing her temples with her index fingers. Michael stayed silent, listening intently.

"Carlos caught me in there. I hadn't done anything yet, not really. I had just picked up the bag when he came in and saw me. And what was I supposed to tell him? A ghost told me her brother was being framed?" She laughed humorlessly.

"Carlos wasn't wrong in getting me suspended. There was an investigation, and though no harm was really done, they couldn't keep me around. The trust was gone. And so was I." *And so was the one thing I did well*, she added to herself. Sketching hadn't been the same since she left. She had tried to recapture that feeling, watching people from her loft window, sketching random passersby with their bikes and phones and godawful crocs, but the passion was gone, replaced with bitterness for the dead.

She ended her story abruptly, staring unseeingly out the window.

For the rest of the ride, neither spoke. Michael continued to scan the cabin as the Coaster made its stops, people filtering in and out.

Eventually, he stood up and offered his hand. Claire hesitated, then grabbed it, hoisting herself onto her feet. She expected them to be thick and calloused, but was surprised to find them warm and soft. Michael looked down at her, his lips slightly parted as he decided what to say. His gaze trailed from her eyes to her lips. Claire noted gold flecks dotting his blue eyes and thought painfully about the last time she was eye-to-eye with Carlos. And his unseeing gaze as he lay in the pool of his blood.

Finally, Michael cleared his throat and spoke. "We must get off this transport before we miss our stop." He let go of her hand and walked off the train. A little deflated, Claire followed him onto the platform.

The sky was overcast in Encinitas, though that never stopped the beach-goer crowds from visiting. Claire noted several apparitions on the far side of the sandstone cliffside wearing wetsuits, some missing parts of their limbs, and others with broken surfboard straps around their ankles.

Before they could notice her arrival, Claire pulled Michael alongside her and began walking north. She wasn't pleased to be so close to the water after what had happened earlier that week, but she figured keeping her feet firmly planted on land would keep her safe. Still, she kept Michael on her left side, acting as a barrier to the water. Just in case.

It was a short walk down the 101 to reach "Madame Courtney's Astrological Readings." The storefront was snug in between a vintage vinyl shop and a seafood restaurant, both with smiling customers filing in and out in abundance, locals and tourists alike. Occasionally, the Coaster would rumble past, shaking the storefront windows that hadn't changed since the '60s.

As Michael and Claire walked toward the entryway, the doors flew open, and several young women stepped out, speaking excitedly to each other. A large, tan-skinned man with dark purple eyeshadow and precisely lined lips ushered them out, speaking in a deep, velvety voice.

"Yes, yes, girls. I look forward to seeing you again next week. And Jess, remember to stay away from large concert venues; the chaos and noise won't do you any good this week."

One of the girls, Jess, pouted. "But I'm supposed to see Pearl Jam on Friday with Mark!"

Madame Courtney clicked his tongue and waved a finger. "And what did I tell you about Mark? That boy is no good for you; your signs are just too incompatible."

Jess's friend snickered. "That's what you get for dating a Gemini."

Jess shoved her friend with an elbow but laughed

good-naturedly. Both girls thanked Madame Courtney and slunk away, chittering in fast, low voices.

Madame Courtney turned and noticed Claire for the first time. Clapping his hands together, he rushed forward, picking Claire up in a tight embrace.

"Clarissa, darling! What a surprise! It's not every day you catch me unaware of your visitation. I should have known; the moon is settled into the eleventh house, but I thought that might have been Lloyd demanding the rent early. Rat of a man, but you already know that." He gave a deep, booming laugh and placed her back on the ground. Claire couldn't help but smile as she bent forward, rubbing her ribs and doing her best to restart her breathing.

"And who is this tall glass of fine?" Madame Courtney looked Michael over, one hand on his hip, rubbing his thumb and index finger together with the other.

Before Michael could respond—likely to detail how "fine" was merely a concept and not a drink—Claire answered. "This is Michael. He's from out of town and visiting for a little while." Michael tried to speak again, but Claire tightly squeezed his arm in warning. Now was not the time to be candid. At least, not outside.

Madame Courtney extended his hand, palm down, his fingers ending in long, ornately painted fingernails. "An absolute pleasure. It's about time I met one of Claire's relatives. Or lovers." He winked, and Michael looked puzzled, ignoring his hand and choosing to bow instead. Madame Courtney frowned.

"He's a family friend." Claire's face turned pink under her freckles. Madame Courtney *tsked* and pulled his hand away.

"Well, that's too bad, Clarissa. For you, too, my dear Michael. Clarissa is quite the catch. And I can tell you two Scorpios would be explosive together." Claire sucked in her cheeks; Madame Courtney had an enigmatic way of noting her clientele's signs. But before she could confirm with Michael if it were true, Madame Courtney laughed and said, "But do come in; I just finished a session." Without waiting, he turned on his heels and reentered the store.

The lobby was small and crowded; dozens of dangling quartz and amethyst hung from metal tree sculptures. Oriental tapestries stretched across the walls, and plush chairs were scattered beneath. They passed through into the backroom where they sat at a table like the one Claire used for her seances. Their services both relied on a similar, dramatic aesthetic, though Madame Courtney preferred to be heavy-handed with his theatrics.

Claire had met Madame Courtney several years ago when she first moved to San Diego. Her mother had spoken highly of Madame Courtney and insisted that she visit him the moment the train stopped in Encinitas. Claire had no desire to meet any of her mother's friends—the few she'd seen over the years had varied between claiming her freckles were a mark from the devil to trying to get her to buy a motley of strong-smelling essential oils to protect her from the fae folk. Nevertheless, she needed a place to stay until she found an apartment, and Madame Courtney had been her only lead. It was a bonus that he had some considerable sway in the community.

Madame Courtney closed the door and sat across

from them at the table, his presence taking up most of the room. Michael took up most of the rest. Claire felt grateful she wasn't claustrophobic.

"How did the two of you cross paths?" Michael asked politely, taking a seat across the table. Madame Courtney raised an eyebrow and eyed Claire reproachfully.

"You didn't tell him?" he said.

Claire shrugged. "It never came up."

Madame Courtney winked at Michael. "How do you think she got such a deal on her place downtown?"

Michael looked at Claire, clearly not understanding. She clarified. "I met Courtney when I first moved to San Diego, and she convinced the shop owners to rent me both levels in the building."

Madame Courtney rubbed his hands together, moving a deck of tarot cards to another table as he cleaned up. "A lovely couple; I had the unfortunate opportunity to read the stars and tell them of their mother's passing."

Michael leaned in. "You can predict deaths? Are you a Seer? A teller of fortunes?"

Madame Courtney waved his hand nonchalantly. "No one can predict death. I prefer to say I predict concepts and abstractions. It should all be taken with a grain of salt." It sounded like something he'd repeated many times, a legal catchall recited ad nauseum for his clientele. Michael sat back, contemplating what Madame Courtney had said.

Claire took advantage of his silence. "Courtney, we need to ask you some questions. They're going to seem a little . . . strange, I guess."

"We all have our reasons. It is not my place to judge

your questions, and you are not to judge my responses. Too harshly, anyway." He turned and pulled out a file, placing it in his lap. From there, he fished out a chart and dropped it in the center of the table. From what Claire could tell, it was a map of the stars, with various planets and their orbits outlined throughout the sky. The map was split into twelve sections, each representing the key astrological houses.

"I have been looking forward to this day for a long time, Clarissa! I knew you'd come around eventually." He began to turn and reach for her hand.

Claire rolled her eyes. "No, Courtney, I'm not asking you to read my astrological sign." Madame Courtney frowned, then turned to Michael.

"How about you, Michael? Shall I read yours?"

"I was born in a time when *signs* had not yet existed."

Madame Courtney turned back to Claire with a raised brow. "Where did you find this guy?"

Claire winced apologetically. "Um, he's the son of a friend of my mother's."

Courtney raised an eyebrow, clearly unconvinced, but said, "I see. You're lucky you're cute." He narrowed his eyes at Michael as though he'd say more, but instead sighed and addressed Claire. "Alright then. Ask away."

"Okay, I need to know about a particular sign." She glanced around furtively before adding, "Sagittarius."

Madame Courtney's eyes lit up, and he smiled widely, revealing a gold tooth. "Ah! The Jupiter sign, our 'planet of expansion.' What would you like to know?"

"Um," Claire looked to Michael and back at Madame Courtney. "Everything?"

"Finally taking an interest and putting aside your childhood prejudices, aren't you? Let's see." In a flurry of efficient action, Madame Courtney moved various tiles around the star chart, indicating the different planets and moons that related to the current house of Sagittarius. To Claire, it seemed nonsensical, but she didn't dare interject. She needed this information, for once.

"Sagittarius, as you should know since it is your ninth house of philosophy," he said with a meaningful look at Claire, who cringed, "is based on the legendary Chiron, son of the Titans Cronus and Philyra. He is a centaur and archer extraordinaire. His archery prowess represents passion, strong will, and adventure." He adjusted tiles as he spoke, entranced by his own words. "Those born between November 22nd and December 21st will have a strong desire to travel, to explore our world and worlds beyond. Many of history's famous travelers were born under this sign.

"Flexible and adaptable, those in the House of Sagittarius yearn for knowledge to aid them in their journeys." Madame Courtney was getting into his story now, his eyes bright. "A fire element at heart, Sagittarius is a being of passion and *joie de vivre*. Something you could use a little bit of, mind you." Claire nodded, ignoring the jab.

"I'm guessing someone like that doesn't like sitting around home all day," Claire said.

Madame Courtney waved a hand. "Absolutely not, but take a look at yourself. Can you honestly tell me you're happy trapping yourself in that closet you call an apartment all the time?" Claire opened her mouth to argue, but Madame Courtney plowed onward.

"Being trapped is one of the worst nightmares an individual of this nature could think of. It goes against the very nature of their desire for expansion; they would be doing everything in their power to leave, whether literally breaking down walls to escape or at least biding their time to gather the knowledge they need to architect their departure."

Madame Courtney readjusted in his seat and added thoughtfully, "I do find it interesting that you're asking about this particular sign. I've noticed some strange vibrations over the last few days." He gazed off toward the far wall, his expression clouding.

"Vibrations?" Michael pulled himself out of his reverie. "What do you mean?"

"It is the time of Sagittarius, so this sign will naturally be stronger than its brethren. I noticed a surge of power twice in the last week, and Jupiter is also much brighter than normal. It's curious."

"Twice?" Claire asked. She shared a look with Michael. Carlos and the driver in the accident. Two deaths by Sagittarius's hand. An image of Carlos on the sidewalk forced its way back into her mind; she could feel hot tears threatening to betray her. Claire pinched her arm underneath the table, trying to keep herself distracted.

"Alright! I answered your questions; now it's my turn." Madame Courtney pulled out a new, thinly translucent chart and set it atop the current map.

"What's this?" Claire asked.

"This is your star map, my favorite Scorpio." Madame Courtney smiled, and Claire groaned.

Michael arched his head to view the map. "The

orbital lines and planet placements are different," he noted.

Madame Courtney nodded. "Yes, the pathways and alignments will differ depending on your star sign. I see this is all new to you, but I'm sure you'll hang on just fine." Claire stifled a laugh at Michael's affronted expression.

Madame Courtney continued, peering down at the chart. He didn't speak for several minutes, murmuring to himself, moving tiles around, and changing the angles of his chart. Finally, he looked up.

"It looks like you might have some turmoil coming your way, Sweetie. Avoid crowded areas of shared thought; it will only bring you knowledge you never wanted. And oh!" Madame Courtney shot her a sly smile and surreptitiously cocked his head toward Michael. "You have Venus in the fifth house this month; you'll *love* that."

Claire could feel Michael shift beside her, and out of the corner of her eye, she thought she saw the corner of his mouth lift.

Cheeks pink under her freckles, Claire pinched the bridge of her nose, "Are you done yet?" The last thing she wanted was for Madame Courtney to pry into her love life— or lack thereof—especially in present company.

Madame Courtney grabbed Claire's map and tucked it away again. "Yes, yes, there you have it, darling. Free of charge, of course, for my favorite Medium."

Claire grinned and pushed herself up from the table. "Thank you, Courtney. We really appreciate it."

Michael stood up and bowed, a fist across his chest. "We thank you for your assistance. Your service has been more vital than you may ever know." He turned around and left the room. Madame Courtney raised an eyebrow to Claire. She just shrugged.

"You know what? I kind of like him. It's nice to meet somebody who recognizes my worth." Madame Courtney gave Claire another lifting, breath-stealing hug before she left the shop.

As they walked back to the Coaster, Michael spoke. "We still need more information."

Claire turned to him in disbelief. "No shit, but it's a start. It's customary to say 'thank you' when someone helps you before you immediately move on." She grinned at him, throwing his words from the previous day back into his face.

He frowned. "I thanked your friend."

"I meant *me*," she said, kicking a pebble from her path.

He continued to walk in silence, and then stopped suddenly, Claire nearly bumping into him. Michael turned around and looked down, locking his eyes on Claire's, his hand resting on her shoulder.

"Thank you," he said after a beat.

Claire swallowed. "You're welcome."

More silence, though Claire could hear the rush of blood pumping in her ears, her heart beating faster.

"We *still* need more information," Michael continued, removing his hand from her shoulder and walking onward.

Claire couldn't help but roll her eyes. She walked

alongside him, still feeling the imprint of his palm on her shoulder.

"I'm well aware of that, thanks. What do you suggest?"

They stepped back on the Coaster as he answered. "Your friend Carlos had more information, did he not? About the attacks?"

Claire nodded slowly, the threat of tears reemerging. "Yes, but he wouldn't tell me. I'm not exactly on good terms with the SDPD." She sucked in her cheeks as though drinking something sour.

"I think he would tell you now, would he not?" Michael said.

His words hung in the air between them.

She stopped breathing and focused on the scenery in green and brown blurs. They passed the Cardiff Kook statue, dressed in the local high school's cross-country jersey, before she responded.

"You're not saying—"

"You could ask him," he interjected.

She shifted in her seat, still avoiding his gaze.

"I don't know if that's such a good idea."

"Why not?"

"I've never called anyone I actually knew before. I just . . . I don't know if I can handle seeing them not alive."

"You mean *dead*."

"Yes, I mean dead. You don't have to say it." Something in her stomach curdled at his words, and she wondered how someone who could show such softness could also be so callous.

The Coaster lurched to its first stop, and they braced themselves on the benches.

She didn't want to see Carlos. No, that wasn't true. She desperately wanted to see him, but not like this. She could imagine seeing his translucent form, the wound on both sides of his head. She felt shaky at the thought.

"We need his knowledge," Michael reiterated, more gently.

"And I need to think."

They sat without speaking as commuters filtered on and off the train. She watched absently as one of the attendants argued with a half-naked man carrying a skateboard. Her mind was elsewhere.

It was too much: the attacks, the deaths, the onslaught of information. Only this morning, Carlos was alive and well. She had yet even truly to process his passing, and now she was supposed to call him? To see him as an apparition?

His words echoed in her mind. *You joined the force to help people, and that doesn't just go away.*

He was always right. She supposed that didn't change in death.

"Not today," she said to Michael, who watched her intently. "Tomorrow."

He opened his mouth as if to argue, but taking in her expression, snapped his mouth shut, and they continued their journey back to the loft in silence.

chapter NINE

Claire was still not entirely convinced that calling Carlos back from the dead would be a good use of their time, nor did she truly feel up to seeing him again. Still, Michael was true to his word and left for the evening to allow her to "rest," something he did not need.

When she asked him where he was going, he said he needed to reinforce the city's perimeters, though he did not elaborate on how he'd accomplish that. Before she could question him, he was gone in a blaze of light and heat.

Mind buzzing and a freshly poured drink in her hand, Claire fixed herself dinner from Michael's groceries and sat on the couch. For a moment, she simply stared at the piles of dirty clothes surrounding the room. She decided she wasn't hungry and set aside her plate. She wandered around the room, picking up various shirts, underwear, and socks and piling them by the door. She emptied the laundry basket she'd used for CD storage and filled it with dirty clothes instead.

She headed back to the kitchen and put the food

away. Turning to the sink, she scrubbed the mountain of dishes and felt a sense of catharsis. It had been at least a month since she had hunkered down and cleaned the apartment. Despite everything that had happened, or maybe because of it, she suddenly wanted to get her life in order. Very few people ever came to visit, apart from Henry, and she didn't care if he saw her in disarray. She ignored the realization, however, that she cared what *Michael* thought of her place.

Claire moved to her bed, tucking in the blankets and repositioning the pillows, when she heard a knock at the storefront below. Making a mental note to find a way to restuff her busted pillow, she placed it back on the bed and headed downstairs to see who would be trying to contact her this late in the day. The sun was nearly setting. Occasionally, someone would be desperate enough to speak with her that they'd stay at the front door, thudding their fists incessantly until she answered, no matter what time it was. Those visits, however, were few and far between, and even so, she would refuse to open the door for that sort. The desperate were dangerous.

She stopped short when she reached the foyer, wishing she had closed the curtains so no one could peer in and spot her. A short, stocky woman stood at the door, her hair tied in a tight bun on the top of her head, the rest slicked down, not a strand out of place. She wore a dark blue uniform with a golden badge prominently on her chest. Claire rubbed her eyes, a wave of exhaustion and stabbing pain emerging behind her eyes. *Of course, she'd show up.*

Claire hadn't spoken with her old commanding

officer since she was let go, and her appearance on her doorstep meant nothing good. Her ex-captain immediately locked eyes with her. The woman stoically pointed a terse finger at the lock and waited for Claire to open the door. Without waiting to be invited in, the woman pushed her way through and immediately walked up the stairs to the loft, her black boots leaving scuff marks on the wooden floor.

Grimacing, Claire locked the door behind her and followed, trying to quickly and subtly replace the salt lines the woman had smeared as she entered.

Upon setting foot into her loft, Claire saw that her visitor had already sat at the small table in her rickety wooden chair. She'd be irritated at the audacity of the intrusion, but Claire could see the woman's tongue rubbing against her teeth, a warning sign Claire knew from the interrogations she observed back in the day. Captain Elizabeth Núñez was readying to strike.

"Water from a bottle, unopened." No greeting. No niceties. The captain's voice was strong and commanding, rich tenor tones ringing throughout the room. Claire knew better than to decline or to shoot back a snarky retort.

Silently, she placed one of the bottles Michael had bought in front of the captain, who, after thoroughly examining the cap, decided it was safe to consume. She drank, finishing half the bottle in one go. She deliberately twisted the plastic cap back on the bottle before placing it on the table.

"Officer Santos died earlier today," Núñez said.

Claire had known this was the reason for the captain's appearance, but hearing it confirmed slammed her in the gut anyway. Dampness surged to her eyes, and she cleared her throat.

"I'm very sorry to hear that. Carlos was a good man." Her words came out in a pathetic squeak, and she cursed herself mentally for sounding weak. She tried to cover it up by leaning against the counter in pseudo-relaxation.

"Yes, as you know, Officer Santos was a decorated leader in the force. His loss is a blow to the entire community." She pulled out a notepad and pen from her shirt pocket. "I'm here to ask you some questions."

Claire nodded and moved to the adjacent couch. The captain flipped open the notebook and poised the pen's tip over the paper.

"Where were you at 10 a.m. this morning?"

Claire paused before answering, unsure how much she wanted to reveal. If the captain was here now, it must mean that she knew that Claire was involved somehow. So, she decided on the truth. Or most of it.

"I was at the convenience store on B Street. I ran into Carlos there."

The captain nodded, jotting something down in her notebook.

"What did you and Carlos talk about?"

Claire bit her lip, thinking back to their last conversation.

"Um, not a lot. I had to return to my office, but mainly pleasantries, I guess? How work was, things like that."

More notes.

"Are you aware of an accident across the street from your establishment?" Claire almost laughed, incredulous.

"You mean the one yesterday? Kind of hard to miss.

I heard the driver died; I'm sorry about that, too."

"Did Officer Santos tell you that?" *Crap.* It wasn't an important detail, not in the grand scheme of things, but Claire felt like she'd let something slip, something she should have kept to herself.

"Uh, I think so? He might have mentioned it. Honestly, I can't imagine the driver making it out alive from how the crash looked to me."

Núñez scribbled on her sheet.

"Tell me, Ms. Reed. Have you and Carlos spoken since your departure from the force?"

Claire shook her head and clasped her hands to stop them from shaking. "No, I haven't seen him in over a year. It's not like we wanted to stay close after what happened."

"Did you hate him for it?" The captain's eyes remained on her notebook.

Claire leaned back in alarm. "Hold on, are you accusing me of something?"

"Just answer the question, Ms. Reed. There's no need to get upset."

"My friend is dead; of course, I'm upset."

"I thought you said you weren't close." She lifted a gaze of ice to Claire.

Claire snapped her mouth shut. Why wouldn't she stop talking? She should have requested a lawyer to be present, and never let her enter her home. She decided to change tactics.

"Since when did the captain of the force go out interviewing people? Shouldn't you be in the office, delegating busy work?" So much for avoiding a snarky comment.

Núñez paused in her writing to shoot her a glare. The stocky woman hadn't lost her severity in the last year and a half. If anything, the glare felt sharper, honed in on her intended target. It used to be reserved for criminals. Now, it was for Claire. To Captain Núñez, they were the same.

"One of my officers was killed. This is personal."

Claire understood. If she'd been captain, she, too, would have led the charge against any witness or suspect.

Captain Núñez cleared her throat and returned to her notepad. "It seemed that Officer Santos and our driver, Jeffrey Davis, had something in common. Would you like to know what that is?"

Claire's heart rate picked up, but she remained silent.

The captain leaned forward. "You were in the vicinity of both deaths. Tell me, what were you doing yesterday around 1 p.m.?"

"I was working in my office. You can't seriously believe I'd be involved in either of these cases, do you?"

"You have a record, Ms. Reed."

"Claire. My name is Claire. You know this, *Elizabeth*."

Captain Núñez tightened her jaw.

"It's 'captain' to you, Ms. Reed."

A stab of sadness sliced the back of her throat. The woman in front of her was the reason she had gotten the job in the first place. They'd first spoken on the phone while Claire was still living in Arizona, several weeks after Claire had sent in her resume and a portfolio she had haphazardly thrown together. When she arrived for an in-person interview, Claire was enraptured by the strong, assertive woman who passionately discussed her duties in the force, and Elizabeth laughed at Claire's dry sense of humor. They made a formidable pair of friends between Claire's wit and Elizabeth's sharp tongue. It hurt to see how she now looked at Claire with such loathing and disgust.

"Ms. Reed," Núñez continued, regaining her composure, "you are not in any trouble, for the moment. I'm here to check in on witnesses to see if anything comes up. Any patterns, maybe clues." She peered around the room as though seeing it for the first time, and Claire felt a small wave of relief, glad she had tidied up, even slightly.

"What exactly is it that you do, Ms. Reed?"

Claire did her best to look confident and unashamed. "I'm a Medium. I conduct seances and speak to the dead for those who are grieving."

The captain snorted and wrote something down on her notepad before putting it away. "Still a criminal, I see."

Red flashed in Claire's vision, and she stood up. "I am not—and was not ever—a criminal. I was found not guilty at the end of the investigation, and I still devote my life to helping victims, something you no longer let me do on your goddamn team. I will not sit here as you come into my apartment and throw insults at me like I'm a fucking dartboard."

Claire strode over to the door and opened it, repressing a wince as she heard a *crunch* from the handle hitting the fragile drywall.

"Unless you have any other questions, I want you to leave. Have a good rest of your evening, and good luck with your investigation. I hope you catch the asshole that murdered my friend."

Núñez sat unmoving momentarily, as if trying to prove that she was leaving of her own accord and not because of Claire's indignation. Then, she headed down the stairs.

As she descended, she added, "I will need the names of the customers you were working with during the crash to check your alibi."

Claire barked their names at her as they crossed the storefront. As the captain opened the door to leave, she paused and turned back to Claire. "I told Carlos he could do better than you, and you know what? By the end, I'm sure he knew that."

Before Claire could respond, the captain stalked to her car and drove away.

W hat a bitch, if you don't mind me saying." Henry had returned, circling the office downstairs as Claire readied the table for her next séance.

"Actually, I do mind. I don't like that word," she said.

"Okay, she's a walking piece of human garbage, rotting refuse in an uncivilized society. If I rolled her eyes like a pair of dice, we'd get two snake eyes and a fistful of debt."

"Much better," Claire smirked.

Henry smiled. She had known Henry wouldn't be gone for long when he stormed out. Most of the time, after their more heated arguments, he would leave and stalk around his old boarding school where he had perished in his senior year before returning to her the next day, pretending he was doing her a favor by coming back. He might as well have been a stray cat; they had the same amount of pride.

"So," he said, examining his nails lazily, "you're going to call for Carlos's spirit? I'm finally going to meet ol' lover boy from romance past?" He cut his eyes to hers.

Claire tossed an unlit candle at him, and he chortled as it soared through his head.

"You know that doesn't do anything to me, right?"

"It's not for you. It makes *me* feel better," she huffed, thinking of her night of restless sleep. She'd woken up clutching the sheets into a tight ball of fabric, her cheeks wet with tears, her face jammed into the blankets as though she were trying to suffocate the pain in her head.

Lighting the candles and using her séance room wasn't necessary, but going through the familiar steps she used to appease her customers was mildly comforting.

"You ready to get the show rolling?" Henry asked.

Claire lit the final candle and sat down. "Not until Michael gets here."

Henry groaned and sat in the chair next to her.

"And he needs to be here for this because . . ."

"Because he needs the same information we do, and I'm not going to be repeating myself." *And his presence calms some part of me.*

"And because you need to show Carlos you've moved onto bigger, better things." Henry waggled his eyebrows at her.

He saw right through her, as always. Claire scrunched her nose at him. "I have a bag of salt in my pocket, and if you keep talking, I'm going to make you well-seasoned."

"Alright, alright, doll face," Henry moved one of his fingers through a flame, causing it to jump, "Well, I hope he'd hurry it up. Where else would he even have to be?"

"Scouting the perimeter of the city, if you're curious, my elderly young apparition," rumbled a deep voice.

Henry jumped and made a face as Michael appeared in the seat across the table. Henry crossed his arms accusingly while Claire felt a heat unrelated to the lit candles in their room.

"If you can just appear as desired, why did you bother knocking the other day?" Henry snapped.

"It's rude to enter without permission."

"And you think this is okay? Turning up like a bad penny in a jar of nickels?" Henry asked.

Claire shushed Henry, who fell into a begrudged silence. She turned to Michael, her heart beating a bit faster. She noticed his stubble was slightly darker than the day before and wondered absently if he ever needed to shave. Her mind then wandered to what his jaw would feel under her palm, stubble or not.

"Did you find anything?" she asked.

He shook his head. "No."

Claire and Henry looked at Michael, who stared back in silence, then at each other with raised eyebrows.

"Enlightening," she deadpanned. Henry snorted and found a seat on the other side of the table, adjusting his tie as he settled down.

Taking a deep, steady breath, she reached into her jeans pocket and pulled out Carlos's photo. Claire placed it on the table and gazed at his face for a beat before closing her eyes. She'd always loved that picture of him: the carefree smile, the relaxed arm over her shoulder, the bright California summer making his eyes glow like two miniature suns. She hoped she was about to see it again.

Claire closed her eyes, and the Gate appeared in her mind, steely and closed up tight. *Carlos Santos,* she called silently into the ether. *Can you hear me? We need to talk to you. Please, come to me.*

"Are you doing something? Nothing is happening." Henry murmured.

"Shut up!" she whisper-yelled and tried again.

Carlos Santos, this is Clarissa Reed, speaker of the dead. I'm calling for you. Please, come.

She opened her eyes only to see Michael and Henry waiting in anticipation.

"He has moved on," Michael said quietly. His eyes seemed sad as he looked at Claire, but she felt a second wind of defiance rise inside her.

"No, hold on. I got this." Claire closed her eyes again, squeezing them tightly against the tears that threatened. *Carlos! Talk to me!*

No answer.

A deep well of disappointment opened up in the pit of her stomach, a cavern of grief and pain. He was gone. Truly and completely gone.

"He was a brave man to move on so quickly. I wish him all the best this earthly realm and The Beyond can offer." Michael pressed a fist to his chest and bowed his head.

Claire held her head in her hands. "How can he be gone? You're *here*," she pointed at Michael, "aren't you the one letting them through?"

Michael placed his hands in his pockets. "There are others in my place as I am here dealing with the escaped. My compatriots must have let him through the Gate."

Claire said nothing, feeling hollow. Aside from being unable to see Carlos again, she was out of leads. The last person to know about the intricacies of the deaths—the last person who would be willing to talk to her about it—was long gone. Or at least, one of them was.

She felt a hand gently raise her chin. Claire looked into Michael's face, the stubble ever more apparent up close. "We'll find someone," he said, his breath warm on her cheeks. "There's going to be another chance, another spectator, another—"

A name popped into her head, and Claire gasped, pulling back slightly to collect her thoughts. She struggled to remember the name Captain Núñez had shared and sat up straighter.

"Jeffrey Davis," she muttered.

"Who?" Henry asked. His chin rested on his fist, the other fingers drumming the table in mock boredom.

Claire ignored him and closed her eyes once more. All she had was his name, but it would have to suffice. Envisioning the Gate, she called out. *Jeffrey Davis! This is Clarissa Reed, speaker of the dead. We need to converse with you. Please come at once.*

Only a moment later, Claire felt the energy in the room shift.

"Where am I?"

With a surge of satisfaction, Claire opened her eyes

to see a man in his late forties sporting slacks and a bloody shirt. The side of his head was badly scraped, but the most intriguing injuries were the small holes on both sides of his head, puncture wounds from a thin silver arrow.

Michael and Henry looked him up and down. Henry floated over to the picture Claire had placed in the middle of the tablecloth and examined the man in the image before looking at the new apparition in the room.

"That's not Carlos," Henry pointed out.

"And the circle gets the square," Claire said dryly. "This is Jeffrey Davis, Sagittarius's first kill."

Jeffrey took in the scene: the table, the candles, the three people circling the table. "Do I know you?" His voice made the inside of her ears itch in a way she couldn't quite scratch. She pushed past it.

"Your death is under investigation by the police. It seems that they believe you may have been the target of a murder. Do you believe your death was intentional?" Claire asked him.

She had expected Jeffrey to widen his eyes in alarm and place both hands on his head as though fighting against hyperventilation despite being unable to breathe. Yet, his voice seemed monotone, almost emotionless, like a part of him was missing.

In her mind's eye, Claire could see the milky substance of his soul draining from his body, consumed by the creature with the gaping abyss of a gullet.

"Murdered?" he asked, unsure what the word meant. He might as well have been questioning her about the weather. His eyes glossed over her and traveled around the room. Claire was unsure if he was taking anything in at all.

Michael crouched down to eye level with Jeffrey, eyebrows furrowed. "What makes you special, Jeffrey Davis?" Michael took the reins, and Claire gladly handed them over.

"Special?" He rubbed the back of his neck, his head tilting to the side as though moving in slow motion.

Henry jumped in. "What's wrong with this fella? I get he got hit in the head, but I've met enough regular Joes with half their brains missing that could understand just fine." He stood up, snapping his fingers in front of Jeffrey's face.

"Henry, knock it off," Claire chastised, but Jeffrey didn't notice. He stood and swayed like a vine in water, slow and constant.

"Sagittarius took a portion of his soul," Michael said, his eyes hard. "Some of his humanity has been lost. No one should ever have to suffer in this way." He took a deep breath and tried again. "What is it you did to benefit humanity?"

Jeffrey's eyes landed on Michael, but he said nothing.

Claire interjected. "He's asking what you do for work."

"Oh," Jeffrey said. "I helped plan . . . yes, I planned for the city. I planned . . . planned . . ." His voice was dreamy as it eventually trailed off.

Claire glanced at Michael, who was still frowning at Jeffrey. It is evident that Jeffrey had little more to share. Whatever Sagittarius had siphoned from him was lost to the Caretaker's hunger.

Claire wondered if Carlos would have been the same if she had contacted him. It was a tragedy to think these two skilled and competent people would be reduced to husks of what they once were. And with that thought, she knew the significance of the caretaker's selections.

"Sagittarius is gathering intelligence by devouring its victims," Claire burst out. She sat back in silence, thinking it over.

Henry looked at Claire and then Michael. "That's a bit of a leap, don't you think? I know you've said Carlos was a hell of a guy, but this poor sap doesn't seem to have much left in him."

Claire rolled her eyes. "He probably did before his mind was drained. Madame Courtney claims that Sagittarius values exploration and wisdom. It's feeding on victims with ties to the inner workings of the city. What I don't get though, is why this is the information it's looking for."

"I can answer that." Michael stood and strode to the window, looking toward the coast, though the city blocked the view. "None of the Caretakers can travel far from the Pit. They are chained, intangibly forced to remain close to the opening."

"The Pit?"

"The portal from which they escaped. It may have closed for the moment, but its presence lurks beneath the waves. It keeps the Caretakers in orbit near their entry point like a magnetic force. I imagine the more they feed, the stronger they get, the more easily they will be able to fight the pull, until eventually..."

Michael stopped, turning to Claire. He took out the Tome and opened it to a page in the middle of the massive book. He held it out to Claire, who accepted it, reading the page aloud.

The Beginnings 1:2

> *To be a Caretaker is to be both matriarchy and patriarchy, monarchy and oligarchy, guardian to their human wards.*
>
> *However, as the duties to their human charge require constant vigilance, a steady hand, and a consistent omniscient presence in their afterlives, it is vital that each Caretaker stay within their realm.*
>
> *As such, so shall The Beyond be sliced into twelve equal parts, one for each of the Caretakers and the lost souls of their realm. Here, they are the leaders of their terrain, their authority only surpassed by the Superior. They determine the fate of their charges, the consequences derived by the decisions in their lives, the rewards reaped by their actions, and the time it takes for their wards to move on.*
>
> *The Superior, however, knew the toll the responsibilities would take, and the Caretakers are not without fault—only the Superior may glean the precipices of perfection. As such, for the Caretakers to maintain their focus, it was determined that they may never leave their given kingdoms. They are not shackled, only compelled to remain, as is the desire and need of humanity.*
>
> *Should any attempt to shirk the duties as Caretakers of their human protégés, their consequences will be swift and severe, their ethereal forms pulled back into their given realms by The Beyond's intangible, indefinable, unbreakable chains.*
>
> *As are the duties of The Guardian.*

Claire stopped reading and looked at Michael, confused. "Wouldn't this mean they shouldn't have been able to escape?"

Michael nodded, eyebrows furrowed in restrained anger. "Yet, it has been done. We will discover how they succeeded in this feat, but we currently have greater issues at hand."

"And they're just going to keep killing," Henry whispered, racking a hand through his hair. His eyes were unfocused, lost in his thoughts, his imagination undoubtably weaving scenes of terror and carnage. Claire knew the living were in danger, but she hadn't considered the peril of the dead.

She was certain Henry was wondering the same.

Michael nodded. "Like a plague. Soon, Sagittarius will be strong enough to leave the city limits, along with the others, and gathering them back into The Beyond will be close to impossible."

Claire sucked in a shallow breath, imagining the demons traveling throughout the state, the country, and possibly the world, feeding to their hearts' content.

It would be cataclysmic, the beginning of the end of civilization.

"How long do we have?" she asked Michael.

He continued to look out toward the ocean as he answered.

"Not long enough."

c h a p t e r TEN

W ho would Sagittarius's next target be? They needed to create a list of people to identify, find, and protect. Henry and Michael sat with Claire in her loft, brainstorming. Doctors, architects, officers of the law, local politicians?

"Not much wisdom in those heads," Henry said.

Ignoring him, Claire paced the carpet. "There are too many of them in the city. Do you understand that downtown San Diego alone has nearly 40,000 citizens? And how do we know that Sagittarius hasn't already acquired enough knowledge to push its boundaries?" She absently twirled a pencil in her hands as she spoke. Michael leaned against the window, the afternoon sun limning his figure, rubbing his chin in thought.

"Sagittarius won't go for just any human doctor or official. It is looking for the gold standard of civilization within this city's limits, the paramount of intellect, philosophy, and wisdom contained in a single soul."

Henry gave a wheezing laugh. "Scraping the bottom of that barrel with a city planner," he snorted.

"Perhaps he had more information than we realize. As for the area it can travel," Michael said as he pulled a map from his duster pocket and laid it on the table, "with only two confirmed kills, it is improbable it is able to go any farther than these locations. I've been circling the county, and to my knowledge, this is the circumference Sagittarius can plausibly travel." He took the pencil out of Claire's hands—"Hey! Ask first!"—and drew a circle. Claire and Henry hovered over the map. Henry's forehead wrinkled.

"That's about a 15-mile radius," Claire noted.

Michael bowed his head in agreement. "Yes, the space Sagittarius can travel is minimal at best."

"Minimal?" Henry crowed. "It could be attacking anyone in what, 700 square miles?"

"At least we have a general area," Claire said. She turned back to Michael. "How are we to know who the 'gold standard of civilization' is? It's fairly subjective, I reckon."

"Not particularly," Michael said. He handed the pencil back to Claire. For a moment, she thought he held onto it longer than he needed as they both gripped it from either side, but he let go, and she disregarded the notion. "I'm sure you have a list of people whom you can find and contact, do you not?"

Claire looked toward the ceiling, exasperated. "Sure, let me get out the yellow pages and comb through the thousands of people nearby. Or maybe I could use my phone, if only I hadn't lost it when one of your Caretakers tried to drown me." She sat down, rubbing her eyes. Sleep had been elusive, and the hours she did happen to doze were fitful and filled with visions of demonic creatures. Michael and Henry stared at her.

She sighed, rubbing her temples. "I'm sorry. Okay, so we need a list of people who could be likely to be the next victims of an attack. I don't have a phone, and there's no computer in my apartment. So," she stood up, stretching her back, "I guess I'm taking a trip to the library."

"I have never seen you go to a library," Henry said as Claire pulled her shoes on.

"Well, I haven't had a reason to, have I? Closest one outside of downtown is Clairemont. I personally don't want to hang out here in the city if I can help it." She looked at Michael as she grabbed her earplugs. "Are you absolutely certain you can't just teleport me over? It would save me a lot of time."

"The risk is too great. Should your flesh become compressed, or your brain expand outside the surface of your skull—"

"I get it. I'll take a taxi." As she descended the steps, she called over her shoulder, "You two coming?"

Henry floated over. "Sure, I'll join you."

"Henry," Michael said, "I'd like you to join *me*." Henry raised his eyebrows.

"Me? Join you? For what?"

"I second that. Why?" Claire asked. Michael walked past her into the office, and Claire followed, trailed by Henry.

"I would like Henry to join me as I survey the area. His body is incorporeal and unlikely to be damaged in our travels. The information we gather will be useful for him in case I am indisposed." Claire turned to Henry, expecting him to decline, but was surprised he was considering it.

Since meeting Henry, she had never seen him prefer to stick around anyone living other than herself. Hearing him decide to go with Michael sowed an unexpected seed of jealousy.

And a little bit of envy for Henry.

Henry nodded, looking pleased. "Well, I guess I'll leave you to it, doll. I've got some surveying to do." He floated over to Michael and stood beside him. Without him by her side, Claire felt uneasy. She shifted back and forth on her feet, feeling the iron rod bounce against her hip in her bag.

"And you're just going to let me go? On my own? What happened to protecting your Gateway?"

Michael thought for a moment, then pulled out a small pocket watch, handing it to her. "Press the button to open this, and I will come to you." Claire brought the circular watch close to her face. It was pale gold, cool and smooth to the touch. Pressing a small button on the side, the top popped open, revealing an ornate watch face, its numbers in Roman numerals, the hands thin and fragile. It would be too difficult to read in a pinch.

"So, I just open it, and you'll come? Does it have a homing beacon?"

Michael cocked his head. "I do not understand that reference. This is one of my personal effects; I am connected to its form and will feel when it is being opened."

"You'll show up? You're sure?" She hated the

desperation in her voice.

Michael bent down, his face close to hers. Claire craned her neck backward to meet his gaze. "My word is my bond. I will always come for you."

Neither moved, like two statues, only a breath of space between them. Claire felt something vibrating inside of her, something she couldn't quite grasp. Michael made no sign of breaking his gaze.

Finally, she nodded and stepped away, placing the watch in her bag, the iron rod, and a small canister of salt she'd found in the back of the pantry. She hoped she wouldn't have to use it. Hope was a flimsy thing recently.

They left the store, and when Claire turned to the others to say goodbye, both Guardian and apparition had vanished. "Perfect," she sighed.

It took her close to thirty minutes to hail a cab. Most cities used apps or car services, but without a phone, she had to resort to searching, waving, and begging. Claire nestled into her seat, enjoying a brief moment of solitude without Henry's snark and Michael's insistent gaze. A moment where the world wasn't ending, just her sitting and looking forward to an afternoon at the library.

"Got a bit of a plan going, do you?"

Claire looked up at the driver.

"Yeah, just heading to the library for some research," she replied.

"What's that?" the man said, his voice deeper than the one she had heard. Claire cocked her head to the side.

"Sorry, I thought you said something."

He grunted and continued merging onto the freeway.

"We're up here, love. You know how We hate being ignored." A sudden stillness arrested her heart, and her eyes landed on the review mirror. The top half of the driver's face was reflected, but rather than his eyes on the road, he was staring at her, pupils large and black, most of his irises blotted out. She plunged her hand into her pocket for Michael's watch.

The voice in the mirror *tsked* and narrowed its eyes. "We're just here to chat, don't you worry. There's no need to signal your knight in ethereal armor now."

Claire paused and waited for the voice to continue. When it was clear that the reflection was waiting for her response, she spoke low so the driver wouldn't hear.

"Who are you?"

"Who am I? Who are *We*, you mean? You know who We are. We are everyone and yet We are no one. We are your soul, personality, and essence, yet We are opposed to you all the same."

The reflection in the rearview mirror disappeared and reappeared in the window beside her. She could see her entire face—her own complexion and features—fixed with the same contorted, exaggerated smile she had seen back in the hospital and on the bus. *Gemini.* The reflection brushed a strand of wavy red hair out of its eyes and tucked it behind her—*its* ear.

"That's not an answer," Claire whispered. The reflection rolled its eyes.

"It's not the answer you *want*, but it is the answer we gave. So, tell me, Clarissa Reed, how goes your plan to capture and send us back to the grand Beyond? Hmm?"

Claire swallowed. "How do you know my name?"

The reflection laughed, her stolen voice amplified, cold and piercing. "We told you! We are you, we are everyone, we are ourselves. That is the wrong question to be asking."

"What is the right question?" Claire asked.

Her reflection tapped its nose. "A good inquiry at last! Clarissa Reed, do you not wonder why Michael chose *you* as his Gateway? Why did he not choose any of the other talented mediums in the area?" This thought had briefly occurred to Claire, but she'd shrugged it off.

"He said I've been marked. I don't need to explain any of this to you."

The reflection wagged its finger at Claire, clicking its tongue.

"So he says. Yet, he chooses a young woman who only knows how to Call but not to Send? A broken Gateway. Dear Michael is no fool, so We ask again, why did he pick you?"

"Do you already know? Or are you really asking me?"

The reflection smiled widely, revealing a bottomless, dark pit behind its teeth.

"Do you actually want to know?" it drawled.

Before she could respond, the car jerked to a stop, and she fell forward, nearly hitting her head on the back of the driver's seat.

"I'm sorry about that; some damn PT cruiser cut me off. This is why most people shouldn't be allowed to drive," the driver muttered.

Claire looked back to her reflection, and it stared back. Gemini was gone.

Claire fingered the watch in her pocket, wondering if she should summon Michael, then thought better of it. She would tell him about the visitation when she returned to the apartment. Maybe.

Something told her to keep it to herself—some kernel of doubt. Michael was still a stranger, someone she barely knew. A bit of suspicion and caution was wise. Why *did* Michael pick her, the "broken Gateway?" She wasn't truly broken, but she was untrained. So, why her?

"Alright, we're here. That'll be $23.50."

Paying the fee was painful, knowing that what little money she'd made over the last few days was dwindling fast.

"Is there any way you could come back in two hours? I don't have a phone, and I'm not sure I'll be able to grab a cab here." The man glanced at his phone, his schedule glowing on the screen.

"Yeah, I suppose. But if you're late, I'm doubling your fee."

She agreed, making a mental note to be outside early. She turned and entered the library.

It was how she remembered every library she had ever visited: spacious, quiet, and comforting. The smell of books filtered through the open floors above, and she could see a few librarians pushing carts filled with novels through the stacks. A mural along one side of the building displayed a rainbow sprouting from an opened book, mythical creatures and fantasy characters smiling and parading about, and above: "If you can dream it, you can read it!"

Most of the books her mother kept at home were reference guides of incantations, tarot manuals, or aura readings. Her father used to bring her novels and poetry books from the different towns he visited during his travels. If only this trip were for enjoyment, too.

She stood for a moment, lost in memory and the tranquility, then walked briskly to the open computers. Cracking her knuckles, she logged into the computer and set to work.

As she was sifting through a list of professors at local universities, she felt a light tap on her shoulder. Looking up, she faced a young woman, college-aged at most, her hair a severe bob just above her shoulders. She pushed up her thick-rimmed glasses and smiled.

"Hi! Library not quiet enough for you?" The girl's voice was in a forced whisper, her eyes resting on Claire's ears.

"What? Oh, right. Forgot I had these in." Claire pulled out the earplugs and placed them in her bag, surreptitiously looking around for any lurking spirits nearby. The girl continued to smile.

"That's alright. Do you need help with anything?"

"No, I think I'm alright. Thank you, though."

The girl didn't leave. Instead, she bent low, looking at her screen. Claire felt the urge to hide her searches, though from an outside perspective, her tabs were perfectly innocuous.

"Going to UCSD?" she asked.

"Hmm? Uh, no. Well, maybe. I'm thinking about applying," Claire lied. To Claire's dismay, the girl pulled out a chair and sat next to her.

"I used to go there! Great school, excellent computer science programs. What are you studying?"

"Er … social sciences."

"Really? That's wonderful. The humanities are truly underrated, you know. Are you going to the seminar they're holding next weekend?"

Claire's ears perked up. "What seminar?"

The girl grinned and leaned over, taking Claire's mouse and clicking on one of the event links. From the corner of her eye, Claire saw a small tattoo on her collar bone: crab claws, the Cancer zodiac. The girl noticed Claire's gaze and grinned.

"You like it? Got it when I was 17 to make my mom angry, which really isn't a 'Cancer' thing to do, but," she shrugged. Then the girl tapped her tattoo lovingly and clicked a link on the screen.

A program flyer appeared on the screen, detailing an upcoming event.

"Dr. Richard Stevenson and Dr. Rahmed Vishwanath to lead a seminar on the California ecosystems and how their biospheres were affected by California's urban development," the girl read aloud. She stood up straight; even at her full height, she was barely taller than Claire sitting down.

Claire recognized the second name from her search. "Dr. Vishwanath? He's a big deal, isn't he?"

The girl giggled, pushing her glasses up her nose again. "I guess you could say that. Frankly, he—"

"Ms. Lo! Are you helping this young woman or are you socializing?" An older woman with greying hair shuffled over, one hand on her waist, the other on an empty cart. The girl's face remained unfazed.

"Helping, Mrs. Gertrude. Jamie here asked for help researching her university, and I showed her how the site worked."

Jamie? The old woman let out a quick breath of frustration and addressed Claire.

"If you need any assistance, please feel free to call for me. You don't need to work with the felon."

At this, the girl's face burned a light shade of pink, and the woman walked away. Claire raised an eyebrow.

"Felon?" she said. It seemed wildly unlikely.

"Sorry, I didn't know your name, and I panicked. I'm Maisy." She stuck out a hand, which Claire shook.

"Claire. Felon?" she repeated.

Maisy shrugged one of her shoulders and rolled her eyes.

"Mrs. Gertrude exaggerates. Volunteering here is part of my community service. Not everyone is completely onboard with the rehabilitation process."

She motioned to the cranky old woman shuffling away with the cart.

"What'd you do?" Claire asked and immediately regretted it. Maisy bit her lip and looked away. "Sorry, that was too personal. Forget it."

"No, it's okay," she sighed. "It's just a little embarrassing. One of my professors wasn't completely impartial with the grading—everyone knew it, not just me—so, I found some personal information on his hard drive and let him know."

"You blackmailed him?" Claire was mildly impressed.

"It's not blackmail if he doesn't fully encrypt his passwords and uses public Wi-Fi," she quickly added.

"I don't think that's how that works, Maisy."

She gave a one-shoulder shrug again. "To each their own, I suppose. Just know if you ever send any pictures or video you'd rather others, ah, not see, you're shit out of luck, because it doesn't take much for someone with a grudge and tech background to find them."

Claire leaned back in the flimsy computer chair, fully eyeing Maisy up and down. She certainly didn't carry herself like someone who'd hold a professor's personal life hostage. The girl smiled easily, her cheeks rounding like the chipmunks Claire would see dogs chasing at Balboa park. She played with the several earrings studding her ear, thin silver chains swinging slightly, before pushing her glasses back up the bridge of her nose.

If this girl was a felon, then Claire considered herself the devil.

"Tech background, huh? Were you close to graduating?" Claire asked.

Maisy shook her head and sighed, hopping onto Claire's desk and swinging her legs. "Only made it about two years in. But my dad was an electrical engineer for years, and I grew up watching him mess with timing paths, IR drops, the works. He'd be working on the floor planning in his office and quiz me on the best size, power, and performance optimization. You know, typical father-daughter bonding time."

"Yeah, I wouldn't know about that," Claire muttered. Maisy paused, opened her mouth to speak, and then changed her mind, choosing to jump down from the desk.

"Well, hey, I'll be here for the next," she counted wordlessly on her fingers, "seven weeks if you need anything: school, tech, killing time." She winked. "I don't get many college-aged people around here, usually just older folks or young kids doing book reports."

Claire nodded. "I'll keep that in mind. And thanks again for showing me this." She gestured to the seminar still on her screen. "It'll be helpful."

Maisy—already smiling widely—seemed to brighten more. "Glad I could help! I'd go, too, but I'm not welcome back on campus yet. Maybe ever." Claire barked out a loud laugh, and Mrs. Gertrude shushed her from across the room. Maisy turned and stuck out her tongue. Mrs. Gertrude recoiled, eyes flashing.

"I better get back to work. You take care of yourself, Jamie."

"Claire."

"Ah, yes," Maisy tapped her temple, "I'll remember that." She shoved her glasses up her nose again, then turned and left.

Claire printed out the digital flyer and dashed to the front of the library to meet the cab driver before he asked triple his price. She felt a surge of adrenaline; she may have found Sagittarius's next feeding.

chapter ELEVEN

O n her way back to the apartment, the odious (yet punctual) cabbie pulled out a cigarette and took a deep pull. He let out a cloud of smoke that settled into the upholstery. Coughing, Claire opened a window.

"Windows stay closed, lady."

"Bite me," she spat back between wheezes, and he glared at her through the rearview mirror before returning his gaze to the road.

As San Diego whizzed by the windows, Claire read through the flyer Maisy had shown her, the edges fluttering in the wind. Both doctors had PhDs in the environmental sciences and had spent much of their time analyzing the biosphere of the western coast. Most of what she read went over her head, but she knew a lot of university students and other guests would attend the event. This would be the perfect vat of knowledge for a demon to feed on, desperate to break free from the chains of Purgatory.

As they drove closer to the Gaslamp, the car slowed to a stop. Ahead of them, a long line of red brake lights extended down the street toward them.

"What's going on?" Claire asked, sticking her head out the window to see the commotion.

The driver blotted out his cigarette in his empty paper coffee cup. "Some sort of holdup. Probably some idiot ran out of gas in the middle of the road, or someone hit an e-bike. Maybe we'll finally get the regulations we need against those things." He sounded almost hopeful at the idea that someone might have gotten hit if it meant the motorized bikes would be banned.

Claire considered how each minute in this cab equaled another dollar on her tab. She recognized the area; she was less than a mile from her loft. She'd gone on foot much further than this. She thanked the driver, privately hoping never to see him again, and handed him some cash. Dodging several pedestrians and apparitions on the sidewalk, she headed steadily down the street before taking a right and nearly walking directly into a translucent man.

She cringed and took a step backward. She clutched the bag over her shoulder and reached inside, curling her fingers around the iron rod she'd packed.

"Help me, please," he moaned, his voice hoarse. A trail of intangible saliva dribbled in a thin, lacy line out of the corner of his mouth in a long, unbroken string. She tried to pretend she didn't see him and walked around, but the man in the dark-stained overalls had seen her panicked expression. He knew she saw him.

"I know you can see me. Please, you have to help me. It's been so long; I can't remember where I am. My name . . . what is my name? Why am I still here? Why are you walking away? Stop!"

She sped up, lengthening her stride. This was a generational apparition, one who'd denied moving on for so long that his knowledge of self was gone. He was confused and afraid, like so many she'd encountered before. She knew his desperation made him dangerous, and a prickle of fear ebbed in her chest.

"I told you to stop!" His voice grew louder and harsher, an otherworldly reverb tinting his words.

She told herself to go faster and keep moving, still clutching the iron rod in her bag. She turned left down an alley, the apparition hot on her heels. Halfway down, she spun, her red hair whipping her cheeks. She ripped the pipe out of her bag and slashed through the man with a cry she felt she'd been bottling up for the last few days, maybe months. With a shriek of both fear and rage, she imagined striking down the monster that killed Carlos, resisting Captain Núñez 's advances, tearing away the guilt and anger and pain that pooled in the acidic depths of her mind.

"Leave me alone, damnit!" She bellowed

The apparition screamed, the sound echoing off the narrow brick walls and into her head as he burst into mist. Claire didn't know where spirits disappeared to when the iron rod separated their incorporeal form from the realm of the living. Perhaps she gave them a second death. The idea of murdering the already deceased did not sit well in her mind; she used the rod as sparingly as possible.

Panting from the exertion, she rolled her neck and hurried down the alleyway, her body still vibrating from the excess of emotion she'd tried to let go with her swing. Claire knew she'd acted more intensely than needed but couldn't find it in her to care.

Maybe I'll order a punching bag for the loft, she thought wearily as she turned another corner. She'd never gone this way before; it wasn't often she traveled on foot just outside the perimeter of the Gaslamp. Turning another corner to find her way back to the main street, she stopped short again when she saw a homeless person huddled on the ground, an enormous dog pawing the blankets atop him.

She paused, considering whether to turn around and go a different direction. While most of the unhoused she ran across in the city were docile, it was getting late and dark. The night bred savage thoughts, sometimes bleeding into savage action. She needed to get back to the apartment, and this was the fastest route.

Summoning up the last dregs of bravery, she walked down the damp alleyway toward the bundle of grimy blankets on the ground, eyes trained on the light of the main street beyond. *Don't make eye contact,* she reminded herself, a mantra she had developed upon first moving to the city. The last thing she needed was to be accosted by the living; she got enough of that from the dead, as it was. As she got closer, however, she noticed that the bundle wasn't moving.

And that enormous dog above the man wasn't a dog at all.

Her heart plunged, and she gaped in sheer terror at the form of Sagittarius leaning over its latest victim. An unnerving sucking noise came from the scene, its head bent low over the figure on the ground. It was wholly focused on its meal.

As slowly as she could, she moved backward. She stepped on a hamburger wrapper slick with grease, and as it slid out from under her foot, she stumbled, falling backward onto her hands. Sagittarius lifted its head at the sound and feasted its yellow eyes upon her.

From a distance, Sagittarius was terrifying.

Up close, it was horror incarnate.

Silvery drool dripped from its mouth. Its skin, which she initially thought was gray and purple, was a mottled pastel blue. Its head rose at least three feet above her own. His massive body blocked out the light of the moon. The fur on its hindquarters was matted, and the spotty hair on its head revealed dented and rotting portions of its skull. It held a silver bow in one of its hands, roughly half the size of its bearer. With its other hand, it lifted the lifeless victim by the neck as though he weighed nothing at all.

At that moment, she was its next target.

Claire planted her feet firmly into the ground. She should run, kick, scream, anything except be still, but she was frozen, her mind blank.

Sagittarius opened its mouth, and a voice of gravel and cavernous depth spilled from its putrid, blood-coated lips. Wisps of its victim's cracked soul slivered into his mouth and out of sight. "Human girl, what knowledge do you have for me?" It dropped its victim back onto the ground in a heap and wiped its mouth with the back of its chafed hands.

She didn't respond. Claire was unsure she could let out more than a whimper if she tried.

Sagittarius drew a deep breath through its nose, closing its eyes and swallowing a long line of saliva back into its mouth with a nauseating slurping sound. "You converse with the dead, young one. You have abilities that others do not possess. Not what I need," it sucked in more air through its teeth, "but satisfying nonetheless."

Claire slipped her hand into her pocket as it spoke, fishing for the watch.

Slowly, Sagittarius lifted a muscled arm to the leather quiver on its back and drew a long, silver arrow. The glint of moonlight on the deadly weapon sent a bolt of fear through her spine. Its arms were thick, muscular barrels that would seem challenging to move, let alone lift and aim an arrow with any precision. The arrow seemed solid, but it ebbed and flowed like fog. The Caretaker notched it in its bow and pointed it directly at her head.

"I must taste what you know."

Claire pressed the button in her pocket.

A bright burst of orange and yellow light illuminated the alley, and Sagittarius roared in surprise and anger. Flaming sword in hand, Michael ran forward, arcing the blade high above his head and swinging it down toward Sagittarius's neck.

Despite its size, Sagittarius was less than cumbersome. Lithe on its feet, Sagittarius leapt to the side, rearing on its hind legs and aiming its bow at Michael. Michael disappeared in a spiral of flame and reappeared throughout the alley, fighting from one angle to the next.

"This is my realm now, Guardian! Be gone from my presence," Sagittarius roared. Michael ducked low to the ground, sweeping his sword at its back legs.

He hit his mark. Black streams of liquid spilled from

the wound, and Sagittarius shrieked. Slinging the bow over its back, it tore down the alley, hoofbeats pounding the pavement out of sight.

The pounding echoes of its retreat quickly died away, and Claire rushed to Michael. He moved toward her, grasping his arm.

"You're hurt." Claire eyed the cut on his shoulder, oozing a dark black liquid.

"Cuts heal. Death does not," he said casually, looking her up and down. "More importantly, are you hurt?"

Claire flushed. "I wouldn't say 'more importantly.'"

A line creased down the center of Michael's forehead, and Claire felt a rush of heat as his eyes trailed over her body. "You are the Gateway; you cannot get injured. I won't allow it."

The heat left her body in an icy rush. His words stung as much as she knew they shouldn't.

Michael nudged her forward down the lane, away from the newest victim. Claire paused briefly by the body Sagittarius had dropped. She knelt, turning it over, searching for a pulse. It was a woman, her eyes milky white, a trickle of blood and wisps of silver leaking from the wound in her head. Bits of mud and sewage painted her neck and clothes. There were no signs of any defensive injuries.

"We need to leave," Michael said, placing the palm of his uninjured hand on her back. The blood in Claire's head thrummed loudly to the beat of her heart, but Claire let him guide her out of the alley.

They hurried down A street, Michael with his long strides and Claire with her short, quick steps. As they neared her loft, Claire took a deep breath and turned to Michael.

"Thank you for coming."

He bowed his head. "I told you I'd come when called."

"Yeah," she said, giving him a small smile, "you did." Michael caught her eye and mustered a slight grin in return.

Claire hurried up the steps, and Henry jumped up from the couch upon her entry. He searched her face.

"There you are, doll! You okay?"

Claire nodded as Michael entered the room behind her, walking to the sink to clean the cut on his shoulder.

"Yes, I'm okay, Henry. Someone else isn't, though."

Henry gave her a questioning look, and she described what had happened in the alley. Henry's expression tightened as she spoke, and he whistled.

"Another one bites the dust. Any idea who it was?"

As Claire shook her head, the movement sending a wave of queasiness through her stomach, Michael answered, "Rachel Kemdrock." Claire looked up in astonishment.

"How do you know that?"

Michael fished an ID from his pocket and slid it over the counter to her. A young woman's face stared back at her, the portrait revealing the collar of magenta scrubs.

"A doctor?"

"She seems to be a healer, yes." Michael finished up by the sink and retreated to the window, pressing against the frame. "Sagittarius is growing stronger and more desperate."

"Desperate?" Henry asked.

"This woman was knowledgeable and honorable in her field, I am sure. However, she is far from the top of the profession. Sagittarius is growing concerned and choosing victims at random."

"Well, it won't be for much longer. Check this out." Claire pulled out the flier she had printed from the library. Michael read the summary while Henry floated over his shoulder to follow suit.

"Keep away from crowded areas of shared thought," Michael quoted.

"Excuse me?" Claire asked, folding the flyer and placing it back in her pocket.

"Your friend, the Seer. He said to keep away from areas such as these. That it may be risky, dangerous." Michael gestured to Claire's pocket, where the flyer was stuffed away. "It does seem likely that Sagittarius will strike here next." He paused for a moment. "Good work."

Claire grinned. "Did you just compliment a mere mortal?"

He returned the smile and bowed his head, fist over his heart. "It is well-deserved."

"You should have heard him the entire time we were traveling around the county's perimeter," Henry piped up. "'Humans are so primitive,' this and 'why must they be so emotional and inefficient' that. He's got quite the low general opinion for someone in service to us." Michael glowered at Henry, but Claire choked out a laugh.

"The old man speaks out of context," Michael corrected.

"And what context would that be?" Claire asked as Henry shook his head, smirking.

Michael cleared his throat and changed the subject.

"This event is scheduled in only four days. We have until then to plan and get ready." He turned to Claire. "You must get some rest. Tomorrow, we will practice your Sending."

Claire's laughter died abruptly, remembering her conversation with Gemini in the car.

A broken Gateway, it said. She opened her mouth to speak and then closed it.

"What is it?" Michael prodded.

He'd just saved her life for a second time—third, if she counted Pisces in the sea that day. He gave her the watch, he came to her aide: she should trust him.

She took a deep breath. "Nothing. I'll be ready."

chapter TWELVE

T heir practice was not until the following evening, and Claire was grateful for the respite. She was short on cash and needed to spend some time conducting séances. Saturday in the shop was slow-moving, but she didn't complain. A day without needing to run from demonic apparitions—ghosts, Caretakers, or otherwise—was a good day in her book.

She had several people show up for a reading that day: a young man asking to contact his recently deceased mother, an elderly man wanting to speak to his wife, and— most notably—a teenage girl and her brother asking if she could call back their dog.

As the siblings sadly left the storefront at the end of the day (Claire was unable to reach little Peaches) and she locked up behind them, Claire returned to her séance table to find Michael relighting the candles. The glow of the flames seemed to revitalize him, his face younger with each flickering spark. Maybe he was made of flame.

Claire sat, waiting for Michael to finish. Finally, the room glowing a pale yellow, he walked to her table and removed the handkerchief from atop the crystal ball. He picked up the sphere and examined it.

"You know that doesn't actually work, right? I bought it at a HomeGoods store when I first opened up. Ties the room together."

He glanced at her. "Why do you keep it covered?"

She bit her lip. She'd taken care of covering all reflective surfaces since Gemini had appeared. "Why do you want to know? Gonna try to read my fortune?"

He didn't respond, instead peering into the ball, whispering under his breath. Claire was about to say something, but the ball began to glow. A faint, ghoulish green light emanated from within the glass. She sat up straighter, dumbfounded.

"How'd you do that?"

Michael brought the sphere closer to his face, causing eerie green shadows to hang down his cheekbones like bats. "As Guardian of the Beyond, I can maintain some of the forces that—at least for the last hundred centuries—kept the Caretakers in their realm. I have embedded some of these forces into this sphere as a temporary prison for our captured Caretakers. I will release this conjuration upon our return."

"Okay," Claire said, working to understand. "So, each time we capture a Caretaker in this crystal ball, I'll just Send it back into the Pit?"

"Not quite," Michael said. "The Gateway to the Pit can only be opened once per solstice. It makes the most sense to send all the Caretakers back at once, which means we need a place to put them in the meantime." He lifted the ball higher. Entrancing, shimmering emerald fog rolled within the orb.

"Alright, I think I'm getting it," Claire said. "As you capture each one, you will imprison them in my sphere until I can unlock the Gateway?"

"Almost," he said, putting the sphere back down in the center of the table. "*You* will be capturing them in the orb, and when the time comes, *you* will also open the Gateway and send them back to Purgatory."

"I'm sorry, what?" Claire shook her head in disbelief, wishing she'd taken more aspirin.

"Was I unclear?" Michael walked over to the window and drew the curtains shut, shrouding the room in darkness against the lights from the crystal ball and candles.

"I thought it was your job to capture the Caretakers. I just come in at the end and send them home."

"I can only do so much. I am more from the Beyond than from the Earth's realms. To truly capture them, I must secure the Caretakers and sedate them, while you Send them into the orb."

"You never explained that."

"I just did," he replied evenly. "Now, Henry will aid us in our practice." Claire turned to see Henry float into the room and sit across from her.

"If she gets me in the ball, she'll be able to get me out, right?" Henry asked. He played with his tie, feigning nonchalance. Claire saw the tightness around his eyes.

Michael nodded. "She is a Caller by nature; she can

easily free you anytime. What we need to focus on," he continued, making eye contact with Claire, "is getting her to Send you."

"Send?" Henry questioned, poking at the orb. His finger entered the glass, making his hand glow eerily.

"She can conjure the dead. Now she must learn to Send them away."

Claire interrupted. "Is '*she*' going to receive any guidance in this, or will you continue talking like I'm not in the room?" Anxiety welled up inside of her, marking her words with more malice than she intended.

"My apologies," Michael said, resting a hand on her shoulder, a familiar cloak of heat emanating from his hand. Her anxiety lessened but did not go away. "Let us begin." Michael stood by the table between Claire and Henry, gesturing to them both. "Look at Henry and keep him in your field of vision. Do you see him?" Claire resisted the urge to roll her eyes and instead fixated on Henry, who shot her a grin and stuck out a swollen tongue. She looked away.

"No, keep your eyes on Henry," Michael said quietly.

Claire closed her eyes. *Satu, dua, tiga* . . .

She returned her gaze, looking solely at Henry's thin nose.

"Now," Michael continued, "I need you to pull him toward the orb. Imagine grabbing onto his shoulders and forcing him down into the glass. Envision it in your mind's eye and make it happen." Claire huffed and imagined pulling Henry by the lapels of his school uniform and dragging him into the glass ball. She tried to envision him inside, palms pressing to the glass as if trying to break free.

"Is something supposed to be happening? Because it just looks like Claire hasn't used the WC in a while."

Claire shot him a look.

"I can't do it if you're chattering at me. Stop talking, Henry."

To his credit, Henry stopped speaking and examined his nails. He was obviously as on edge as she was. Claire closed her eyes, still thinking of Henry within the orb, but she couldn't focus. Her mind kept circling back to the creature in the alley, its enflamed eyes locked on hers, its drooling maw ready to devour her.

No. Focus. Henry, orb, capture.

She opened her eyes, and Henry remained seated at the table, looking bored. She turned to Michael, whose face was unreadable. "It's not working."

"It's not working *yet*. You simply need practice. Try again."

Claire took another deep breath and refocused on Henry, urging him to transfer to the orb. Still, nothing happened, and it remained this way for over an hour. By the time she was done, sweat trickled down her temple, and Henry seemed as though he was going to burst out of his chair from boredom.

"I can't do this anymore; I need a break." Claire pushed herself from the table and stretched her arms above her head.

Michael pursed his lip, his jaw tightening and accentuating the line of his jaw. He took a breath before he spoke. "We will try again tomorrow. Do not worry; it will happen when it needs to happen."

"If that's the case, we might as well not practice and just jump into action," Claire muttered.

"You're a fighter, Clarissa," Michael said, placing the orb in his pocket. "I've known this from the day we first met. We need you to fight our enemies, not yourself." Head throbbing, Claire retreated to her room, closing the door behind her and lining it with salt so Henry wouldn't follow. She'd spent enough time staring at him; she needed to be alone.

She swallowed another dose of aspirin and rummaged through the cabinets, looking for something to take the edge off. The last bottle stood empty by the waste basket. Why hadn't she asked Michael to pick up some whiskey when she sent him off for food? She knew the answer—she was still embarrassed to ask, as though it was an admission that she had a problem. The real issue at the moment was the fact that she had no liquor.

Debating whether she could sneak out for some, she pressed her ear to the door, listening to see if Michael and Henry had left. She heard the muted voices mumbling through the wall and quietly opened the door to listen.

"What if she can't do it?" Henry was asking Michael.

"She can, and she will."

Claire felt a small surge of pride from his words.

"But what if she *can't*?" Henry pressed. "I'm telling you, I didn't feel a thing. Not even a nudge." There was a pause before Michael answered.

"Failure is not an option." Silently, Claire closed the door. *Failure is not an option.* The sentiment was lovely—if not heavy with implication—but was entirely untrue. Failure was absolutely an option, and one that she was currently facing head-on.

She needed a drink, Caretakers be damned.

Slinging her bag over her shoulder and checking to ensure her salt and iron rod were inside, she opened the window to the fire escape—the cool, mid-autumn breeze wafted in, shifting some of the grains in the salt line. Clare stepped over the ledge, careful not to slip on the metal steps, and closed the window with a quiet *click* before heading down the stairs.

She headed to the same convenience store where she'd last seen Carlos. It wasn't an ideal choice, but it was still the closest option, and she felt—hoped—that Sagittarius didn't hunt in the same place twice. A few minutes later, she was leaving the store with several bottles of richly colored liquor in hand.

Claire disliked traveling on foot in the city, especially in the evening. Nightlife was rife in the Gaslamp, and the bright neon lights and music from the local bars and clubs made the area feel seedy and undesirable. Keeping her head down, she returned to her loft as quickly as possible.

"Need to take the edge off?"

Claire looked to her right and saw a scantily dressed woman leaning against the wall. The woman was shrouded in the alley's darkness, but the nearby bars' neon lights illuminated her transparent figure. The looper threw a cigarette on the sidewalk and ground it under her strapped high heels, the black lace straps of her lingerie hanging loose on her emaciated thighs.

The woman took a step forward, squeezing her arms

to her sides, pushing her cleavage forward. "Or should I say, 'get off?'"

Claire ignored her, continuing to walk past. This wasn't the first time she had encountered this woman. When Claire had first moved to the city, she'd tried to help her break the cycle, but several years later, the woman in red continued her one-sided conversation and untimely end. Claire hurried with increased intensity before the gunshot from years past fired, before she would hear the woman collapse to the ground. The woman repeated her death on a nightly cycle.

Then again, people woke up, shuffled to work, crawled home, swam in a pool of liquor and weed and food and pills and porn or whatever they needed to feel alive, and repeated the same damn thing every single day. Maybe everyone was a looper, not just the dead.

When she returned through her apartment window, the office downstairs was silent, so she assumed Michael and Henry had left. Humming tunelessly, she poured a large glass from one of the bottles and took several sips, sighing audibly. It had been at least a day since her last drink, and she felt it. She took another sip, pretending that the alcohol wasn't the only reason she was able to relax.

Claire plopped down into her seat, swirling the liquid in her glass. She watched it tiredly as it spiraled like a maple-colored tide pool, drawing her in, and tried not to think of the looper she passed. *Need to take the edge off?*

"Don't mind if I do," she said aloud, lifting the drink to her lips.

Then, her reflection on the surface of the whiskey smiled.

She dropped the glass, the drink spilling onto the carpet. She heard a disapproving click of the tongue, and Claire looked up to see her reflection in one of the new bottles, distorted and grinning.

Her breath caught in her throat. She went to toss a blanket over the glasses, but the reflection spoke. "So, Sending is an issue, is it?" Claire paused and inspected the bottle. Her reflection curled around the cylindrical glass, eyeing her up and down.

"And I should speak to you because . . . ?" Claire asked.

"Because Michael is no teacher. We, on the other hand, know exactly what to do." Perhaps it was the exhaustion or the light buzz, but Claire listened attentively, against a nagging feeling in her gut.

She placed the bottle back on the counter and asked, "Are you offering to help?"

The reflection shrugged.

"Maybe We are. Maybe We want to poke fun at dear old Michael and his many failings."

"Well, it's in your best interest to ensure I remain as incompetent as you believe I am." The reflection morphed back into her face and reappeared in the now-empty glass.

"Yes and no. What's life without a little challenge? I daresay that Our brethren won't leave much for Us if they're allowed to continue galivanting through the streets." Claire bit her lip, considering.

"Sagittarius said that it considers Earth its realm now."

The reflection yawned. "Yes, Sagittarius is as

delusional as ever. With a boring, unintriguing goal, as ever."

"Then why are you here? Tired of your old stomping grounds? Need to take what isn't yours?" Claire asked.

Its eyes narrowed, the edges of its smile traveling up toward its temples. "We don't *need* new dominion. Earth has always been Ours, if only from afar. We have other plans in mind."

"Like what?"

"In due time. Until then, you need a little help, do you not? Perhaps We can be of assistance."

Claire nodded slowly, keeping her eyes on her reflection. "Let's pretend for a moment that you were to help me. What exactly would you say?" The reflection opened its impossibly wide smile, revealing several sets of sharp, triangular teeth, a return of the evil Cheshire cat.

"Then We would say you're Sending the wrong object."

"The wrong object? What's that mean?" But the reflection's manic expression turned perplexed, mirroring her own. Gemini was gone.

Sending the wrong object? Claire found a clean glass in her kitchen; she was uncomfortable drinking from the one to which she was just speaking. Claire sat on the couch, deep in thought.

This entire experience felt like one elongated riddle, each thread looping and knotting together. Whenever she thought she understood what was happening, something new was thrust into the mix. It all muddled into one disorienting, gut-wrenching mass of confusion and fear.

The quiet hum of cicadas in her mind began their

orchestra again; Claire could feel her fingertips go numb as a blanket of panic attacked her. Shakily, she took a sip from the glass, dribbling down the corners of her mouth, trying to force the tingling away. What if she couldn't do it? Any of it: sending, trapping, figuring out this entire fucking riddle of a life.

She'd been letting people down for most of her life, but failing this, failing Michael, hit like an anvil to the chest.

Claire thought back to her father, what he'd say when she came home with a D on a test, a letter from the school claiming she needed to stay late for detention, a black eye from when she fought some kid who made fun of her second-hand shoes and hand-me-down clothes.

"The only person you can let down is yourself; take care of yourself, and you'll take care of everyone else," he'd said.

While the words weren't particularly helpful in this situation, they were comforting all the same.

Claire considered going to bed but knew she'd toss and turn all night. Instead, she placed her glass on the table and grabbed a nearby scrap of paper and pencil.

She held the tip of the graphite above the paper, unsure what she wanted to draw. Visions of the Caretakers strobed in her mind's eye: the sinewy skin of Pisces, the stretched smile of Gemini, the snake-like, undulating muscles of Sagittarius.

But then another image came to mind—fiery eyes of molten azure. A burn flowed through her body like a draft of whiskey down her throat, and the numbness in her fingertips and buzzing began to fade.

For the first time in months, she placed the pencil to paper.

The riddle she'd fallen into would have to wait.

chapter THIRTEEN

T he next day went as well as the first, which was to say dreadful. By the time the third day had come and gone, Claire's pulsating headache never entirely dissipated no matter how much she drank, and Henry was just as fed up as she was. Only Michael remained steadfast, reminding them both that "practice was key."

"Yeah, well, we're obviously using the wrong lock because nothing is happening," Henry complained. He sat sprawled across from Claire, both feet hanging over one edge of the chair, his head nearly upside down on the other side. His tie hung loosely over his shoulder.

"Concentrate," Michael coaxed. "Do it again. Keep Henry in your mind and hold steady. Extend your incorporeal self and cajole your target into the orb."

Both elbows planted firmly on the table, head in her hands, Claire forced herself to stare at Henry, who was actively swinging his legs in a distracting manner. Her fingernails bit into her scalp, pulling out several strands of her strawberry hair.

With a great huff, she pushed out her chair, standing and stalking to the opposite side of the room.

"This is insane. We have one more day until the seminar—an event we aren't even one hundred percent sure Sagittarius will attend—and I can't even get a damn child into a glass ball, let alone a demon."

"Watch it!" Henry barked at the jab, but she ignored him with a wave of her hand.

Michael walked up to her and placed a hand on her shoulder. "It's important that you remain calm. Refocus your energies on—"

"Don't you dare tell me to calm down," she snarled, throwing his hand off her. "I haven't eaten in hours; I haven't slept in days; every sound I hear makes me lose my shit. Do you actually care about me, or are you just worried about your damn Gateway?" With a cry of frustration with both him and herself, she thrust her arm toward the ball, wishing she could pick it up and shatter the infernal thing against the wall.

It moved.

Or something did. She stared at the orb in disbelief. Within the crystal, tendrils of fog began to swirl around themselves. She leveled her gaze on the sphere, envisioning the glowing green light enveloping Henry in his seat.

And the orb moved again.

The green glowing light lifted from the orb and hovered in place. Caught off guard, Claire lost her concentration, and the light fell back into the sphere. She looked at Michael, who, for once, seemed speechless. And then he turned toward Claire and smiled, his beautiful eyes alight with the moment of success.

"That's improvement!" he shouted.

"Hell yeah, that's improvement!" Claire pumped a fist in the air. Without thinking, she jumped over and wrapped her arms around Michael. Her hands could barely get around his waist, and his chest felt like a furnace against her own. He stilled, then brought his arms around her, returning the embrace.

Realizing what she'd done, she quickly let go of him, refusing to make eye contact. She could feel his molten gaze burning into the back of her head as she turned to face Henry instead.

Henry broke in, jumping from foot to foot excitedly. "Finally, doll! I was beginning to cramp up from the stress, and I didn't think that was possible nowadays. What'd you do differently?" he asked. He removed his legs from the arms of the chair and leaned forward. Claire rubbed the back of her neck, embarrassed and perplexed.

"I'm not sure. I just thought about throwing the orb and smashing it against the wall, and the light just . . . lifted out."

The wrong object. Not Henry, the orb.

The orb was the correct object.

"Can you do it again?" Michael asked. His voice was as steady as ever. Claire glanced at him as she walked back to her seat and tilted her body forward to the orb again. He was watching her closely, his face guarded, though he seemed distracted, somehow.

Biting her lip, she refocused on the orb. In her mind's

eye, she envisioned the light lifting from the orb again and floating to Henry, coating his body in jade light. After a moment, the light in the orb flickered and lifted, moving toward Henry, who watched, transfixed.

"Okay," Michael's voice speared through her concentration. "Now, slowly cover him with the light. Draw him into the orb."

Claire lowered the glowing light, grinding her teeth in concentration, enveloping Henry's translucent form. Henry grew smaller and less defined, the green hue overtaking his features. Soon, he was gone, wholly immersed in the green light. Her heart gave a worried thump, but she pressed on.

"Good. Deposit him in the orb."

Claire struggled to move him; the light somehow seemed heavier than before, as if Henry's spiritual body had suddenly gained the mass it would have had in life.

Losing focus and collapsing in exhaustion, Henry shot out of the light, the glowing ball returning with intense speed to the glass. Henry stood next to the table, swaying like he'd been spinning. He pressed both hands to his head, steadying himself.

"Are you okay, Henry?" Claire asked, lifting a drained gaze toward her partner. He nodded woozily.

"That was quite the ride there, doll. Didn't expect to remember what nausea felt like. Not exactly something I'd like to do again. At least, not right now."

Both Claire and Henry turned to Michael, who nodded.

"This was an excellent improvement. We can try again tomorrow. For now, rest. Then, we plan." He leveled a heavy gaze at her, his eyes glowing with pride.

They all left the room, and Claire's thoughts lingered on the feeling of Michael's chest against her own.

The rest of the evening was filled with practicing Sending Henry into the orb, despite the promise of a break. Henry returned shaky with vertigo, but neither complained, just readjusting his tie with each successful Send. Eventually, she was able to capture Henry in the crystal ball three times in a row.

Michael was over the moon. Though he did not emote the same way he did when Claire first succeeded, he did, however, smile on occasion, which was equivalent to Henry's whoops of joy and Claire's snorting laughter.

Claire did not try to hug him again, though she could have sworn he edged closer, waiting for her to embrace him again.

Later that night, Claire went to the kitchen sink, plugged the drain, and filled it with water. She had debated this for the last hour, but curiosity got the better of her. Once the sink was full, Claire turned off the tap and leaned forward, her reflection wearily staring back at her. Claire cleared her throat.

"Can you hear me? Are you there?" she said in a whisper.

Silence. She tried again.

"Hello? Gemini?"

A gurgling voice rose from the water.

"A pleasure to be called by you, Clarissa Reed." The reflection changed, her face manic once more.

"You keep referring to yourself as 'We.' Is there more than one of you?"

Her reflection gave her a coy smile.

"As We've told you before—if you were listening—We are you, you are Us, We are the mirror to all things. A twin to your soul, if you will."

"Right," Claire said, unsure how to respond. "I just wanted to say thank you for your help. With the Sending."

The reflection nodded.

"Improved, have you? That's good; We are glad. We appreciate a challenge. You will be a formidable opponent when it comes to our turn."

"Turn? What's to stop me from taking you now?" she asked, perplexed.

Gemini didn't seem to mind her tone. "Another good question! You may not know much, but you know how to follow a line of inquiry." Gemini gave a laugh, the sound gurgling in the water. "No, Clarissa Reed, it is not yet our time. It will come, We promise. Until then, keep a wary eye out for our brothers and sisters. Sagittarius has spoken about you; you are known among the Caretakers. You have no element of surprise to save you."

In a flash, something shot up into the air from the water below. A hand of water gripped her throat and dragged her into the tub. In shock, Claire inhaled a mouthful of water and struggled to pull herself free. Her hands gripped the sides of the sink as she thrashed. She could hear laughter echoing from all around her, the water crashing in waves as she bucked to break free. Residue of soap mixed with the water burned her eyes, a froth churning on the surface. Claire plunged her hand into the water and pulled out the plug, the water rushing down the drain.

As the water emptied, the hold on her throat loosened, and Claire fell backward, coughing up water and soap. "Fucking piece of—" she spluttered aloud.

She should have known better than to call one of the Caretakers. What had she been thinking?

Nothing, she cursed. *I didn't think at all.* As a child, her teachers had called her impulsive, and her family had laughed it off, reframing her as "energetic" and a "free thinker." So much for that.

She climbed to her feet, steadying herself on the wall to avoid falling on the slick floor. She was completely drenched. Hiccupping, she hobbled over to the bed and fell onto her back, drinking in deep gulps of air.

Never again, she thought to herself as she closed her eyes and tried to fall asleep.

chapter FOURTEEN

Claire did not speak of her violent conversation with Gemini. Embarrassed by her naivety, she kept the near-drowning to herself. Deep down, she knew she needed to tell Michael; keeping such important information under wraps made no sense, especially when they'd eventually need to capture all of the escaped Caretakers, not just the centaur beast.

She promised herself that she'd tell Michael after they'd caught Sagittarius. Aside from its disconcerting smile and obvious danger, Gemini had been helpful thus far. *Perhaps not all of the Caretakers were utterly evil.* That was the justification Claire told herself as she readied for the seminar.

The morning of the event, Claire forced down some eggs and orange juice, knowing she'd need her strength. Hunger eluded her, however, and the food sat like a lump in her stomach, sitting in tandem with the knots of fear and anxiety.

Henry came by first, waiting by the window for Claire to let him in. He entered, vibrating with nervous energy. Sitting on the couch, he stood up and moved to the chair, where he almost immediately got up again and began pacing.

"Nervous?" Claire asked.

Henry gave a lopsided smile. "You're one to talk. Taking up tap dancing?"

Claire glanced down and noticed she was bouncing her toes against the floor. She forced herself to sit still and looked out the window.

"Michael should be here soon," she said.

Henry nodded, still pacing. After a moment, he stopped and asked, "Can we trust him?"

Claire stopped tapping her feet and squinted at him, confused.

"Who? Michael?" she said incredulously.

Henry pursed his lips in response.

"You're joking, right? We've been working with him for days, and now you're asking if he's trustworthy? We are about to go face some demonic creature from the depths of the world in a couple of hours, and now you're questioning things?"

She could feel the hypocrisy coating the words on her tongue; her mind flitted briefly to her secret tryst with Gemini.

"Well, I'm sorry I'm a little behind the eight ball," he shot back. "I'm just saying, we're about to do something foolish and dangerous, and we put a lot of blind faith in him."

"You'll be fine," she said dismissively.

"I'm talking about you, doll. I'm already dead; you still have some life left in you."

This thought had occurred to her, but she'd refused to dwell on it like the rest of the recent unpleasantness.

"Well, it's a little late now. Don't worry; if I die, I won't leave you hanging," she said with a lightness she didn't feel.

His shoulders seemed to relax slightly, and only then did Claire realize that he was afraid of being left alone, fearful that Claire would choose to move on and leave him behind. She looked at him with fresh eyes and saw him: a young boy scared to lose his friend and return to isolation.

"It's going to be okay, Henry. Try not to worry about it."

He nodded and opened his mouth to reply when Michael popped into view, preceded by the sound of a crackling flame. He dusted his hands on his coat before placing them in his trouser pockets.

"Ready to leave?" He posed his question to them both but kept his eyes on Claire. She squirmed under his stare.

Henry's bravado returned in full gusto, his secret vulnerability out of sight. "Born ready, sir. Let's get at it."

Michael asked Claire again, "Are *you* ready?"

Claire nodded, opting to stay silent in case opening her mouth allowed her partially digested meal to reappear on the floor.

Michael nodded. "Alright. Let's begin."

I t was a little less than an hour's commute via the Coaster to UCSD. It took more time than they expected to find the correct hall, and most of the seats were taken by the time they arrived.

Michael nodded to Henry, who remained outside, watching for Sagittarius's arrival. Michael gripped Claire's shoulder briefly as Henry left, whispering in her ear. "Good luck, Clarissa." His warm breath danced along the shell of her ear, and her heart skipped a beat. They locked eyes. Before she could respond, he let go and moved to a seat along the wall.

Claire walked unsteadily to a seat on the other side of the room. She could see Michael scanning the room if she arched her head just so around a large man in a tweed coat. She did the same, noting serious-looking older men and women dotted here and there, but mainly college-aged students littered the auditorium. Most of the crowd spoke in low, respectful tones; others tapped away on laptops, while others still scribbled in their notebooks. They were all so blissfully ignorant of the danger that surrounded them.

Remembering she was supposed to be a student, Claire pulled out a notebook of her own, pen poised over the paper. She had a flashback to her university days, recalling the doodles that etched the corners of her paper when she should have been taking notes and listening to the professor.

The crowd suddenly hushed into a respectful silence, and a young woman stepped on stage, grabbing the microphone and speaking in a quick, perky voice.

"Thank you all very much for coming to be with us

today. My name is Jane Garner, and I will be hosting today's seminar." She paused as a muted applause rose and died from the crowd. "As you know, UCSD is holding Doctors Stevenson and Vishwanath here to discuss their joint thesis on California's diverse ecosystem and its advancement and deterioration due to the development of our urban landscape. Please join me as we give a warm welcome to our esteemed guests." Another polite round of applause sounded, Claire joining in, as two well-dressed men walked onto the stage. The crowd fell silent once more, and the lecture began.

Claire struggled to pay attention as she thought about Henry keeping watch outside and Michael patrolling elsewhere. She felt agitated and vulnerable without her earplugs, but they had already agreed that she needed to keep all her senses uninhibited. Her eyes bounced around the auditorium, looking for anything unusual. Everyone seemed thoroughly engaged. She tried to mimic their rapt, attentive expressions, but nerves got the better of her. She tried calming herself by sketching absently on her paper as the speakers droned on, but her hands shook.

Two hours crawled by, and Claire was lulled into a sense of complacency. She turned her head to the doorway and saw Henry peeking in. They made eye contact, and he shook his head and shrugged. No sign of Sagittarius. He went back outside, and she refocused her attention forward. The speakers were wrapping up, taking questions from the crowd. They had been wrong; this wasn't the place. Sagittarius wasn't coming.

The sound of applause pulled her out of her disappointed spiral, and she remained seated as the audience began to disperse. Sighing, Claire got to her feet and started to make her way over to Michael, but he raised his hand to stop her, his eyes on the stage. Puzzled, she followed his gaze. Both speakers were perched on their stools, deeply immersed in quiet discussion. One adjusted his glasses, content after a successful presentation, unaware of anything awry. Claire looked back to Michael, who pointed to a glass window on the upper level.

Behind the window, to Claire's horror, was an immense silhouette, its arms raising.

Michael disappeared, reappearing in front of the two speakers in a burst of flames. The men leaped from their stools, shocked by his sudden appearance. Recovering himself, the first man's expression turned offended.

"Excuse me! No one is allowed up here," one of the men said, his accent thick and commanding. Claire marveled that he was more concerned with propriety than the honest-to-God flames Michael conjured when he materialized. Michael ignored him.

Time seemed to slow. In one moment, Michael had conjured the burning sword in one of his hands, the other reaching a clawed hand toward where Sagittarius towered behind the glass. Claire's stomach dropped as Michael shouted something in a language Claire didn't understand, and Michael closed his fist, thrusting it downward.

The window broke in a downpour of glass shards on the seats below. Sagittarius fell from the jagged hole as if pulled by an invisible hand and landed in a crumpled heap on the stage. Students still filtering out of the lecture hall shrieked as they saw glass fly through the room, and the speakers staggered backward.

"He's got a gun!" One of the college students yelled and pointed accusingly at Michael, unaware of the creature slowly getting to its feet on stage. Panic ensued, and everyone rushed toward the exit in a scene of chaos. Michael ran in the opposite direction and stabbed the blade into Sagittarius's hindquarters. The centaur let out a roar of rage and agony, writhing as Michael used the blade as a pole to swing himself up onto its back.

Sagittarius bucked and kicked, hands scrambling at its unwanted rider, but Michael held fast.

"Do it now!" Michael's voice was strained from the effort of holding on. His coat billowed chaotically with each kick of the mighty beast beneath him.

Claire blinked, remembering she wasn't a mere bystander in this, watching the terrifying epic battle unfold onstage. She sprang forward, scrambling closer to the stage, and removed the glowing green ball from her bag. Ignoring the hammering of her heart trying to beat out of her chest, she held it up and focused her attention on the light.

Move, she begged mentally. The light wavered and vibrated, slowly rising from the orb. *That's it; focus,* she thought, *just like we practiced.* The ball of light floated all too slowly toward Sagittarius, who was still thrashing on stage under Michael's grip.

"Help me," a voice croaked beside her, cutting through her focus. Her attention faltered as she felt an icy grip on her shoulder. Turning her head, she saw a translucent young man only a few inches away from her face. His eyes were bloodshot and bulging, his neck purple and bruised, a rope burn encircling his Adam's apple. He spoke again, and she could see his tongue, purple and swollen, just like Henry's. Her mouth went dry.

"Help me; I don't want to die," he croaked again. Claire clambered away from the apparition, gripped with fear and revulsion, bumping into one of the chairs. Her hand slipped, and the orb fell to the ground and rolled away.

"Clarissa!"

Claire looked up in time to see Michael lose his grip. Sagittarius flipped over, and Michael's body was thrown across the stage. He slammed into a row of chairs with a reverberation she felt in her feet and fell still.

"No, no, no," she repeated to herself, her panic growing exponentially. Falling to her hands and knees, she crawled away from the apparition toward the orb, which had lodged underneath one of the chairs in the front row.

"Young girl, you have returned."

Claire heard Sagittarius address her, but she kept her eyes on the orb, trying desperately to unstick it from the seat.

"You've traveled many distances to see me, to know me. I am honored by your pursuits," it continued, closer now.

Claire's fingers gripped the side of the glass, yanking desperately. It moved slightly.

"I must know what you think of the world. I must know your travels, from the intellectual to the physical. There will be time for that. But first, I must feed."

Claire yanked again, finally dislodging the orb and prying it free. She shot to her feet and spun to face Sagittarius, expecting to see a silver arrow aimed directly at her skull. She heard two *thwacks* of the mighty bowstring. Two shots fired.

Claire's heart stopped, expecting to feel the arrows pass through her skull before blackness consumed her.

But she felt nothing.

Her eyes traveled across the room, and to her horror, she watched the two speakers collapse on the ground, just barely at the entranceway, so close to escape. But not close enough.

Claire backed away, her spine pressed firmly against the wall, surveying the destruction: the confetti of glass, two dead men, Michael crumpled against the far wall, the apparition moving steadily closer to her. A panicked buzzing like cicadas sang in her ears, her hands growing numb. It wasn't supposed to have gone this way; it was supposed to be over by now.

It still could be.

Claire gripped the orb, focusing on it, trying to Send the light out again. But her concentration was waning. There was too much going on, too much going wrong.

She had failed.

A broken Gateway.

It's okay, Claire, just try again. A memory bubbled up inside Claire as she fought desperately to focus. Her father, hands holding her waist, as a nine-year-old Claire tried and failed to balance her feet on the pedals of a rusty, one-geared bike. The Claire in her memory pouted, her eyes brimming with tears as she clutched the handles, the grip digging into her tiny hands.

"I can't; I can't do it, Daddy. Don't let go; I'm going to fall!" Little Claire was blubbering, eyes fixed on the asphalt, imagining bloodied knees in her near future. Julian continued to hold on, his voice calm yet stern, as steady as his hold on his daughter.

"Wherever you look is where you'll go. If you look at the ground, that's where you'll end up. Don't be afraid; just look forward."

Claire lifted her stinging eyes in the auditorium, oscillating between the orb and the bleeding Caretaker. She frantically tried again and again to call the light. Sagittarius made its way toward the two dead speakers, hunger gleaming in its eyes. On the stage, Claire could hear Michael stirring, bringing himself back to consciousness, back to her. A small part of Claire breathed a sigh of relief to see Michael coming to her aide soon, but it wasn't fast enough.

Work faster, she chastised herself.

"Oh, Sagittarius, brother. Hungry, are We?" A cold, multi-layered voice echoed throughout the auditorium.

Sagittarius stopped short and looked toward the piles of broken glass in the concert hall.

Claire, too, regarded the glass shards and saw in the pieces hundreds of reflections of Sagittarius, each one baring its teeth in a threatening, manic smile.

"You are not welcome here, Gemini," Sagittarius responded, a growl lacing his voice.

Gemini "humphed" petulantly, sounding like hundreds of voices speaking at the same time.

"You can't mean that. We're siblings, after all. If We're going to be technical, *none* of Us is welcome here. But that's not going to Us stop us, now, will it?"

For the first time, Sagittarius looked uneasy, its eyes darting between the reflections and his victims.

"Leave me to my feeding."

"Oh, you know how much We'd love to do that, but We can't have you leaving Us too soon. We need you to stick around for the family reunion."

Sagittarius furrowed its brows, anger bubbling to the surface.

"Do not speak to me in those condescending tones. I am your elder, your intellectual superior, and you will treat me as such," he huffed, stamping a hooved foot upon the floor.

"Are you sure about that?" Gemini asked.

Sagittarius made to respond, then cried out in sudden pain. Michael appeared behind the centaur, pulling the sword from its back and bringing it down again in a powerful slice against its body. The gash sprayed a black swath of blood across the row of chairs beside him. Michael angled himself between the beast and where Claire stood.

Sagittarius flailed and then, with a final withering look at Gemini, galloped out of the room, leaving Claire, Michael, and the two dead professors in its wake.

chapter FIFTEEN

"Well, that was a disaster."

Henry crossed his arms and tapped his foot like a teacher chastising his student for not completing her homework. Claire, indeed, felt like a child in detention. She sat in the chair back home, legs tightly pressed together, making herself look as small as she felt.

"You don't have to say it out loud," she muttered.

Claire had failed so abysmally she could barely look at herself in the mirror, even while they were still covered. Two more men were dead because she couldn't focus when it mattered most. She couldn't shake the sound of the heavy silver arrows releasing from the Caretaker's bow. *Thwack, thwack* … the moment played over and over in her head on repeat. Their blood was on her hands.

Henry turned toward her again, as he had been doing since they arrived at her apartment.

"I just want to make sure we're clear about the part you played in Sagittarius getting away."

Claire glared at him. "You were the one who was

supposed to be the lookout."

"And you were supposed to capture him, doll, not freak out like you've never seen a ghost before."

"Enough," Michael said, his voice quiet, his tone hard. Both of them fell silent, and Claire resumed hugging her chest, keeping her eyes on the carpet.

"We did not succeed this first round," he began, slowly alternating his gaze between Claire and Henry. "We will have another opportunity. To be successful next time, we must regroup and remain vigilant, undeterred, and united."

He addressed Henry. "Insults and blame only fracture us. They have no place in this partnership."

Henry looked sheepish. "Apologies," he muttered, "we'll make it right." He stuffed his hands in his pockets and kept his eyes to the ground.

Michael turned to Claire. Claire couldn't look at him, couldn't allow herself to see the disappointment, maybe even fury etched in his face. "He is right, though," Michael said, "Your fear of the dead let our chance slip away, and now two men are dead."

Claire pinched her arms to keep from crying. Dr. Stevenson and Vishwanath were dead. She lost focus because she panicked.

Because she was a failure.

"I'm sorry," she whispered, her eyes still downcast.

"Apologies do not bring back the dead," Michael responded, his voice not unkind, but low, grounded. At his words, Claire felt as though she had been punched in the chest, the air leaving her lungs in a single blow.

Michael crouched down in front of her. When she

refused to meet his gaze, he reached out, softly lifting her chin so her eyes met his. He blinked slowly, his long lashes brushing his cheekbones. "We must conquer these fears if we are to succeed."

She was touched when he said 'we.' Finding her voice, she muttered, "It won't happen again." She wouldn't let it happen twice; she couldn't let it interfere with their mission again.

Michael nodded, something shuttered in his eyes. He stood and walked to the window, lost in thought. Claire wondered what he would say about their next steps, but instead, he said, "Tell me about your affiliation with Gemini." He was still facing the window.

A trickle of sweat dripped down her back. "What do you mean?"

He turned back to her, his features harder than before. "I have noticed how you cover the reflections in your home and avoid looking too long at mirrors and shining surfaces. Gemini only comes when there is a game to play."

Claire lowered her eyes to the floor again. It was time to come clean.

She took a deep breath and recounted the times she'd seen and spoken with Gemini, from the hospital to the kitchen sink attack. When she finished speaking, no one moved. Claire and Michael's breathing was the only sound in the room.

"I know insults aren't allowed, but am I allowed to curse?" Henry asked.

Michael nodded, and Henry let out a stream of angry words, kicking the wall only to have his foot harmlessly float through it.

When he finished his outburst, he settled back down in his seat. "Doll, you're a piece of work."

Claire didn't bother disagreeing.

"Gemini is not to be trifled with," Michael finally said. "I would be more careful with your dealings in the future. And it *will* happen again; Gemini does not let Their playthings go so easily, not when they still provide the entertainment They're looking for." He paused for a moment. "However, it seems that little harm has been done in this particular regard, and there is no need to pursue it further."

For the first time since she began her confession, Claire willingly looked up. Michael's face had softened, and Claire felt her chest beginning to thaw.

"Not to change the subject, but what should we do now? We have no leads and two more dead victims." Henry pointed out. He was crabby, but he wasn't wrong; there was no clear way forward, not without any new information.

"I guess I could go back to the library and look up more events like that one," Claire suggested.

"Perhaps. I must go and ponder our next move. Do not leave your home for the rest of the day. I will return tomorrow." With that, Michael disappeared.

"I don't know what's ruder: when he suddenly pops up or decides to leave," Henry griped.

"The former," Claire answered, and Henry gave her a reluctant grin.

He left soon after Michael, stating he had some "spiritual business to attend to," which she knew meant he would meander around his old school to collect his thoughts.

Taking Michael's command to heart, Claire switched into a mostly clean sweatshirt and some fraying sweats, the ankle bands torn and loose. If she didn't find a way to occupy her mind, however, thoughts of the two dead men on the ground would torture her all day. Settling under the blankets in her bed, she plucked a book from her pile—a Russian novel featuring a man with a taste for murder and names too long to pronounce—and tried to focus on the words on the page.

You have the right to remain silent. Everything you do can be used against in you in the court of law—"

Claire bolted upright; the book she had been reading before she nodded off fell to the ground. It took her a moment to understand what she was seeing: nearly a dozen officers crowded her little apartment, lifting the couch cushions, opening drawers, and searching through boxes of her belongings. Two officers pulled Claire from her bed, forcing her onto her knees and wrenching her hands behind her head.

"What the hell is this?" Claire yelled, fighting against the grip of a particularly bulky officer.

The man continued reciting her rights as she heard one of the women speak into her walkie-talkie: "Suspect is being detained as we speak. Some resistance. Over." The device crackled with static, and a voice confirmed the receipt of her message.

Claire tried to speak again. "What's going on? I didn't

give you permission to come in here! Let me go!"

The man lifted her roughly to her feet, and she tried unsuccessfully to break his grip. "We knocked several times before entering. Clarissa Reed, you are being arrested for the murders of Jeffrey Davis, Richard Stevensen, Rahmed Vishwanath, Rachel Kembrock," he lowered his lips to her ear, breath hot and humid with malice, "and one Officer Carlos Santos."

Her stomach lurched. "On what grounds?" Her voice fumbled over her words, making her sound guiltier than she liked.

Another officer across the room shouted, "Foster! Look what I found."

Claire craned her neck to see what she meant, and the color drained from her face. The officer was holding the ID of the dead woman in the alley. She'd left it lying on the counter.

The officer holding her—Foster—tightened his grip on the hood of her sweatshirt, his other hand clicking the cuffs closed and tight on her wrists. "How's that for grounds?"

"No, please. It's not what you think. I—"

He didn't let her finish, which was fine because she didn't know what to say. How could she explain away the dead woman's ID in her apartment? It was evidence for their case—solid evidence—covered in her fingerprints.

"We finally found something that'll stick," Officer Foster said gleefully as he paraded her down the stairs. She saw that her shop was also filled with officers searching every corner of the room. He pushed her outside, and she winced in pain from the chafe of the cuffs. Lights flashed blue and red, just like the crash last week. Onlookers gathered to watch the proceedings, many taking selfies and recording with their own commentary. She'd be a trending social media hashtag in no time.

As she was shoved into the car, bumping her head on the door opening, she caught a glimpse of the driver. The woman looked over her shoulder and gave her a cold smile. "I couldn't miss this, now, could I?" Captain Elizabeth Núñez turned back to the road, and they were on their way to the precinct.

chapter SIXTEEN

Camera lights flashed endlessly, and reporters shouted questions as Claire was dragged into the station, doing her best to keep her head down, hair covering her face. Though she hadn't been reading the paper lately, she could only imagine the story that had developed: multiple deaths within the same general vicinity, three of whom had been highly prominent fixtures of the community.

Cheers and jeers erupted from all sides as she was dragged through the station doors. Officers she recognized and others who must have joined after she'd left catcalled and shouted vulgar insults as she was led into a holding cell. Officer Foster uncuffed her wrists and shoved her inside, locking the cell door behind her before leaving. Claire leaned against the bars, gripping the steel.

"Listen to me! People are in danger! Let me out!" Even as she yelled, she noted how she sounded: guilty and desperate, and a little crazy. She had heard similar convicts yell the same comments in years past, all of whom were later found guilty of their crimes.

Giving up, she sat on the beige cot suspended from the wall, a wave of fatigue and stark incredulity coursing through her.

Shit.

Fucking shit.

Goddamn son of a bitch fucking shit, we're screwed.

That was an understatement. Try as she might, Claire could not think of a way out. Why hadn't she seen this coming? Maybe she could make a run for it when they took her out for interrogation. But then what? Live life on the lam until Sagittarius and the rest of the Caretakers destroyed the world?

She could tell the truth. Immediately, she discarded the idea. The truth was worse than their current theory about Claire's serial killing spree. Plus, this was personal. Everyone at the station believed that not only did they catch a cop killer, but they would finally get true vengeance upon the ex-employee who'd attempted to tamper with evidence.

They were going to see her found guilty, no matter what.

She groaned and lay down on her stomach, face pressed into the plastic cot. It was uncomfortable, but she deserved it. How could she have been so stupid as to keep that ID? Why hadn't she returned it to Michael to return to the body? If she'd successfully captured Sagittarius at the lecture, maybe she wouldn't be here now. At the least, those men would still be alive. She had been making mistakes left and right, and now she would finally receive the comeuppance she deserved.

As she miserably contemplated the past few days, a harsh male voice drawled out of the cell across the hall. "I'm gonna get out of here, you know. One way or another."

She pushed herself up with a grunt and looked over.

A man in worn jeans and a metal-band t-shirt stood behind steel bars, looking in her direction.

"Yeah? You sure about that?" Claire said, nonplussed.

They always believed they would get off scot-free. Claire remembered watching an interrogation with Captain Núñez —*Officer* Núñez at the time—and the meth-head kept repeating the exact phrase over and over again: "I'm gonna get out of here, you'll see." He ended up being correct, though he died of an overdose a week later. He wasn't wrong, though. He got out. One way or another.

The man across from her reached down and picked something up. "I'm not going away for this, no, sir. No one ever believes the innocent; the guilty are much more interesting."

Claire watched as he jerked his knee upward, as though breaking a piece of wood.

But there was nothing in his hands.

"No, please, not here," Claire moaned, averting her eyes away from the looping man. She didn't need to watch what would happen next; she already knew.

After she was suspended from the station, the officers dusted the prints on the gasoline canister, finding the young man's fingerprints. They brought him in for questioning, tried connecting him with the string of arson attacks. Claire had heard how the man struggled in his cuffs, bellowing his innocence.

They found the boy later that night, his wrists torn and exsanguinated, his corpse curled like a sleeping child, but in a pool of crimson.

He never made it to court.

Over the next few hours, she heard the man reappear every twenty minutes or so. "I'm gonna get out of here, you know. One way or another." She kept her eyes focused on the wall in front of her, refusing to look at yet another reminder of how she'd failed.

After the twelfth time she heard him repeat himself, she turned and yelled at him, "Philip Larkin! You are dead! You hear me? Gone! Deceased! Six feet under! Wake up!"

For a moment, she thought he heard her. She was almost sure of it, the way he paused before breaking the non-existent tray. But then he shook his head, as if warding off a bothersome fly, and brought his knee up again.

She sighed, turning back to the wall. This wasn't the first time she'd tried breaking a loop, but it never worked. They were too entrenched in their own traumatic ends.

A metal door opened, and Captain Núñez sauntered in, Officer Foster in tow. She stopped by the cell lock and eyed her up and down as Foster opened the door and cuffed her.

"We heard screaming," Núñez said, her voice monotone and uncaring.

Claire shrugged. "Ok."

She could see the captain gritting her teeth, and Claire almost smiled, if only to see her reaction. But over her shoulder, she caught a glimpse of the loop, lying on the ground, unmoving. Her impending smirk disappeared abruptly.

"We're ready for you. Follow me, and don't speak unless you are spoken to. I want to save our delightful conversations for the interrogation." Captain Núñez spun on her heels and led the way out of the holding cells, Claire and Officer Foster following.

The walk was short and quiet. The other officers had grown weary of yelling taunts and insults. The thick-faced Foster cuffed her to the table, nodded his regards to the captain, and left the room.

From what Claire could tell, the interrogation room hadn't changed, except she was now cuffed to the table instead of watching from behind the two-way mirror that covered the expanse of the wall in front of her.

Captain Núñez sat down across the table and poured a glass of water. Claire began to reach forward to take the offering, but Núñez immediately drank the entire glass before refilling it. Claire tried to cover up her movement by pretending to sweep some dust off the table, but Núñez smiled.

"I'm sorry. I should have asked if you'd like some water." Claire waited for the offer to follow, but it never came.

Figured.

"Ms. Reed, do you know why you are here today?"

"I know I won't speak until I am given a lawyer."

Núñez nodded.

"Yes, I thought you might say that. And a lawyer will

be assigned to you; I will make certain of it."

"So, I can go now."

Núñez laughed, her gaze cold. "Oh, I think we should just chat before we place you back in your cell." She braced her forearms on the table. "Why'd you do it?"

Claire kept her mouth shut. She knew Núñez was goading her, trying to get her to speak, let something slip. If she didn't speak, she wouldn't give anything away.

Núñez spoke again. "Come on, you're a smart girl. I know you want to share how you did it. Were you jealous? All these people in their successful careers and lives, and here you are, running cheap scams out of your apartment for a quick buck."

Don't respond, Claire told herself. She could feel her hands flexing as she tried to keep her mouth shut. It was harder and harder to bite her tongue and deny defending herself.

Núñez could tell. "I could give you a deal, you know. We've known each other for quite some time. Confess, and I'll do my best to minimize the sentence. You might see daylight again by the time you're eighty."

Claire involuntarily kneed the bottom of the metal table, wincing in pain.

"She's getting to you. You're going to let her do that?"

Claire startled and looked over Núñez 's shoulder, and Gemini stared back, her own eyebrow raised in challenge.

"Go away," Claire growled, and Núñez scoffed.

"I'm not going anywhere. Tell me, what do you think, Ms. Reed?" Núñez prodded. Claire tried to focus back on their conversation, but Gemini was making faces in mirror, teeth bared in a taunting smile.

Núñez turned and looked at the mirror, and Gemini morphed into Núñez instead. The real Núñez turned back to Claire, but Gemini kept Núñez 's assumed features.

"Are you listening to me, Ms. Reed?' Núñez said, irritability leeching into her tone.

"What? Yes." Claire refocused on Núñez and chastised herself for breaking her silence. Núñez frowned.

"You should be taking this offer more seriously. You won't receive the same deal after you leave this room."

Claire took a deep breath.

"What're you going to do, Clarissa Reed? We hope you look good in orange." Gemini said in an oily voice. Gemini shifted back to Claire's features, wearing an orange jumpsuit, her name emblazoned on the front. It winked, and Claire's face in the mirror lost its manic smile.

Gemini was gone.

Claire shook her head. She locked eyes with Núñez. "I'll be seeing my lawyer now."

Núñez sucked in her breath. "We have eyewitness accounts of your presence at the deaths of nearly every individual, along with the ID of Rachel Kembrock, found inside your residence."

"It's all circumstantial," Claire couldn't help but say. *Shut up,* she scolded herself.

Officer Núñez shrugged and snapped her fingers. Officer Foster returned to the room. "Maybe, maybe not. All I know is that things aren't looking too good for you."

Officer Foster lifted her roughly from her seat and

ushered her toward the door. As they took a step toward the door, Núñez called after her. "One last thing, Ms. Reed."

Foster twisted Claire around to face his captain. Núñez 's expression was filled with hatred, but Claire could see a fraction of the sadness she was masking behind her eyes.

"We have direct evidence indicating your part in the death of Officer Santos. Consider that while you wait."

Officer Foster yanked her from the room and pushed her back down the hallway to her cell. Claire knew it would be her home for the indeterminate future.

chapter SEVENTEEN

I'm gonna get out of here, you know. One way or another."

No matter how many times the loop repeated itself, Claire couldn't find it in her heart to ignore his practiced, final words. Perhaps this was her penance for being unable to stop his capture. There was no proof he was innocent aside from the desperate claims of his sister, but that was little consolation to dull the guilt that had long settled into her memories. Layers of guilt just seemed to keep building, thin coatings of film atop film, permanently calcified.

The fingerprints.

The ID card.

The direct evidence Núñez allegedly held in her back pocket.

The mere fact that she was always nearby whenever Sagittarius shot his arrow and claimed another victim as its own was damning enough. Having the entire force—its captain at the helm, leading the charge with ever-increasing intensity—was the nail in the proverbial coffin.

Possibly her literal one, too.

The sound of crackling flames roared to existence in the silence. Surging to her feet, Claire took in a stoic-looking Michael and a frazzled Henry by his side.

"You look terrible, doll. What'd they do to you?"

The insult was softened by the sheer relief of seeing them both. Michael, meanwhile, was inspecting the door of the cell.

"Simple lock and key. A fool's defense," he muttered. Another flash of heat and orange flame, and Michael was gone.

"Nice to see you again, too," Claire said sarcastically to the place Michael had just been. Henry stepped into her eyeline.

"I mean it. What have they been doing to you? You look like you've been down for the count and kicked around. No mercy from the men in blue, I reckon. Not for you, anyway." Henry eyed her up and down, attempting to ascertain the department's preferred method of torture for suspected traitors.

"Not much, just showing off the indisputable evidence against me that's going to land me in prison for the next few decades. Or hours, if one of the Caretakers gets to me first." Bitterness and sarcasm seeped into her voice.

"It's all circumstantial, doll face. We'll get you out faster than a cat out of a bag."

"That's not how the saying goes."

He grinned and shrugged, perusing the room,

clicking his tongue in distaste.

"Okay, your turn. It's been hours; what took you so long to show up?" Claire asked.

"Well," Henry attempted to dust off the cot, his hand floating through the flimsy plastic, and then sat down. "It took us a while to realize you'd been taken. I came back to argue more because my fuse was still lit, but you were gone. Honestly, I thought maybe one of the demon beasts got to you, by the looks of the mess; someone ransacked your place and enjoyed every minute of it."

"Yeah, my old buddies on the force didn't seem to give a shit about tidying up," Claire muttered, a brief flare of anger igniting and dying in her stomach.

He grew quiet for a moment, rocking on his feet as though fighting the words that wanted to come out. "I was real worried about you, doll. I thought you were a goner, and I'd turn the corner and find you . . . you know . . . and after everything I said earlier—"

Claire interrupted him. "It's okay, Henry. I'm not dead; you're not stuck with me yet." Henry gave her a weak grin, and Claire said, "Go on; what happened?"

Henry cleared his throat and continued. "Michael showed up, and we went out looking for you together. Wasn't too hard; with the hordes of yellow-bellied journalistic vultures looking for a morsel of information about the 'Gaslamp Murders,' we just followed the noise."

"Gaslamp Murders?" Claire groaned.

"Yeah, and with your luck, your face is probably plastered with that moniker all over the web by now."

"Perfect. That's just . . . perfect." The marketing

wrote itself: *Madame Clarissa, the Murdering Medium*, she thought bitterly.

Another flash, and Michael reappeared, a set of keys in his hands. Reaching one of his arms through the bars, he inserted the key, twisted, and the cell door popped open with a small creak.

Claire rushed forward, slamming the entry shut again. "What do you think you're doing?"

"Relieving you from this prison. We have work to do." Michael made to reopen the gate, but Claire held fast, her arms crossed in front of her chest.

"And how do you think that'd look? How am I supposed to explain how I escaped?"

Michael narrowed his eyes, then shrugged. "You won't need to explain. You will be freed, and we can focus on the capture and return of our immortal foes." He reached out to unlock the cell again, and Claire grabbed his arm, clutching at his coat. She shook her head, exasperated, a few strands of unkempt hair tickling her face.

"You can't expect me to be on the lam for the rest of my life. What am I supposed to do if we successfully capture all the Caretakers? When you're finally done and gone? It's not like I'll be able to reenter society as if nothing happened."

"We will deal with that when the time comes," Michael said.

Claire had enough. She threw her hands in the air and paced the room. It was the same size as her bedroom, yet the storm-gray concrete walls seemed to close in tighter. It was much like her future: bleak, cold, and isolated.

Admittedly, that description wasn't terribly different

than the week before this chaos had entered her life, but at least she hadn't been trapped. At that thought, she felt a prickle of pain behind her eyes. She wondered when she last had a drink and immediately felt ashamed.

Pinching the bridge of her nose, Claire responded to Michael, trying and failing to keep the frustration, bitterness, and blame out of her voice. "No, we will deal with it now. Believe me, the SDPD and the world don't take kindly to alleged murderers walking around scot-free. Unless you can suddenly make me invisible, I will attract attention."

This finally gave Michael pause. He frowned at the lock as though that was the primary source of their misfortune. Claire felt a sense of pride in stumping this ancient being for a moment, but it was short-lived. If he couldn't think of a way out, how could *she*? A buzz sounded, and the doors at the end of the hall reopened. She heard Officer Foster making his way to her cell, his footsteps echoing.

Claire shared one last glance with Michael before he nodded, drew in his coat, and disappeared, the flash of heat and campfire scent immediately swallowed by the cool, dank air. Henry, however, remained and placed a hand on her shoulder.

"I'm not going anywhere, doll."

She smiled at him.

Officer Foster sneered. "Not sure why you're so pleased. The captain needs to see you again, and I've never seen anyone make it past round two with her." He unlocked the cell and snapped the handcuffs back on Claire's wrists, tightening them until she felt the circulation slow in her fingertips. She gritted her teeth but refused to acknowledge the pain. Henry, on the other hand, attempted to kick the man in the groin. His foot simply soared through Officer Foster's abdomen, but Claire appreciated the gesture.

Everything was the same in the Interrogation room as it was before. The empty metal table was reflected in the spotless two-way glass; the other walls were a painful white. Núñez had yet to arrive.

Officer Foster clipped Claire to the table and leaned forward to whisper. His breath was hot, smelling of stale coffee and less than two hours of sleep. "Carlos was a friend. The station's friend. Your friend. And now we've got your cornered, you fucking bitch." His eyes glittered with rage. Claire repressed a shiver.

He left, and the moisture of his breath still lingered on her face, an uncomfortable, wet cloth against her skin. Henry sidled over and half sat on the table, glaring at the door.

"What a piece of shit," he spat.

Claire shook her head and looked down at her cuffed hands. "No, I'd probably do the same thing if I thought someone killed my friend. Worse, actually. Gotta admire his restraint." She twisted her wrists, trying to move them into a more comfortable position, but the metal dug into her bones. Already, sore red lines were appearing at the edges of the cuffs. It was a reminder of what she'd done. What they thought she'd done, anyway.

Claire and Henry waited. And waited.

Minutes slid by, heavy and viscous. Claire tapped her foot, the *tap tap tap* out of sync and rhythmless. Captain Núñez wasn't the kind to dally, even to intimidate perpetrators. She should have already been at the table, teeth displayed in a hungry snarl disguised as a smile.

Henry broke first.

"What in God's sake is taking so long? Is this what they do? Bore you into confessing? If I had known that bird would be taking her sweet time, I would have gone with Overcoat Jones. Whatever he's doing has got to be more interesting than what's happening here."

"You young people have no patience, do you?" Claire joked, turning her head in time to avoid seeing him stick out his tongue again. He was right, however; this was beyond the usual wait time, even as a tactic to break her spirit.

Muffled sounds closed in at the door. Claire raised an eyebrow; the doors and walls were nearly soundproof. If she was hearing anything outside of the room, it had to be close to a thunderous commotion.

"Henry, why don't you go out there and see what's going on?"

Henry nodded, eager for something to do.

As he reached the door, it burst open with a crash, swinging through Henry's body. He stumbled back from the shock, moving out of the way for the livid-faced captain who lunged to the table and slammed her palms down with an ear-ringing smack.

Claire jolted backward and sucked in a gasp as the cuffs cut into her wrist. Alarmed, Claire searched Captain Núñez's face and thought of the first earthquake she'd ever experienced in California: the deep, earth-shaking vibrations and tilt, the violent agitation of the world around her. It seemed that a personal earthquake of her own was happening in Núñez 's face, her visage a dark plume of maroon fury.

"What did you do?" Less of a question and more of a statement.

Claire leaned as far back as she could without pulling on the metal cuffs again. She swallowed.

"Can you be more specific?"

This was not the answer Núñez was looking for. The captain gripped the front of Claire's sweatshirt and lifted her to her feet. Claire felt her upper back jolt forward as the cuffs restrained her posture.

"You think this is funny? Do you see me laughing? How did you do it?" A mist of saliva coated Claire's face, droplets flicking into her eyes. She flinched as Núñez shook her. "Look at me when I'm talking to you!"

Claire opened her eyes to see her old captain nearly nose to nose with her. She tried again. "Look, I don't know what you're talking about. I've been in the holding cell and then here this entire time."

Strike two. Núñez lurched her grip downward, and Claire fell forward, her forehead hitting the table with a sickening thud. The room swam in front of her, and when she tried to open her mouth to speak again, something warm and tasting of iron dripped into her mouth. Henry roared a string of expletives as he tried to stand between the two, a transparent, useless barrier.

Núñez interjected before Claire could refocus. "It's gone. Where did it go?"

Claire didn't bother to respond. It was apparent that unless she was giving some sort of confession, Núñez didn't want to hear it. Not that it mattered; she was dazed, and her headache had spiked tenfold from the slam into the table. She struggled to form words.

"You blister of a woman," Henry continued to howl, throwing his fists through Núñez 's chest. "I don't hit a dame, but I will give what's what to a fucking wench." Claire could see his clenched hands push through the other side of the captain's body to no effect.

Núñez let go of her shirt, and Claire slumped in her chair. A roll of nausea billowed in her stomach, and she kept her mouth shut, afraid of what might come out if she were to try to speak. The captain trailed along the edges of the room, eyes trained on Claire like a lion deciding how best to devour its prey. This creature had been starved, and Claire had no plans to help it feed.

After a few minutes of wheezing breaths, Claire could barely hear over Henry's stream of curses. Núñez finally sat down on the other side of the table, face still dark and blotchy.

"Who are you working with?

"Nobody," Claire gasped, only able to get out a single word. The trickle of blood tickled her chin as it dripped down her face. Núñez pursed her lips and sucked in her cheeks. Claire half expected to be thrown on the table again, but it seemed that Núñez had come to her senses.

"The footage of you in your cell is missing, along with the evidence. You couldn't have gotten out to swipe it, so someone had to help you. Who are you working with?"

Claire kept her face as purposefully blank as possible while the room swam around her. She had a guess as to what might have happened.

"I've got a guardian angel. Maybe you can ask him," she said, head pounding.

The anger Núñez had loosely tamped down reappeared. Henry narrowed his eyes at Claire, who ignored him.

"I can keep you here for as long as I need. And I can't promise that other footage won't go missing once I leave this room. You better pray your guardian angel shows up fast enough." A tremor ran down Claire's spine at her implications.

"I know my rights. You have 48 hours to file a charge, and from what it sounds like, all you have is your supposed 'witness.'" Something flickered behind Núñez 's eyes, and Claire took a leap.

"Except I'm thinking that was a bluff. You may hate me; you may think I'm a murderer and a thief and the scum of the earth. But I also know you, and despite everything you've been doing, you're not going to let your officers assault me more than you just have. You've got more honor than that."

Núñez stopped moving and stared wordlessly at Claire. If she looked hard enough, Claire thought she could see the officer she once knew before everything went south: hard-working, honor-bound, loyal.

To a fault.

And now that fault had opened into a cavern, its depths as immeasurable as her grief. And Claire saw that she had miscalculated. Grief and rage had changed Núñez to her core.

Slowly, Núñez stood up and walked to the door.

Pulling the handle, it swung open, and Officer Foster walked in. He held a short, heavy baton in his hands.

"Honor does not bring back the dead." Núñez left, the door clicking behind her.

225

When Claire was ten years old, she witnessed a pack of coyotes attack a rabbit. The sun had nearly settled in for the night, the top of its curve sending out its last rays of warmth before extinguishing beneath the weight of the horizon. She had learned that when the sun went down for the night, creatures averse to the light crept from their caves and crevices for the hunt.

The coyotes, skinny and malnourished, bent low to the dirt trail, their yellow eyes trained on the little ball of fluff chewing on a stray bit of browning grass. The rabbit was unaware that when the sun winked its final beams, it would also be its final moments of life.

Claire thought back to this moment as she sat, still chained to the table, watching Officer Foster check the lock on the door, the baton still firmly gripped in his hand. Satisfied, he looked up at the camera in the far upper corner of the room. A small red light had been illuminated each time

Claire had been dragged for interrogation. With a nod, the light turned off.

And took her beating heart with it.

Panic bloomed inside her chest as she watched Officer Foster circle the table. With each step, he tapped the baton into his open palm, the muted pat of the weapon coinciding with the tap of his uniform-issued boots. Claire had once seen an officer apprehend a criminal, shoving him down onto the ground with the heel of his shoe. She had instinctively winced in pain, imagining the sharp crack of her nose and jaw.

In mere moments, she wouldn't need to imagine it anymore.

She tried to swallow, but her mouth was dry, like the desert surrounding her childhood home. That poor rabbit. Would she ever see her home again? Her father never saw their home again.

Don't think like that.

"I'm going to enjoy this," he said.

Officer Foster stalked behind her chair, and Claire watched him through the mirror. Henry stood in front of Claire once more. "It's alright, doll; I've got you," he growled.

Claire appreciated the gesture, however fruitless.

Foster placed a hand on her shoulder and crouched to speak directly into her ear. His grip was tight, and the hair on his knuckles brushed her neck, creating an unpleasant ripple of goosebumps on her skin.

"Don't worry," he continued. "It'll only hurt. We have no plans to end your life. We're not murderers, unlike you."

In a flash, Claire lurched her head sideways, the top of her skull colliding hard with his mouth and connecting with his front teeth. He stumbled backward, one hand cupping his chin. A stream of blood trickled from a split in his lip and dripped into his open palm. Now, they had matching injuries. Droplets seeped between his meaty fingers and splashed onto the floor. His cut lips pulled back to reveal a red-painted snarl, and Claire was pleased to see she'd knocked out one of his teeth.

"You bitch!"

He raised the rod above his head, the fluorescent lights glinting off its surface. The baton swung down in a practiced arc aimed directly for the center of her crown, and Claire dodged sideways, falling off the chair, her arms forced straight by the cuffs. The blow glanced off her shoulder, and she grunted. Officer Foster jerked forward with his momentum, momentarily off-balance.

"I know you're angry," Claire spat, her words coming out fast and raspy, "I know you think I'm a criminal and a murderer and a lowlife and maybe a hundred other terrible things, but I swear on my life that I didn't kill anyone."

He ignored her.

Claire tried again. "Are you going to make me suffer while Carlos's actual murderer roams free?"

Officer Foster spat a mixture of saliva and blood on the ground. "I don't ever want to hear his name come out of your mouth!" He swung the baton again, this time making contact with her wrists. Claire screamed and instinctively tried to kick and pull away, but she was held fast in place. Through her cries, Claire could hear Henry shouting, and through the blood and sweat in her eyes, she could see him trying to fight. Foster's voice was thick with frenzied fixation.

"I'd like to see the public empathize with a cop-killer face like yours when I'm done with it," Foster spat. Bleary-eyed, Claire watched as the large man lifted his foot to stomp down on her face. Claire slumped, readying herself for the landing strike. The pain in her wrists was too much, the day was too much, everything was too much. She closed her eyes.

Officer Foster let out a sudden gush of air, and Claire opened her eyes to see him careening backward as though something large and heavy had crashed into his abdomen, sending him flying. His back hit the wall with a thud, and he fell to the ground, groaning.

Henry stood over him, fists balled by his side, his face a mixture of fury and shock. He lifted his hands and surveyed them, but they seemed as pale and transparent as ever.

"Henry?" she slurred, confused.

The apparition started out of his reverie and hurried to her, his eyebrows raised in concern.

"I saw him coming for you, and—I don't know—I just ran at him, and he fell like a bag of bricks." Claire turned her head side to side, attempting to clear the pain-addled fog.

"Didn't know you could do that," she mumbled.

"That makes two of us." He tentatively reached his hands to her cuffs to grab them, but this time, they slid right through. He was back to being a whisper in the wind.

"Can you pick up the keys from his pocket?" Claire asked, and Henry bit his lip.

"I can try." He walked over to the groaning officer and tried searching his pockets, but his fingers slipped through his body, intangible as ever.

Claire's head was clearing. "Maybe it has to do with speed. You know, go fast enough, and you can break through some sort of material barrier?"

"I know you're hurting, doll, but I'm going to need you to try using your brain a little harder." Claire tried to roll her eyes but stopped when the nausea hit.

"Okay, okay. How about—"

"Who are you talking to?" Officer Foster pressed his palms to the wall, heaving himself upward with a grunt. With increased desperation, Henry began to punch and grab at him, trying to either hurt him or procure the cuff keys. Both were unsuccessful. Whatever had allowed Henry to attack Foster was now gone, and she was back to where she was before: hurt, powerless, and in very immediate danger.

"You think you're so clever?" Officer Foster stepped forward, looking worse for wear. Blood from his missing tooth stained the front of his uniform, several droplets coating his badge. He was hunched slightly, his breath still recovering from the tackle into the wall.

"Clever?"

"Kicking me when I wasn't looking." Claire shook her head.

"Kicking you? How could I have possibly done that? I'm sure you already noticed, but I'm not in any shape to attack you right about now."

"Always with the lies."

"That doesn't even make any sense!"

He's insane, Claire thought wildly. It didn't matter what she said; everything would be her fault, one way or another.

"Let's try this again." Officer Foster readied himself, and Claire saw Henry barrel forward, only to pass harmlessly through the officer's chest. He spun back and tried again, like a bull charging a matador, only to miss its target.

Brandishing the staff, he pulled it back, focusing now on her knees. "Teach you to fight back," he muttered, tensing to strike.

Then his face changed. His eyes clouded over. His pupils and irises faded before disappearing completely. The tension tightening his jaw slackened, the bags under his eyes sagged, his shoulders drooped. Milky and unfocused, his unseeing gaze settled on Claire's face.

What the hell? Cautiously, Claire stood up. "Foster? Are you still in there? Henry, are you seeing this?"

Henry opened and closed his mouth, lost for words, eyes wide in shock. "I don't—I mean—did I do that?" He reached out a hesitant hand toward Foster and immediately jerked it back as the officer's body twitched madly.

Foster's head jerked sideways, his ear nearly hitting his shoulder. It then tipped forward, his chin stabbing the top of his sternum before twitching his head in the other direction. Claire shuffled backwards as far as she could manage as the officer's head jerked and turned, his face and hands twitching uncontrollably. Henry floated over to Claire's side, watching wide-eyed and fearful.

"Henry, is there any way you can find Michael?"

"I have no clue how to find him. Don't you have your pocket watch?"

"They emptied my pockets when they were

processing me." Henry cursed and stepped in front of Claire, the top of his head reaching just above her chin, hands raised in defensive positions, more performance than practicality.

The officer's body suddenly went still.

Something flashed next to him, and Claire swore she saw someone standing by his side: skeletal and pale as ivory. Its mouth was pressed to his ear as though sharing a secret in hushed, whispered tones.

But then it was gone.

"Clarissa Reed." The gravel of his voice was gone. Officer Foster's words echoed within himself, his voice slightly out of sync with the movements of his slackened jaw. He raised both hands, palms to the ceiling.

Another pause, and then his hands began to move up and down like buoys in the ocean. His blinded eyes held a level gaze at Claire. She didn't dare move. Foster's anger and abuse were dangerous but predictable. This, on the other hand, was no longer Foster. Whoever—or whatever—it was posed a new kind of unknown danger, but she knew it would be worse than a few broken bones.

"Clarissa Reed," the thing inside Foster repeated. Its hands stopped, and its left hand was higher than the other. "You have been found innocent of these crimes. You will be set free." For a moment, it looked as though it was done talking. Then, it turned to Henry, and its hands began to undulate again.

"Henry Faulken." Claire felt the coolness of Henry's body as he moved backward and bumped into her.

"Y-yes?" Henry frowned and watched as the hands slowed to a stop, the left hand higher than the right, though only by mere centimeters.

"You have been found innocent . . . of *these* crimes." Foster paused. "You will receive penance for your other indiscretions when the time comes. For now, be released." Henry tensed as Foster began to turn, this time to stare into the mirror. For a third time, Claire and Henry watched as the hands danced and swayed higher and lower.

His right hand stopped far above his left.

"Antoine Foster. You have been found guilty of your crimes. Punishment will be swift and severe. Consequences must match the catalyst." With its final words, Foster's head slumped to his chest, and he stood in place, the vision of a sleepwalker gone still.

Claire cleared her throat. "Officer Foster? Have you come back?"

With a gasp as though he'd been held under water, Foster lifted his head in alarm. He spun around to face her and swayed in place, looking faintly dizzy.

"I ... uh ..." he stuttered, searching the room as though he'd lost something but couldn't quite place what it was.

Finally, he rubbed his hands on the sides of his pants, drying the sweat coating his palms, before pulling a set of keys out of his pocket. He strode toward her, and Claire pulled away from him. However, he simply unlocked the cuffs. The metal clinked as they released from the table, and Claire rubbed her wrists, feeling the circulation of blood into her hands once more.

Foster turned and opened the door to the hallway. "Follow me as we collect your effects. I reckon we will want to be quick about it." Cautiously, as though any sudden movement would remind him of his burning desire to leave her bloody and bruised on the interrogation floor, Claire crept past him and started toward the front lobby, Foster and Henry on her tail.

In sharp contrast to the cheers and jeers of her arrival, Claire's reentry into the front of the station was met with an eerie, stoic silence. Officers stopped mid-paperwork, and visitors followed suit and paused their conversations. Claire was a single-float parade procession, and everyone watched as she forced herself to keep her head high and her eyes trained on the front desk.

She imagined she was quite the sight: covered in drying blood, the bruises on her arms deepening a darker purple with each step. Officer Foster didn't look much better himself.

The man at the desk was slightly younger than her, and from what Claire could remember, he had not been around during her expulsion. However, anger and resentment are easily spread, like a disease. Despite being strangers, he viewed her with the same contempt as his colleagues.

"I'm here to pick up the items taken from me." She had no idea why exactly Foster was allowing her to leave, but she certainly wasn't going to question it. Whatever creature had overtaken his body in the interrogation room was powerful and dangerous.

The man cleared his throat, crossing his arms and making no apparent move to fetch her effects.

"You sure about that, Ms. Reed? Seems to me that you only just got here; be a shame to let you go so quickly."

"Twelve hours hardly constitutes a short visit. My belongings, please." Still no movement. Their glares held steady, waiting for the other to break. A few steps behind her, Claire knew Officer Foster had finally caught up.

"Jack, give her the bag and be done with it." The man—Jack—raised an eyebrow and leaned back. Jack uncrossed his arms and settled his hands on his hips. "Sir, I don't think the captain would—"

"Are you questioning me, rookie? I said, let her go. That is an order." Jack's expression lost some of its initial hardness, chipping away into uncertainty until he finally reached under the desk and picked up a plastic bag. He emptied the contents individually, placing each on the counter for Claire to take.

"Pocket watch, wallet, house key. We tossed the bag of salt." Claire glowered as she snatched all three items and shoved them into her pocket. Without thanking the man, Claire sped through the front doors, eager to leave.

Early morning air was wonderfully brisk against her face. The workday traffic had already begun to creep through the streets, the only honking of pre-work road rage perforating the city. Claire glanced backward and saw Officer Foster watching her from the front steps. He nodded at her, and his face hardened into a quizzical expression.

Placing one of his hands on the door frame, he clenched his fist as his other hand gripped the door handle. He looked as though he had no control over what his own body was doing, and panic flooded his features. Officer Foster pulled the heavy door closed with as much strength his 200-pound body could muster. Even from a distance, she could hear the crack of the bones in his hand. Someone inside screamed. Claire watched through the glass as Officer Foster fell to the ground, cradling his mangled hand in anguish, the lost gaze drained from his face, replaced with agony.

Claire had seen enough. She sped away, the words that had come from Foster's mouth repeating in her mind: *Consequences must match the catalyst.*

chapter NINETEEN

L ibra may be a dangerous adversary, but it knows how to operate within the boundaries of morality and justice," Michael said.

When Henry and Claire returned to her apartment, they tripped over one another to describe everything that had happened. The entirety of the update might have been quicker if Henry had stopped interrupting Claire to make comments about the digression of the police force.

"Back in my day, the men in blue—"

"And women," Claire added. Henry shot her a look.

"Women weren't coppers back in the day. In any case, corruption like this didn't exist in the same way it does today. It's an outrage, a complete lack of respect for the badge." In frustration, Henry swatted at a candle they had lit upon their return. The flame flickered but remained bright and warm. Since the walk back to the Gaslamp, Henry had been attempting to make physical contact with various items:

kicking at litter, slapping the tops of garbage cans, poking Claire in the shoulder. None indicated they'd been disturbed besides Claire, who threatened to douse him with salt if he tried to poke her again.

As they'd walked, Claire wondered about what Libra had said: *"You will receive penance for your other indiscretions when the time comes."* What indiscretions had the Caretaker been judging? Despite their many conversations in the last few years, Claire knew very little about Henry's life. She'd always felt it was rude to ask and chose to wait for Henry to reveal his past when he felt comfortable. She watched him rant. The time, it seemed, still had yet to come.

Michael's voice interrupted her thoughts. "There has been corruption in all systems and institutions since the beginning of society. It is inevitable."

Henry ignored Michael's comment, choosing instead to try flicking an old receipt off the coffee table. It remained still.

Claire offered. "Maybe it only works when danger is involved. The receipt isn't going to do anything to you, except maybe a paper cut if you can make your little trick work."

"I can do without your comments, thanks," Henry shot back, not looking at her.

"You were commenting constantly when I was practicing my Sending!" Claire said, indignant.

"Now is not the time for arguments," Michael cut in as Henry opened his mouth to retort. "Our next step is to regroup, decide on Sagittarius's next plan of attack."

Claire turned on Michael, hands balled into fists. "Speaking of 'time,'" she growled, "when exactly were you thinking of showing up when Foster was beating me within an inch of my life?"

Michael frowned. "I was taking care of the evidence you needed removed. And I was . . . unaware of what was happening at that time."

Something seemed to catch in his throat, and he turned away. The back of his neck had turned pale, and the muscles seemed to be pulled taut. But Claire wasn't ready to let him off the hook. *She* was the one who'd been beaten and tortured, not him. She gritted her teeth.

"Since returning from our disastrous attempt at UCSD, I have been arrested, stuck in a cell with a looper, interrogated, beaten, and crossed paths with yet another Caretaker. I need a break." *And a drink.*

Standing up, Claire grabbed a used glass from the sink and poured some whiskey. Without pausing to recap the bottle, she took a long draft, relishing the burn as it ran down her throat and settled into her stomach.

"Clarissa, I need you focused," Michael said, his voice low and eyes fixed on the glass in her hand. She raised it in salute.

"Then you're going to have to give me a minute. I don't know exactly how *you* function, but my face hurts, my wrists hurt, my head hurts." She downed the glass, refilled it, and then settled back into her seat across from where Michael stood. "I know the humans you meet are dead, but living ones need to eat, use the bathroom, and occasionally rest. And this," she raised her glass again, "is the only way you're going to get me relaxed enough to listen to you drone on yet again about this impossible situation." Already, Claire could feel the liquor dulling some of the ache in her temples.

Michael frowned, eyeing the glass in her hand. "There are other ways to relieve your pain besides searching for the bottom of the bottle."

"I'm not looking for your opinion; I'm just looking to survive another day." She wouldn't let him make her feel more guilty than she already felt. And this issue was the least of their concerns. It wasn't even an issue to begin with, she decided.

"Alright, while Henry and I were having a nice little chat with Libra after almost getting my brains beaten in," she said, "I assume you were out finding Sagittarius. So, what'd you find?"

Michael pursed his lips, his hands clenching and unclenching in his coat pockets. "I know you are changing the subject," he pointed out.

He walked to the window and looked out to the crowded street, resting one of his forearms horizontally on the frame. Silence.

"I enjoy watching the e-bikers at war with the car commuters as much as the next person, but maybe we can leave the people-watching to another time?" Claire said with more snark than she felt.

Michael ignored Claire's jab.

"Sagittarius has gone into hiding. I don't know where it is," Michael said.

"Lovely," Claire muttered, resting the glass against her temple.

Henry kicked through the table leg. She closed her eyes and rested the back of her head on the chair, allowing the buzz to weigh her down. Perhaps a bit of sleep would do her some good.

"Even if we do find Sagittarius, we would need a way to capture it," Michael added, tapping on the glass window, lost in thought.

"We do have a way. I Send it into the ball, right?" Claire was met with silence. Opening her eyes, she saw Michael still looking out the window. Henry, too, was purposefully avoiding her gaze. "What? You don't think I can do it, do you? I've done it several times, remember?"

Henry cleared his throat. "Of course, doll. It's just that maybe some more practice would do us some good, you know?"

"We've already practiced; we know I can do it."

"It is not a matter of 'can,'" Michael interjected, "it is a matter of control and focus. You lost control. Your fears cost you your focus, and you paid the price. Those human men paid the price. It is too heavy a cost to pay again." Claire could feel her face growing red and was embarrassed to feel her eyes grow damp.

She placed the half-full glass on the table and stood, the room slightly unsteady. "It was one time, okay? I wasn't expecting any apparitions to be there. We'll be better prepared next time. I won't fail again. Now, if you'll excuse me," she strode to her bedroom door, "I'm going to take a nap for the next century. When I wake up, I'm going back to the library to see what might be catching our Caretaker's eye. Until then, go away."

With that, Claire slammed her bedroom door behind her.

She woke six hours later, her head still foggy, but the pain muted. Lying on top of the blankets, she stared at the popcorn ceiling, unwilling to get out of bed. She knew Michael and Henry were right; she had let fear take over, and that allowed two people to die and Sagittarius to escape, likely leading to more deaths that would ultimately be her fault. Childishly, she wondered if she could pick up and leave. Sure, she had sworn she'd never return to Arizona and live under her mother's roof again, but at least it'd be secure, albeit tedious and unbelievably exasperating.

She brushed the idea away. For the short time he'd been around, her father hadn't raised someone who passed the buck. "You take ownership of your achievements," he'd said, "and failures. They're both yours."

She had failed the last time. It wouldn't be repeated.

Groaning, she stood and stretched her arms upward, popping her shoulders and back with a series of satisfying cracks. She splashed some water on her face and walked out of the bedroom. Both Michael and Henry were gone. She hadn't expected them to stay, but still, a prick of guilt poked the back of her mind.

The glass of liquor, still partially full, was left on the table. She stared at it, then picked up it, emptied it in the sink, and refilled it with water. She sipped as she plucked an apple from a bowl on the counter and headed downstairs, reluctant to see the mess the police had left behind. She knew she'd see that wax had spilled and been pressed into the carpet, pages of shredded books had covered the floor, and chairs were upturned and scattered. It would take hours to clean up, and even then, she'd need to buy new assortments of candles, books, and accoutrements.

Taking a deep breath, she opened the door to her shop and halted in surprise. Henry was sitting on the table, directing Michael as he walked around, picking up the last bits of clutter that had been strewn around the room.

"Place the books over in the far corner; it's much better than where she had them earlier. She's sweet but has no sense of interior design." Henry barked out a wheezing laugh and noticed Claire enter the room. "Well, good morning, doll face. Well, afternoon, anyway. What do you think?"

Claire's mouth opened and closed wordlessly, trying to think what to say. The trash was gone, the broken items replaced with items much newer and nicer than the ones she'd had before. The supposed "ancient manuscripts" she'd kept for ambiance were replaced with real books, their bindings leather with gold printing of Latin titles she couldn't read. Candles of various sizes and colors encircled every nook and cranny in the room. The carpet was clean, free of embedded wax, the shredded paper was gone.

"Where did you get all this?" Claire looked to Michael, who placed the stack of books in the position Henry had pointed out. She begrudgingly agreed they did look better in their new spot, and she saw Henry grin from the corner of her eye.

"It's a gift," Michael said. Claire frowned, remembering the bags of food Michael had stolen the week before.

He seemed to know what she was thinking. "We went to your friend in Encinitas and told him of your plight. He gathered these for you." Claire felt her eyes grow damp again. She'd have to visit Madame Courtney soon and thank him. Claire surreptitiously wiped her eyes with the back of her hand.

"You guys went to see him?" Michael nodded, and Henry walked over, attempting to rest an arm on her shoulders, instead allowing it to hover just above.

"You're doing your best; we know it's been tough. We appreciate you, kiddo," said Henry.

Claire sniffed. "Don't call me kiddo; I'm older than you," she said with feigned indignancy.

"We both know that's not true, sport." Claire snorted and shoved his arm away; he moved it as she sailed through. "Anyway, this was all Michael's idea."

"Really?" Claire redirected her attention to Michael, who surveyed the room. It was the first time she'd seen him slightly sheepish. It was almost … human.

"A Gateway cannot focus in a cluttered environment. It was only prudent," he muttered.

Claire smirked. "Sure thing, Michael. Thank you. Both of you."

She gave them each a watery smile. Michael took a step forward, paused, and then walked to Claire, pulling her into a quick embrace. His coat enveloped her shoulders, making her feel like she was swaddled in a heated blanket. Warm and safe.

"You're welcome, doll," Henry said from behind them. Michael let go, taking several steps away.

Claire cleared her throat. "And I'm sorry. You're right; I shouldn't have been so defensive."

Michael waved a hand in dismissal. "We look forward, not backward." Michael strode to the shop's front door and opened it, gesturing for both of them to follow.

"Where are we going?" Claire asked.

"The library, as you requested. We have more research to do."

Henry floated through the door to the sidewalk, and Claire followed suit, pausing next to Michael.

"Are you coming?"

"Sagittarius has left my scope of awareness," he said. His voice betrayed an edge of annoyance. Claire figured Michael had never experienced any failure in his abilities before; it obviously unnerved him. "So, it may be best that I join you for now. Besides," he added as Claire locked up the shop, "any time I leave you alone, it seems you are a beacon for trouble. It'll save some time if I escort you."

Claire snorted and thought she saw the corners of his mouth twitch upward.

This time, Gemini did not pay a visit on the cab ride to the library. However, a new level of awkwardness settled in as Michael squished into the backseat beside Claire. The taxi was a repurposed Fiat painted yellow and black like a bumble bee. It took a moment for her to convince Michael that he couldn't sit in the front seat next to the driver, an older woman who looked like she'd rather lose the commission than have this man attempt to sit up front next to her.

"It is easier to defend in the front seat of this vehicle. Nearly 200 years ago, mortals had utilized that seat as the warrior sentinel to defend the driver. Hence, the term 'shotgun' was created for that purpose," Michael had claimed as he settled into the back seat with a frown.

"He's joking," Claire hurriedly told the woman and gave her the address before she could change her mind on accepting their fare. Instead, Henry sat in the front seat, and though he said nothing, he bore a cocky little grin.

Once they arrived and entered the library, they branched off. Claire went to the computers, Henry to the bulletin board for events, and Michael set off to peruse the rest of the building, casing the area for Caretakers.

The room was nearly as empty as the last time Claire had been there. A few college-aged students sat huddled in a corner, studying and chatting in low voices. An elderly man gossiped with one of the matrons at the check-out counter without a book in hand. On the far side of the room, a small group of young children sat cross-legged as the girl Claire had met—Maisy—read from a large, colorful, cardboard-paged book. Claire couldn't hear what Maisy was reading, but judging by the faces she was making and the laughter from the children, it was a hit.

Claire plopped down at the computer she'd had before and opened the web browser to search. She typed in "UCSD" and clicked Enter. Links and images popped up, many of the same as the last time she searched the university. This time, however, multiple news articles had been added, with titles like "Honorary Guests Lecturers Dead After School Shooting; Suspect in Custody."

Glancing around to see if anyone was looking her way, she clicked the link, and a short article popped up. For a moment, the picture refused to load—it seemed that these computers hadn't been replaced since the late 90s—but as soon as it did, Claire scrolled down the page to hide it.

The image was of her in handcuffs being ushered into the station. Her face was hidden under her mane of orange and red waves, but it was unmistakably her. Captain Núñez was captured mid-stride beside her, a look of wild pride in her foxlike leer. Claire wondered what had happened after she was freed. If anything, Claire wouldn't have been surprised if Captain Núñez had broken his other hand in retaliation for letting Claire go. She was sure she hadn't heard the last of the SDPD.

Claire scanned the article, looking for her name.

Dr. Richard Stevenson (47) and Rahmed Vishwanath (49) were killed in a school shooting at the University of California, San Diego, on December 8th. Both men were guest lecturers regarding the effects of city development on California's biosphere and have been praised for their research in the California education system over the last five years. Allegedly, an individual shot both Stevenson and Vishwanath toward the end of their presentation. No other casualties have been reported at this time. According to the San Diego Police Department, an unnamed individual had been taken into custody but has since been released due to lack of evidence.

Claire felt her shoulders relax; aside from the photograph of the back of her head, she was still as anonymous as ever.

"I thought that might have been you, but I couldn't be sure. Didn't think of you as the murdering type, but what do I know?"

Claire whipped her head around and saw Maisy standing behind her, a cardboard book under her arm. The children were bouncing around the room with abandon, free from their read-aloud, much to the older librarian's chagrin. The shawl-shrouded matron was vacillating from child to child, trying to keep them quiet while simultaneously shooting glares of malice toward Maisy, her criminal colleague.

"It was all just a big misunderstanding," Claire said.

Maisy smiled, her hazel eyes squinting behind her thick-rimmed glasses.

"Darn. I was kinda hoping you were found guilty of *something*. Not killing or anything, maybe just trespassing, then you could keep me company as I finish up my hours. I still have," Maisy made a production of counting on her fingers, examining an imaginary calendar, "168 hours left to go."

"Sorry to disappoint; innocence can be irritatingly inconvenient."

Maisy nodded in mock understanding. "Being guilty isn't so convenient, either." She pulled out the chair beside Claire and sat down, surveying the screen. As she did so, Henry floated up to Claire, one hand in his pocket and shaking his head.

"Nothing on the boards, doll. Just some fliers about an open mic where you can pretend to enjoy some poetry from people who enunciate all the wrong words." He snickered and, upon noticing Maisy, immediately stopped. He raised an eyebrow, and Claire could see his hand inching toward his tie. "Well, that's a sight for sore eyes. No offense, doll face." Claire bit her lip and tried to keep a straight face as Maisy piped up.

"So, are you here to Google yourself? Couldn't do that in the privacy of your own home?"

"No computer," Claire said absently. It wasn't easy to keep her focus on Maisy, with Henry standing directly next to the girl, who was a couple inches taller, ruffling his hair. Claire decided to remind him that Maisy couldn't see him after their visit, though it didn't seem to bother him.

Maisy looked startled, like she couldn't fathom not owning a computer. "You should take one of mine; I've got loads. Bit of a collection I've got going on."

Maisy didn't strike Claire as the computer-collecting type: wrapped in the same plaid scarf from the other day, it hugged the collar of her jean jacket. She looked more likely to kick up her combat boots on a nearby table and switch between staring off into space and people-watching with the intensity of someone with too much time on their hands.

"Why do you have so many computers?" Claire asked.

"Like I said, my dad was an electrical engineer, my aunts and uncles are software engineers, my grandparents were mechanical engineers. My cousin is a painter, but they don't talk about him. In any case, I grew up around screens and technology."

"Well, you'll have to show me sometime."

"Plan on it. I'll buy you a coffee, and we can talk about getting you a computer, though I guess it'd mean you'd be coming to the library less." Another crinkle-eyed smile.

Claire glanced at Henry, who pursed his lips. Clearly, he wasn't pleased to see Maisy flirting with Claire with him so close.

He pointed at Claire. "Oi, tell her you have a friend who'd like to hear more about her computer whatsits and all that." Privately, Claire knew Henry knew nothing about technology past the 80s; his pre-computer days were too ingrained in his past for him to care about any new tech innovations. Maybe he'd found a reason to care.

Claire ignored him.

"What have you found, Clarissa?" Michael appeared beside her, carrying a book in his hands. She looked down at the cover, but the title was hidden.

Claire sighed. "Not much, really. Honestly, I don't even know where to start."

Michael looked up at Maisy, who shied away slightly at his bright cobalt stare. Frowning, Claire looked between the two and remembered how intimidating Michael looked at first, with his overcoat and towering intensity. Maisy looked like a young child by comparison, barely in her early twenties.

Claire cleared her throat. "Michael, this is Maisy. She works here."

Maisy let out a small laugh. "*Volunteer*, actually. Maisy Lo, at your service." She held her hand while Michael inclined his head in a slight bow.

"Thank you for your service to the arts, Ms. Lo." He gave her a smile that she returned, unsure.

Claire turned her laugh at Maisy's confusion into a cough. Maisy's hand dropped to her side.

"Thank you? I reckon you're quite the old soul,"

Maisy said, chancing a smile.

"You have no idea," Claire muttered. The corners of Michael's mouth twitched upward, and Claire felt a twinge of pride.

"She likes old souls," Henry crooned, poking Claire through the shoulder. Claire waved him away, pretending to brush her shoulder.

"So," Maisy stood straighter, resetting herself, "is there something I can help you both with? This is sort of my job, after all. Besides, Mrs. Gertrude will throw another fit if she sees me idly chatting and not throwing down knowledge like my life depended on it." She cast a glance to the elderly woman across the room.

"Honestly," Claire said, "we're not even sure what we're doing." She sighed.

Michael rested a hand on her shoulder, and Claire could feel the skin of his knuckle graze her neck. She suppressed a shiver.

"We are searching for an individual," Michael said.

Maisy nodded. "Okay, well, we've got loads of biographies upstairs. Who is it?"

Michael shook his head, rubbing the stubble on his jaw. "Allow me to rephrase. We need to know where this individual will be within the next 24 hours." Maisy took Michael in, turning her head slightly in growing suspicion. Her eyes darted to Claire as if trying to see if she was on the same page.

Claire broke in. "One of our . . . friends hasn't been answering his phone. We're worried about him, and because it's been less than 48 hours, the police won't help us. Besides, they're not in a position to listen to me now. I think you can relate to that." Maisy nodded gravely, eyes on Michael's hand that cupped Claire's shoulder. "Anyway, we think we can narrow down where he'll be if we just know what's going on in the county; he likes lectures, talks, stuff like that."

"And you're certain he's still here in the city?" Maisy asked, deep in thought.

Claire inclined her head.

"And you're positive he's missing? Like, not just has his phone off and been asleep for the last 12 hours?" she added.

Claire nodded, and Maisy bit her lip, her hands wringing together absently. Henry placed a hand on her shoulder, and when Maisy didn't react, Henry looked disappointed. Claire felt a twinge of pity for him; he'd died so young, and she'd never asked him if there were someone special he'd left behind. She sometimes forgot how lonely he must be, just like the rest of the departed.

"I think," Maisy said quietly, glancing around, "I can give you a better option than searching for random events and hoping for the best."

"What's that?" Claire asked.

Maisy shuffled in place, obviously uncomfortable with what she was about to say. Michael bent forward to get closer to Maisy, who stepped back in alarm, the small chain on her earring swinging.

"It is a matter of life and death. Whatever service you can provide is immeasurable to our plight." Michael's eyes were starting to shine, the blue radiating unnaturally bright. Claire reached a hand and placed it on Michael's back, silently urging him to calm down, to reign himself in. She felt his heartbeat slow beneath the coat, and Claire kept her hand on his back, warm and comforting like a flame.

"What Michael means to say," Claire distracted Maisy from Michael's gaze, the girl seeming more resistant than ever, "is that this is really important. But if you can't help, it's okay. We'll figure it out." Maisy rocked back and forth on her feet, shooting furtive looks at Mrs. Gertrude, who had finally herded the kids back to their parents and was tidying the book-strewn tables.

"Okay," she finally said. Maisy took off her glasses and rubbed her eyes. After placing them back on her face, her demeanor turned resolute, the same defiance Claire had seen when they first met. "Alright, I'm off in about twenty minutes. Just stay put until then." With that, Maisy walked to the front desk to help a mother check out a book for her giggling daughter. Henry floated after her without a word. Claire sighed inwardly; Henry could have his fun, but Claire wasn't looking forward to the emotional crash when he remembered what he was.

She turned to Michael. "Any idea what she has in mind?" she asked. Upon noticing his gaze, he stared at Maisy, who turned a pale shade of pink and shuffled into the back room and out of sight.

"The young girl is capable and resourceful. She will be an adequate addition to our mission." Appeased, Claire turned her attention to the book in his hands.

"And what do you have there?" Michael held up the book, and Claire examined the cover: *The Intricacies and Idiosyncrasies of Astrology*. Claire smirked and looked up at him.

"Really?" she deadpanned.

"I find that this manuscript may be useful for the time being, even if it's based on the deluded human interpretation of the Caretakers and The Beyond."

"I suppose you're right," Claire agreed. "Come on. Let's grab Henry and get ready to head out. We'll need to get you a library card, and I'm sure that'll be an adventure all on its own."

chapter TWENTY

M aisy lived with her parents several miles inland from the library. It had been years since Claire had lived in the suburbs, and the "copy and paste" houses and the lack of constant traffic noise made her feel uneasy. It was too quiet out here. To Maisy, however, this was a comfortable nest she was not quite ready to leave. As Maisy drove Michael, Claire, and, unwittingly, Henry, to her home, she regaled them of the different places in her community. "And this is where I climbed my first tree, and this is where I first broke my arm, both of which was on the same day, mind you. And over there is where I kissed Natalie Smyers, and then Edi Cullen in middle school, but Natalie had cinnamon Altoids beforehand, so I had a major allergic reaction and was sent to the ER. We never hung out again after that, God knows why."

Henry's interest in Maisy grew with every word that fell from her lips. While Claire sat in the back and Michael rode shotgun, Henry leaned himself forward over the center console, responding to everything Maisy said, though she was deaf to his remarks:

"I never bring people home, so Mom and Dad will be so excited."

"A dame like you should only be bringing home the stars, and I'd be happy to be a part of your constellation."

"Are you hungry? Mom is definitely going to make you dinner; I hope you like congee."

"I'd drink the ocean and eat the mountains if that's what you'd want me to do."

Maisy hit a speed bump too quickly, and Claire kicked Henry and mouthed, "Shut the hell up." He smirked but fell silent.

By the time they reached her parents' gravel driveway—slightly carsick and nauseous from Henry's constant chatter—Claire had learned most of Maisy's life story in bits and pieces. She was adopted at the age of two and was given every opportunity. They'd tried athletics, music, and the arts, but nothing stuck until computer camp in sixth grade. She hadn't stopped learning, even when removed from the university.

"Yeah, it's going to go on my record, and maybe it'll affect some of my future job prospects, but I reckon if I'm good enough, my employers aren't going to care," Maisy said as she pulled to a stop. Claire expected Henry to interject— he certainly had opinions about the current generation's code of ethics—but he remained silent, instead nodding emphatically. Claire grinned and looked at Michael, who returned it.

As they walked to the door, Claire felt his hand brush against hers, and the heat stayed long past his touch.

"Hey, Dad!" Maisy called out into the foyer, unlacing her shoes and placing them against the wall. As Claire followed suit, an older man rolled out in a wheelchair onto the hallway tiles.

"You're home early, Mae-Mae. And you've brought guests, I see." He smiled at them and pushed himself forward, extending his hand in greeting. Although it was apparent that Maisy was not blood-related to her father, they shared the same warm mannerisms.

"Hi, I'm Claire. I met Maisy over at the library."

"Oh yes, where she's working. My little Good Samaritan," he squeezed Maisy's arm. Claire tried to catch her eye, but Maisy purposefully looked away.

"And this is Michael," Maisy added to cover the awkward pause. Again, Maisy's father reached out to shake Michael's hand. Hesitant at first, Michael reached out his hand and shook it up and down awkwardly, still bending slightly in a bow.

"Ouch! You've got quite a grip, young man." Michael let go, and her father wiggled his hand in the air, regaining the feeling in his fingertips.

"My apologies, sir," Michael responded, but the latter waved it off.

"Don't fret; people handle me too delicately anyway. I'm Peter, but you can call me Pete. Just don't call me—"

"Late to dinner. Cliché as ever, Dad," Maisy finished Pete's sentence, and he grinned at her.

"Speaking of which, Mom is in the kitchen cooking.

Will your friends be staying for dinner?"

"No, we're just here for a short visit," Claire said.

"Ah," Peter replied, beginning to back away, "perhaps another time, then. Shout if you need anything. And, Maisy, say hello to your mother before disappearing into the den." Maisy gave him a thumbs-up before he left.

Claire gave her a knowing, slightly judgmental look, but Maisy shrugged and looked away.

"Some things are a 'need to know' basis, and what happened isn't 'need to know.' Come on; I need to say hello to my mother." Maisy bounded down the hall, Henry right on her heels.

The kitchen was small but bright. The walls were tiled in pastel yellow, the grooves a deep chocolate: an actual '70s interior. Wooden cabinets were mostly closed, though the doors appeared permanently propped open, filled to maximum capacity with pots and pans. The counters were covered with bowls, plates, and random utensils. A woman with graying hair pinned up in a loose bun was whisking something in a bowl as they entered.

As they clattered into the room, she looked up with a grin. "Welcome home, Mae."

"Hi, Mom." Maisy walked over and hugged her. "These are some friends I met over at the library. I'm going to show them my collection before they head back home." Her mother nodded, her face serene despite the droplets of batter dotting her cheeks like sweet constellations.

"That's nice, dear. Perhaps your community service is doing you some good after all." Her mother gave her a hard stare, and Claire realized that at least one of her parents knew what had happened during her time at UCSD.

Maisy nodded, grabbed an apple from the counter, and took a large bite. In between chews, she asked, "Do you need help with anything?"

Her mother shook her head. "No, thank you, Mae. Enjoy your time with your friends." With that, her mother returned to cooking, and Maisy ushered them into the back of the house.

"Mom and I have come to an understanding about what happened," Maisy said as she pushed open her bedroom door. "We try not to stress Dad out with these kinds of things. He has enough on his plate."

Claire opened her mouth to disagree but snapped it shut as they entered Maisy's room. When Maisy had said she had a collection, she was understating her hobby. If anything, it seemed closer to an obsession, balancing on the precipice of hoarding. One side of the room was filled with glowing, flickering black and gray boxes, creating a whirring buzz of white noise. Through various tangles of wires, they connected to a desk lined and stacked with blank monitors. The third wall held fans of all different sizes, and though they were thrumming and pushing air across the room, it did little to stifle the heat from the electronics. The only area without any technology was a mattress directly on the ground, the blankets unmade.

"An impressive collection, Maisy Lo," said Michael.

"That's the understatement of the year," Henry breathed as he circulated the room, inspecting the different blinking lights and screens. "When this gal wants something, she goes for it."

Maisy blushed with pride, responding to Michael.

"Thanks! Took me years to gather all these beauties. Check this one out." She bustled over to a large, blocky monitor, its screen rounded with a colorful "A" on the side. "Macintosh 128k. I'll still play Zork on a floppy disk occasionally if I'm feeling nostalgic." She spoke tenderly, as if these computers were her children. Her voice sped up the more she spoke. She continued to point out her favorite hard drives and CDs, ranging from the 80s to modern day, for the next few minutes. Michael, Claire, and Henry just stood and stared.

"Of course," she said, pulling out a rolling chair and pressing one of the buttons on one of the large metal boxes, "we won't be using anything from the last century." She laughed at herself.

Six monitors lit, the screens glowing painfully bright in the dim room. Maisy began to click away at her keyboard, muttering to herself as different screens and applications opened, closed, and were dragged from screen to screen.

"Are you going to explain what you're doing, or is it a surprise?" Henry said, forgetting momentarily that Maisy was deaf to his words. He gestured to Claire to repeat his question.

"So, Maisy, what exactly are you doing?"

"Shhh, I'm focusing," she chided, and Claire fell silent.

"For someone who claims to be a low-level felon," Henry said, examining a monitor with a faux wood finish, "she has all the makings of a Boss Baddie in corduroys."

"Do not confuse expertise with personal ethics,"

Michael said, and Maisy hushed him as well.

"And . . . here we go." Maisy pressed a final key, filling the screens with dozens of black-and-white video feeds. Claire bent forward and squinted. After a moment of confusion, Claire recognized a street in one of the images.

"Is that the pier?" she asked.

Maisy grinned.

"And A street, B street, C street, and 1st street. You get the picture."

Slightly pixelated pedestrians and cars paraded in and out of the footage, unaware of the prying eyes that watched them go about their frantic lives.

"Is this in real time?"

"Couple minutes' worth of delay, but yes. Check it," and Maisy tapped on one of the video boxes. The image took up the entirety of the screen, allowing them to view the scene with more detail. Claire took note of the camera's filming direction: above, angled diagonally downward in a partial bird's eye view on an intersection.

"These are footage streams from the traffic cameras," Claire realized aloud. She looked to Maisy, who looked smug. "How are you able to do this? Is it even legal?"

Maisy placed a hand on her hip and gave her a look that reminded Claire of Maisy's mother. "Is that a question you really want answered?"

"No, not really."

"Exactly." Maisy shrunk the image again, and the rest of the boxes reappeared on the screen. "So, if you're certain your friend is still in San Diego County, you'll be able to find him somewhere on here at some point." She waved to the chair next to her, and Claire sat down. Maisy began to stand up and offer her chair to Michael, but he declined the offer.

"He usually prefers to stand," Claire said, eyes on the screen.

"It is a natural readied position," replied Michael.

"Ready for what?" Maisy questioned, but Claire just shook her head.

Michael grunted vaguely and steadied his gaze on the screens, eyes darting from square to square, his training as Guardian resurfacing with practiced diligence and unwavering focus.

"Stay as long as you like," Maisy said, "but if you do, you will be expected to stay for dinner. What does he look like? I can help you search."

Claire hesitated. It was unlikely Maisy would be able to see the Caretaker, much like the other students at the lecture hall.

"He's difficult to describe. Don't worry about it."

"Alrighty then. Let me know if you change your mind." Maisy hopped out of her seat and fell onto her mattress, picking up a nearby book and delving into the words.

"This is going to take forever," Henry grumbled but seemed more than pleased to settle in next to Maisy, attention half on the screen and half on her book. Claire agreed but couldn't think of any other plan of action. Looking to Michael, he ignored Henry's complaint and continued his search.

A sigh escaped her lips, and Claire, too, settled into her seat and squinted at the little slices of San Diego, hoping for a glimpse of their quarry.

Several hours later, Claire's eyes were dry, stinging, and drooping, a painful and distracting combination. Images were starting to blur together. The faces and vehicles all looked the same, and jumping between screens was tedious. If she had seen Sagittarius, Claire wasn't sure she would have realized the Caretaker, perhaps mistaking it for a strange looking pedicab or abnormally large dog, especially as she grew increasingly tired.

At one point, Maisy's mother brought several dishes filled with couscous and salad topped with shredded chicken. Michael declined the dish, but when she pressed him further, he accepted the plate, leaving it untouched on a stack of books. Claire realized she'd never seen him eat and made a mental note to ask about it when they left.

On the other hand, Claire couldn't remember the last time she'd had a home-cooked meal; most of the meals she prepared came from a box with a spice packet and five-minute cooking instructions. Aside from raw vegetables and cans of beans, her family hadn't been one to cook extravagantly, or healthfully. "Ingredient-only households" were meant to force you to cook, but for her, it merely taught her how to eat everything separately and as blandly as possible. This was a nice change of pace.

For a while, Maisy had left to help her mother in the kitchen—"Gotta pay the rent somehow, and there's not a lot of money in forced volunteer work"—allowing Michael and

Claire to speak freely, though few words were exchanged as they sat, eyes pressed to the screens. Henry, reluctantly, stayed in the room, scanning the monitors, his arms crossed, his mind likely in the kitchen with Maisy.

Finally, Claire piped up with the question that had been burning in her mind all day. "So, what happens when we capture all the Caretakers?"

Michael answered, eyes still on the screens. "At the solstice, you will Send them all back to the Beyond. And I, too, will go with them."

"Into the Beyond? I thought you weren't allowed in there."

Michael was quiet for a moment. "I'll go back to the entryway and resume my duties there." A minor fracture of disappointment formed in her chest, and she pushed it away.

"Michael, why can't you enter The Beyond?" she asked. Claire wasn't sure why she'd asked; she hadn't planned on bringing it up since the train, but her curiosity won over her trepidation.

She hadn't expected him to answer, but then she felt a tap on her shoulder and looked to see Michael holding out the Tome, its pages opened.

Taking a break from the screens, Claire turned to the book and read.

The Guardian 2:1

In the beginnings of The Beyond, the Caretakers were diligent in their guidance. They took in their human souls, provided judgment and consequence, and cared for their wards as their own children.

Yet, there was one who felt unsettled in their role.

This Caretaker longed to leave its given realm. It viewed its duties as servitude to humankind, and as such, felt that man was given a pedestal on which to remain. It grew resentful and hateful against the souls that entered its domain, providing longer, extreme punishments and torturing its visitors.

Until one day, it decided to leave.

The Caretaker left through purgatory's unguarded gates, escaping into the human realm. By the time the Superior discovered its disappearance, the creature had ravaged village after village, slaughtered man, woman, and child, and left each town torn asunder in its wake.

With great difficulty, the Superior was able to force the Caretaker back into its realm, melding its limbs to its throne, cursed never to walk its domain again.

Yet, the Superior knew it was only a matter of time before the next Caretaker would desire to flee.

So, the Superior searched for a Guardian, a soul who would spend their days defending the Gateway, to keep humankind and the Caretaker safe in their place. The Superior eventually decided on one lost soul, one who held honor and loyalty coiled round their heart. The soul was told they would never need to leave through the Beyond; instead, they would live for eternity as The Guardian, keeping the Gateway safe, never to pass into the Beyond.

Claire slowly closed the book and returned it to Michael, who took it without a word.

"You're human?" She asked a few minutes later.

"Maybe at one point, perhaps," he answered, his voice low. "It's difficult to remember. Much has changed since that time."

Claire repositioned herself to see him better. The

blue light glowed against his face, his eyes darting in quick motions side to side. He seemed to be paying little attention to anything beyond the screen. "I thought you said you never met the Superior."

Michael nodded. "That is true. The Tome is only as accurate as the author, though that name has been lost to time. My mission came to me as a message, a sudden transformation. There was little choice in the matter. Choices do not matter, as far as the Superior is concerned." His words were bitter, and he fell silent. Claire followed his lead, mulling over his words. He rarely showed so much emotion; Claire burned with curiosity and wanted to ask more but shoved her queries aside.

Several more hours passed, and despite the nap earlier that day, Claire was feeling the precipice of exhaustion and, on the heels of that, panic.

"This is pointless," Claire finally groaned, leaning back precariously in her chair. It groaned loudly and tilted unsteadily toward the floor.

"It is not pointless; it is merely tedious," Michael corrected.

"Oh, my bad. This is *tedious* and pointless," Claire shot back. She didn't care that she sounded childish; the stress clouded her focus, and she was too tired to regulate her maturity.

"What we need to do is narrow our search," Henry said, taking a break from the screens and rubbing the bridge of his nose. "We need to go back to what we were doing before and brainstorm generally where he'd be. The county is too large for us to watch for so long."

"Henry is correct," Michael said.

"Who's Henry?" Maisy piped up from the bed. She had returned, plopping herself down on her mattress, oscillating between her phone and an old vintage computer manual thick enough to be a brick. Privately, Claire thought a brick would be equally as interesting as a computer manual.

"Michael's imaginary friend," Claire answered.

"You're a little old for an imaginary friend, right?" Maisy furrowed her eyebrows, placing a bookmark on her page before closing the cover. Michael looked affronted.

"Henry is not an imaginary friend; he is an essence of what he once was, an apparition belonging to The Beyond."

"You should have left it at imaginary friend," Maisy said, "and I'm going to choose to ignore the sarcasm, especially when I'm going out of my way to help you."

"I don't deal with sardonicism," Michael responded.

"Sorry, Maisy," Claire interjected. Claire returned to Michael and Henry. "Maybe we missed something."

"Well, Michael slashed at Sagittarius pretty good, so I guess it'd probably go somewhere to heal?" Henry offered. Michael nodded in agreement, choosing his following words carefully.

"He would need to heal after our last interaction. It's likely taking him longer than usual, considering he never got the chance to acquire the knowledge and wisdom of his targets."

"Okay, so if he's hurting and didn't get his chance to feed, where would he go?"

"Michael," Henry popped in, "after Sagittarius kills its prey, how likely is it to give up its feeding?"

Michael frowned. "Unlikely. When a target is acquired, it will finish the job."

"Right, but it didn't. Couldn't, anyway. So, those bodies are still out there undrained." Claire felt a prickle of understanding create goosebumps along her spine.

She spun to Maisy. "Can you get up the San Diego County Morgue feed?"

"I mean, sure?" Maisy cringed but walked over and selected a few frames, dragging several images to a new screen. Claire repositioned herself in front of the monitor, the light reflecting on her pale face.

"There!" She shouted and pointed to the upper right-hand corner. Everyone crowded around, Maisy moving to the other side of Claire to avoid bumping into Michael. Sure enough, a pixelated silhouette ambled into focus down a semi-deserted street several blocks from the morgue doors. The figure was limping, moving slower and more deliberately than the last time they fought.

"It's there," Michael announced, straightening to his full height. The top of his head nearly grazed the ceiling fan. Claire could feel the temperature rise from his body as he readied himself for action. "We must leave at once." Michael made for the door as Maisy pressed herself to the wall to give him room.

"You found your friend? Where? I don't see anything." Maisy cleaned the lenses on her shirt sleeve and put them back on, squinting at the video. Sagittarius continued to creep into full view, but Maisy could see nothing.

"He moved out of the screen but was there," Claire

lied. She raced after Michael as he strode for the front door, Henry slightly behind her, looking over his shoulder to Maisy, who stood bewildered.

"Michael! Hold on; we can't just *go*. We need a plan, preparation, something. I'm not ready, remember?"

"There is no time for that," Michael said. "This is the closest we've been to Sagittarius since we last battled; we mustn't lose this chance, and we mustn't allow it to heal." He pried open the door and walked down the driveway.

"And how are we supposed to get there? We don't have a car; I don't know when the next bus leaves, let alone where the station is. Think this through, will you?" Michael finally paused, stopping with a jerk, his coat swaying.

Claire caught up to him and rested her hands on her hips, chest heaving.

"We need transport," he acknowledged, and Claire felt a brief sense of relief. "Maisy Lo, we request your assistance." Claire watched as Maisy stumbled out the door and shivered suddenly, unknowingly tripping through Henry.

"Hey," Henry barked, glaring at Michael, "there is no way we're letting this gal anywhere near that damn thing. I won't allow it." He planted his feet and crossed his arms in defiance.

Maisy, too, was reticent to help. "Look," Maisy started, biting her lip and pushing up her glasses that had slid to the tip of her nose as she'd run after them. "I've been happy to help you look for your friend and all, but this is verging on some sketchy stuff. First, he's missing, then he's hanging around a place for dead people. I don't know; I'm not totally stoked about this, but maybe it's time you contact the authorities." She rocked on her bare feet, sucking in her cheeks, and Claire felt a tangle of guilt knot in her throat.

Is this how she wanted to treat the people who helped her?

"She's right." Claire rested a hand on Maisy's shoulder, looking at Michael for support. "She's done enough. We've already dragged her further into this than we should have. Thank you for your help; we really appreciate it." She turned and hugged Maisy; Maisy returned it after a moment of hesitation. "Come on, Michael, we need to find the closest bus."

Michael opened his mouth as if gearing up his argument, but upon seeing Maisy's fearful expression, his own softened. He bowed his head and then, as an added thought, extended his hand. His palm surrounded the entirety of her hand.

"You have done us a great service, Maisy Lo. This is where we leave you, indebted to your kindness." He smiled, and Maisy turned pink under her black bangs. Michael gestured for Henry and Claire to follow, and they began to walk toward the nearest cross street.

"I'll see you later, dame," Henry said, trying to brush a lock of hair behind her ear, heading after the others.

For a moment, Maisy stood in place, still anxiously hopping from foot to foot. She looked at her home, to Claire, back to her home, and then sighed. "Hold on," she called. They stopped, and Maisy rushed back into the house, returning with her boots and keys in hand. "It's just a ride," she warned, "and that's it. I'm not staying, and I'm not picking you up. I'm not a taxi service; this is the last time I'm helping you. Got it?"

Claire hesitated. "You don't have to do this. It's okay to say 'no.'"

"And I am. Just saying no to any future requests." A smile crept onto Claire's face; Maisy's nose was a pale red from the cold of the evening, giving her the look of an obstinate rabbit.

"Okay," she agreed.

Maisy nodded and unlocked the car. As Michael and Henry settled in, Claire stopped her. "Sorry, can I ask for one last thing?" Maisy raised her eyebrows in question.

"I did say no to any other requests."

"I know, but this one is straightforward."

She sighed and rubbed her neck. "What is it?

Claire felt in her pockets to double-check that they were empty. "Do you have any salt I can borrow?"

chapter TWENTY-ONE

It was only a ten-minute drive from Maisy's home to the morgue. Claire clenched the small Ziploc bag of salt that Maisy had brought from her parents' kitchen in her pocket. Preferably, Claire would have brought an entire canister just in case, but beggars couldn't be choosers, and she was already more than grateful for Maisy's help.

Shoulders tense in the seat next to her, Claire could tell that Michael wanted to discuss strategy in the car. However, Michael remained silent, with Maisy listening at the front and Claire making it adamantly apparent that Maisy should know as little as possible about the situation. She could almost hear the gears whirring in his mind, the blades sharpening in his head as he prepared for battle.

Henry sat in the front seat, unusually quiet. Craning her head to the side, Claire looked at Henry and saw him staring intently at the car radio. His finger was raised and jabbing at the different buttons; however, each time he made contact, his index finger pressed through, and the radio remained silent. Should he have been alive, they would have heard his teeth grinding together in frustration. Claire tried to get his attention and give him a reassuring smile, but he remained intent on the radio, poking again and again, failing again and again.

"Stop the vehicle here," Michael spoke, and Maisy turned on her blinker, slowing to a stop along the curb.

"Thank you, Maisy. We'll talk soon." Claire patted her on the shoulder and clambered out of the car.

"Just," Maisy paused, looking from Claire to Michael, "just, be safe." And with that, she rolled up her window, placed the car back into drive, and left. Claire stood and watched until the little green car sped to the end of the street and turned out of sight into the darkness.

A heavy hand pressed into her shoulder, and she looked up to see Michael, his eyes bright in anticipation, his tone serious. "It's time. We must be quick; it would not be good for Sagittarius to feed before we arrive."

Claire nodded, and Henry floated after the two, still silent. Michael's strides were long and practiced, causing Claire to double her steps to keep up, still hurrying several feet behind. As he walked ahead, Claire turned to Henry.

"Are you okay?"

He didn't answer at first, and for a moment, Claire wondered how lost in thought he was if her question had fallen upon deaf ears. However, he responded, his voice low.

"I'm not sure how much use I'll be in this fight."

Claire frowned. "What do you mean? Of course, we need you. Any extra pair of eyes is worth having around."

Henry replied, "Is that all I'm good for? Watching? I can't even throw a stack of papers at the thing and give it a papercut." He sounded miserable. He continued floating forward, his arms crossed, shoulders hunched. Claire felt a wave of tenderness toward the teen, taken too early in his young life, before he could make a mark on the world. She wondered if all the dead who remained behind felt as purposeless as some of the living.

"Of course not, Henry," she said. "I need you around. Having you around keeps me grounded, even when you're not touching the ground." She lightly punched him through the shoulder. "I trust you to watch my back."

"Wasn't able to do that last time." Guilt bled through his voice.

"That was all me. I panicked and screwed up. We know better now. Just stick by my side, and we'll be okay. When we're done, we'll go home, and I'll let you chill out in the living room instead of kicking you out. Sound good?"

Henry thought about it. "You never finished reading to me the other day."

Claire snorted. "Yes, well, we had an unexpected visitor." She nodded toward Michael, still pressing forward, head moving side to side in constant surveillance. "When we get back, we'll finish the book. But don't expect me to deal with your commentary; I still have some leftover salt in the cabinet, and I'm not afraid to use it."

This earned a smile from Henry. He lifted his head and looked at her. Claire was taken aback by how young he looked in the moonlight, his form limned by the soft white glow of the moon. Sometimes, it was tough to remember that although he was nearly a century old, he was still, in many ways, a boy.

"Okay, I promise to stay mum. But let's read something different; I've had enough horror for a lifetime."

"Wise choice," Claire joked, and Henry punched her back, a cool shock of air drifting through her arm as he made contact.

"Silence," Michael said suddenly. Claire lurched to a stop, nearly running into his back as he stood in place. Across the empty street was the morgue, the glass doors revealing a dark, unoccupied front lobby. The parking lot was vacant, a single flickering streetlight illuminating a mere fraction of the concrete space.

No sign of employees. No sign of pedestrians or commuters. No sign of Sagittarius.

Still watching the opening of the morgue in the corner of his eyes, he turned his body to the others, one of his hands rubbing the stubble on his chin in thought.

"There is no obvious sign of entry. We're lucky; Sagittarius must be more injured than we thought." He pointed to the corner of the building, shrouded in night. "Claire, prepare yourself in the shadows. I will stand at the entryway; when Sagittarius arrives, I will incapacitate it again. When it is time," Michael produced the glass orb from within his coat and handed it to Claire who took it gingerly with both hands, "you will send it into the crystal."

Claire hugged the orb to her chest, noting the warmth that emanated from the glass. She couldn't be sure if it was from Michael's body heat or the orb was generating energy waves. Throat tight, she nodded and began walking toward the shadows, Henry in tow.

"No, Henry," Michael said. "I need you to circle the perimeter and tell us when the Caretaker is nearby."

Henry furrowed his eyebrows. "Not a lot of good that'll do. We already know what's coming; I'd rather stick with Claire and make sure she's safe."

Michael shook his head. "An honorable notion. However, as we learned from our previous encounter, we now have other Caretakers who have taken an interest in our Gateway. We need someone to alert us if any others reveal themselves nearby."

Henry opened his mouth to dissent, but Claire answered instead. "It's fine, Henry. Michael is right. Just stay nearby, check in with me every few minutes, and it'll be okay." For a moment, Henry looked as though he would refuse. However, he leveled his gaze with hers, then nodded.

"Stay safe, doll face." He floated down a nearby alleyway and out of sight.

Claire heaved a sigh, inclined her head to Michael, and started toward the morgue. "I agree," he said. She paused and studied Michael. He rested his eyes on her.

"What are you doing?" she asked, her voice hitching. Michael stepped forward and wrapped a hand around her lower back, pulling her closer. She stepped forward, unable to look away from his eyes, the ochre glowing brighter with each breath they took together. With his other hand, he reached down and gently placed a palm on her ribs. Heat ebbed from his skin through her shirt into her body, the ache and soreness from the last 24 hours subsiding. Despite what they were about to do, the horrors they were about to encounter, she found herself wishing he'd place his hand directly on her skin, traversing her bare torso, healing her in more ways than one.

And then it was over. He removed his hand and instead moved a strand of hair out of her face, tucking it behind her ear.

He whispered, "Stay safe. We need you."

Her body was on fire: his fire. His lips were parted slightly as though he had more to say. But the moment passed, and he closed his mouth. With a nod, he marched past her, taking his position on the steps before the doors.

She stayed in a place for a moment, touching the lock of hair he had moved, and then moved to the shrouded wall, huddling in place. She knelt, one knee pressing into the ground, both hands still curved around the sphere. She counted her breaths, working to slow the blood flow pulsing loudly in her ears, refocusing on what needed to be done.

One, two, three . . .

Yat, yee, sum . . .

Uno, dos, tres . . .

Один два три . . .

And she waited.

And waited.

And waited.

The moon caressed the night sky, slowly traveling westward as time passed. Claire was getting antsy; the heat from the orb was no longer enough to keep her body warm. Her adrenaline was beginning to ebb away, and her legs were developing pricks and needles.

Where is it? Henry had circled back to Claire several times, having seen nothing of interest.

"Hey! There's a car coming." Henry said, reappearing nearby.

Sure enough, bright headlights appeared at the end of the street, crawling toward their lot. The LEDs blinded Claire, and she struggled to see the driver. Perhaps it was an early morning traveler—*very* early morning—or a restless college student needing a drive to let off some steam … with a slow drive by the San Diego County Morgue.

The car, blinker clicking loudly in the silence, turned into their lot, and Claire recognized it. Maisy had returned. Maisy threw the car into park and stepped out of the vehicle, moving toward Michael. She didn't notice Claire in her hiding space as she passed.

What was she doing here? Claire's anxiety returned, and she left her post.

"Maisy! You shouldn't be here," she called.

Maisy jumped and turned, her arms crossed.

"I was worried," she said. "I just got this horrible feeling. And it just seems like you're all about to do something idiotic." Maisy took a step toward Claire.

A *whoosh* sounded through the night air, and Claire's heart skipped a beat. She opened her mouth to scream, to yell at Maisy to move, to duck, to run, but nothing came out.

Sagittarius had arrived.

chapter TWENTY-TWO

Henry dove toward Maisy, his body colliding with her own. Maisy's body flew several yards across the lot, and she tumbled to the ground, bouncing across the asphalt until she came to a stop, unmoving. Henry's translucent body covered her own, still protecting her after his impact. Beneath his form, Claire could see one of Maisy's legs bent akimbo, her knee at an unnatural angle.

Gaping at where Maisy had just stood, Claire saw that an arrow had been lodged into the ground, missing Maisy and creating a thin, precise, and deep notch in the concrete.

Fuck.

She scanned the sky for Sagittarius. She crouched, ready to launch herself out of the way of another projectile, though her joints felt immobile with fear. A loud buzzing filled her head. A dark mass shifted in her peripheral, and Claire snapped her gaze to it.

On the far side of the street, Sagittarius stood, a

gargantuan silhouette against the flickering fluorescent streetlamps. It gripped its bow in one of its calloused hands. A stream of liquid—jagged as lightning, black and viscous as rancid engine oil—dripped in sluggish droplets from the side of his torso; it still hadn't healed from Michael's attack at the auditorium.

The Caretaker started toward Maisy, its monstrous hooves clattering against the street, slow and deliberate. As it got closer, Claire could see its hooves were chipped, and mold emerged from the cracks, as though the host was actively decaying. Yet, though Claire could see Sagittarius was still wounded, every step reverberated with power and menace, creating puncturing echoes under the moonlit canopy.

As Sagittarius moved closer, it reached into the quiver on its back, producing another arrow from the sleeve and notching it in the bow. It lifted the weapon, aiming it at Maisy. She wouldn't survive it.

Claire tried to scream, "*Move your ass and get her out of here, Henry!*" but the words came out in a harsh whisper, the air rushing out of her lungs like a balloon squeezed by a kid's party clown. Maybe she was the clown. She opened her mouth again and took a weak step forward.

"*Praecipio tibi ut desinas!*" Michael shouted, his voice carrying over Sagittarius's heavy steps. Claire turned to see him and froze. His great power was on full display, and Claire watched in awe.

Memories of Michael in her loft converged with the Guardian she saw before her. He had been a man, composed and unyielding, someone who made her body tremble in the best possible way. How he would grasp her shoulder, pulling her gaze into his dusky blue eyes with the heat of warm coals, gave way to this blazing tapestry of power and regality. He was an infernal tornado of smoldering ember, a torch of brilliant white, yellows, blues, and reds. The man she thought she knew was no man at all, but a supernatural being, a guardian, an angel.

Her guardian angel.

His hands lifted upward, his fingers tipped in claws, palms outstretched toward the Caretaker. Air and fire flowed together, flickering in an ethereal spiral around his fingertips, spreading up his arms and across his back. He no longer controlled the fire; he *was* the flame.

Sagittarius halted and looked at Michael, unimpressed. He looked merely as though a dead snake had fallen onto its path, perturbing and harmless. It paused a moment and watched Michael with an appraising look before letting out a guttural choke. Claire thought it was gearing up to roar, but as it stayed in place, she realized it was laughing. A panic attack was growing; the buzzing was returning.

No, it's not. You're fine; focus, Claire thought, trying to shovel the panic away.

Sagittarius's voice carried across the lot. "You seek to capture me," it said, marveling in its formidable essence. Its voice was deep, an unearthly, frigid dampness dancing along its words. Its voice was meant to exist deep within the earth, not on its surface. Claire could almost feel her body plunge into its depths, its voice like sewing needles drilling deep into the many crevices of her body. "Your actions are futile and misguided," it said dismissively.

With a sudden burst of speed that should have been

unnatural for a creature of its size, Sagittarius repositioned its bow and fired it at Michael. He lunged to the side, nimbly avoiding it. Michael shouted defiantly and redirected his flames toward the projectile. The arrow soared through the glass doors of the morgue, but rather than shattering the window, it left a narrow hole the diameter of a small coin.

The Caretaker roared in exasperation and grabbed another arrow. A blinding flash of purple light lit the sky as Michael yelled out an unintelligible command, and Sagittarius stumbled backward as though it had been kicked in the chest. Now, it was angry and finally recognized the threat of its opponent. Its eyes bore into Michael, two pools of bubbling sulfur. Michael's head craned upward to maintain eye contact, unafraid.

That thing will crush him, Claire thought wildly, as a new surge of panic erupted on Michael's behalf. She pressed against the cement wall, forcing herself to stay hidden. *Michael said to stay away.* She bit her lip, a trickle of blood coating her tongue. Hiding had seemed so easy, to let Michael take charge, but seeing Sagittarius tower over him was terrifying. The beast's frame was riddled with broad, powerful muscles shifting under its hide like thick worms struggling to break through its skin. Its expression was pure venom. Claire felt the urge to run into the open, to draw its attention away from Michael to keep him safe. The desire to help was almost overwhelming.

I need to help him; I need to keep him safe.

Biting her lip harder, she forced herself to stay hidden from view.

"These mortals gather precious gems of wisdom,

feasts of knowledge," Sagittarius snarled. "They drink from the nectar of experience, benefit from the ambrosia of travel and journey. Yet, they waste it." Sagittarius spat a gelatinous gob of saliva and black blood on the ground. The flickering streetlight reflected off the spit on the asphalt. "They do not appreciate what they have; they do not know they are merely scraping the surface of what there is to know about the universe and The Beyond. It is not their fault; they are simple, basic creatures. But they are undeserving and unequipped for the opportunities they are given."

Michael trailed a wide perimeter around the beast, turning its gaze away from the mortuary, where Claire stood hidden. Claire thought over the words; they were not unlike things Michael himself had said in the past few days. But he left no room for camaraderie when he spoke to the beast. "Your duty is to those of humankind who have passed from the living into your care in the Beyond. You do as the Superior commands. As the chosen Guardian of the Beyond, you will heed my demand to return."

Sagittarius pressed a hand to its chest. "I am the patron of knowledge, of wisdom, of journey. I may be given the title of 'Caretaker,' yet I am essentially a slave to humankind," he said with disgust. "How am I to believe I have any control if I am forced to remain bound to the confines of the Superior's purgatory?" Sagittarius arched its back, its voice reaching a trembling crescendo. "No. It is our turn to roam this realm of our free will. Mortals will place what they have at my feet, willingly ... or not." In a flash, Sagittarius pulled back the bow and released another arrow at Michael's head.

"Michael!" Claire couldn't contain it; the warning cry ripped from her chest, the fear and panic finally digging its claws in and splitting her ribcage in two.

Michael looked toward the sound of Claire's voice, momentarily distracted. He turned back toward the beast at the last moment and dodged. But the distraction had cost him. He wasn't fast enough. The arrow pierced his shoulder, driving through bone and exiting out of his shoulder blade. A spray of blood propelled from his back, and he stumbled heavily, cursing.

No! Shit, shit, shit, Claire chastised herself. Her warning was supposed to *help* him, not get him injured. With a roar of pain and anger, Michael launched into action, drawing his blade. The streetlights continued to flicker in rhythmless repetition, and Claire saw the fight in strobed flashes: swords arcing, blades piercing, bows drawn, hooves outstretched.

Claire watched desperately for Michael's sign to bring forth the Sending through the cacophony of battle cries and crackling flame from the Guardian's fingertips. She clutched the orb tightly in her hands. Claire watched in horror as Michael's blows came more and more clumsily. He was undoubtedly slowing, each avoided strike becoming narrower than the last.

And the Caretaker knew it, too.

The panicked buzzing of the cicadas in her head suddenly fell silent.

Screw the cue. Claire pushed herself from the wall.

As she did so, an icy chill stroked the back of her neck. Claire's stomach twisted, and a sharp pain in her heart threatened its furious beating. She turned, and bile rose at the back of her throat. As she beheld the sight in front of her, the taste of vomit coated her tongue, mixing with the iron tang of blood.

In her panic-addled mind, she tried to count the figures that had materialized and were swiftly approaching. One, two, three, five—eight—thirteen figures were ambling toward her, their forms seemingly corporeal in the poor light. Spirits had come.

Like cockroaches flooding from a crushed wound in old drywall, more and more semi-translucent bodies emerged, climbing over one another and falling limply to the asphalt before standing again on wobbly limbs.

A woman with ruptured eyes staggered near, sensing Claire's presence yet unable to see her. An old man with a swollen skull blundered her way, speaking gibberish from delirium. Young men and women reached forward with contorted limbs and punctured chests, elderly folk with deep discolored bruises like mottled posies, others whose faces were too shredded and scarred or stretched like taffy to identify. These lost souls who stayed behind with their broken bodies in the mortuary had sensed her presence in the way she felt theirs.

And they demanded to speak to her, their voices layering on top of each other over and over.

"Help me."

"Where am I?"

"I need to get back home . . ."

Claire tried to suck in a breath, but her throat had closed up, just like one of the nearest deceased, his own throat thick and swollen. She thrust her hand into her pocket and gripped the bag of salt there. She tucked the orb under her armpit and ripped the bag open, snatching a handful of granules and scattering it in the space around her, mineral shrapnel in her war against the dead. The spray caught several apparitions, shoving them backward into the masses.

The others continued forward, and she threw another handful and then another. The ghosts hissed and spat, recoiling from the touch. Many began to retreat, preferring the numbness of their deceased corpses to the pain.

Still, others surged onward as the Guardian and Caretaker's battle raged in the background. Claire reached her hand into the bag and drew out empty.

"Shit!" She dropped the bag and pressed her back into the wall, edging down to the corner toward the front of the mortuary, her eyes on her ghostly pursuers. The brick wall scratched roughly at her back as she dragged herself away.

Claire opened her mouth to yell for help.

A pair of translucent hands protruded from the solid wall behind her, clamping over her mouth. She could feel pressure from the incorporeal palms, though she did not know if it was real or imaginary. An intangible sheet of ice wrapped the bottom of her face, and she envisioned the moist mildew of a rotting forest floor, the watery depths of a tepid lake: decaying, putrid, spoiled.

Dead.

And wanting to drag her down with them.

Her spine felt like it was nearly embedded into the wall; her vision was clouded by fingers bent in rigor mortis, eyes vacuous. Faces pressed low against her hips while others hung high above her head. Bodies continued to press in against her until all she could see was a thick fog of white and gray, the colors of her life these last few years.

Claire closed her eyes, squeezing them so tight she could see little dots swimming beneath her lids. She had spent so many years running from these apparitions, replacing the echoes of the dead with the meaningless chatter of the living in her ears, and for what? Some dead-end job, a cheap-ass apartment, a life of struggle to make meet even the *basic* of needs. Who gives a shit if a bunch of underworld demons took dominion over the world outside her office? It's not like the world was doing her any favors, anyway.

Maybe it was time to just let go.

And with that thought, she started to drift.

Something solid pelted her face, and the press of bodies against her immediately released. Claire's eyes stung as she opened them, gasping, her lungs filling in a rush of air. Through stinging tears, she saw Maisy above her, tossing salt from a large Tupperware with abandon.

It was apparent that Maisy couldn't see any of the apparitions; she twisted from side to side, randomly scattering grains of sand in the wind. She called to Claire, her voice raspy in panic and confusion, "Am I doing this right?" as she flicked salt in every direction.

Had the situation been less dire, Claire might have laughed. Claire could see the dead inching away from her, thanks to Maisy's help, and the deep gratitude she felt nearly brought a fresh wave of tears to her eyes. But she couldn't fall apart, not yet.

"Aim that way and just keep going!" Claire

commanded, clamoring to her feet. She needed to return to the mission—to Sagittarius, to Michael—but she wouldn't leave Maisy for dead. "And you keep with her!" She shouted to Henry, who nodded and circled the girl, eyes fierce against his dead brethren.

She skidded to a stop, watching the brawl at the front of the building. To his credit and Claire's enormous relief, Michael was still holding his own. They each had a few more cuts and scrapes, but the two warriors were evenly matched, with Sagittarius still weakened from its injuries at the lecture hall.

Looking up after landing a cut to the beast's massive leg, Michael saw Claire. She noted the flood of relief mirrored in his eyes, either at seeing her unharmed, ready to Send, or both. He turned back to Sagittarius, his brow furrowing with a resurgence of adrenaline.

With a primal cry, Michael leaped into the air and stabbed downward with a burst of energy, pinning Sagittarius to the ground, its front legs collapsing into the street.

"Now, Claire!" he cried over its deafening roar.

Raising the orb, she focused all she had on the glass sphere, envisioning the light within lifting and traveling toward the Caretaker, enveloping its body.

Lift, damn it!

The light within the orb wavered, leaving the glass before falling apart like a popped water balloon. The light returned to the sphere.

Damnit!

Claire's heart thundered in her ears as she tried again to focus.

"It's time, Claire! Do it now!" Michael yelled again, his voice wavering with effort, struggling to keep Sagittarius pinned to the ground. The centaur was writhing in place, bucking against Michael, taking back its leverage inch by inch. Sagittarius focused its eyes on Claire.

"I know you, Clarissa Reed. And you know all too little the risks you take by joining this fight."

Claire ignored its words, her hand cramping from holding the ball so tightly. She tried again. The light fluttered like a radiant jade candle yet stayed in place.

Sagittarius let out another guttural, derisive laugh. "The knowledge you need to complete your chosen task is insufficient. The Guardian has let you down and allowed you to join the fray too soon. You are weak." The Caretaker, emboldened, shook its body, and Michael tightened his grasp, beads of sweat flying off his forehead as he fought through the pain of holding on.

Claire glared, mustering false confidence into her voice. "You're the Caretaker of knowledge, right? I'm the patron of being a smartass, and I bet it will kill you when you realize you're wrong."

Sagittarius growled as Claire tried again to send the light from the orb.

It flickered and died once more.

She was going to fail, and Sagittarius was going to escape.

Again.

Just moments ago, she was nearly ready to give in, to drift away. Maybe that was for the best.

The tendrils of defeat encircled her arms, and the

hand holding the orb began to dip.

"Deep breaths, doll face. One thing at a time." Henry appeared beside her, cupping the bottom of her hand beneath the orb. Although she couldn't feel him lifting her hand, a sense of determined fervor erupted in her chest, a flood of renewed authority and confidence.

Claire lifted the orb and focused again, focusing on her friends' faces, envisioning the floating light—Maisy, who had just saved her, despite her terror. Henry, who was always by her side making sarcastic comments, and Michael, her Guardian.

The glowing, ethereal ball of light rose from the crystal sphere and floated toward Sagittarius, whose expression immediately changed. Panic alighted in its face for the first time. As the green light approached, Sagittarius struggled harder to get free. With a sudden jerk, the Caretaker rose on its hind legs and slammed to the ground, throwing Michael off its back, dangerously close to Sagittarius's stone hooves.

"Michael!" Claire screamed. The Caretaker raised its legs again and slammed down on Michael's ankle. Beneath Michael's yell of pain, Claire could hear the crack of the bone and the grinding as Sagittarius smeared his ankle on the pavement.

At the sound of Michael's pain, the light burst, but rather than dying into nothingness, it expanded outward, a blanket of luminescence smothering the parking lot and all its inhabitants. The orb vibrated in her hand, painfully heating to the point where she could feel her skin begin to bubble and fuse to the glass, yet she held fast.

If this were her last act before walking into the light, she would see it through. She was done with failure.

There was a guttural, inhuman scream, and then the light shot back into the orb, and Claire let go. As her eyes readjusted to the dark, she could see that her palm was red and blistered, with patches of skin covered in blood.

Heart still racing, she looked up and saw Michael on the ground. She ran to him. He was unconscious but breathing. She stroked the hair from his forehead, and he stirred slightly.

Sagittarius was gone.

The first Caretaker had finally been captured.

chapter TWENTY-
THREE

Claire ignored the dull pain of her battered body as she helped Michael sit up. He groaned. The shoulder of his duster was covered in blood, mixed with Sagittarius's oil-colored ichor; it was difficult to distinguish whose was whose. She chanced a glance at his crushed ankle only to immediately look away with a sudden resurgence of nausea. His foot seemed flattened compared to the rest of his body, a 2D sketch attached to a 3D leg.

"Don't look now, but your ankle is completely busted," she said quietly.

Michael stared down his body and then shrugged, wincing as his hurt shoulder moved. "Should be fine in a day or two."

Claire raised an eyebrow and then blinked rapidly as a few stray grains of salt dropped into her eye. "I'm sorry to break this to you, but your foot is pulverized. I wouldn't be surprised if they have to amputate it. I'm pretty sure your bones are just loose change in your skin."

Michael shifted, attempting to get to his feet. The ends of his hair, wild and askew for once, brushed the bottom of her chin. "You forget what I am," he muttered. She could hear him attempting to regain his pompous, authoritarian tone, but the corner of his mouth twitched upward, and Claire felt the tension in her shoulders slacken.

Cute, she thought, and then immediately dismissed the errant thought.

"No, I didn't," she responded. "You're an enormous pain in enormous pain. Would you like some help, or would you prefer to keep struggling to prove how tough you are?" Michael pursed his lips, but Claire could see the flames in his eyes flicker.

"Help would be much appreciated, Claire."

She smiled as she reached under his good shoulder and lifted with a grunt. She suppressed a shiver at the feel of his warm, firm body pressed against hers. She turned her face away, admonishing herself for blushing.

"Hey, what happened to 'Clarissa?'" she asked. Michael looked down at her. From this distance, Claire could see a stray lash dusting the top of his cheek and resisted the urge to delicately run her finger across his cheek to remove it.

He hesitated and cleared his throat. "Claire is more efficient to say," he answered gruffly. With a sidelong look at her, he added, "You prefer it, right?"

Claire smiled. "Yeah, I do, actually." They stood in place, eyes locked, bodies frozen against the other, body heat intertwining.

As though he was caught being unprofessional, he coughed lightly and looked around, eyebrows purposefully furrowed, businesslike now. "Where is the orb? I must investigate it thoroughly to make sure it is safe."

Trying to ignore the unexpected pang of disappointment, Claire led him to the glass sphere and picked it up. Despite its new 300-pound prisoner, the glass felt no heavier than it had when it was empty. She had expected it to give some physical indication of its new inhabitant, but to the ignorant eye, it was a normal, ordinary sphere, a mere prop for a psychic charlatan.

The night had returned to normal; the silence held no danger, only vacancy. The parking lot became a motionless sea of concrete once more, the turbulent waves of violence and death just moments before succumbing to peace. Claire knew, logically, that she should be experiencing a sense of relief, a brief reprieve from life's recent chaotic waters. Yet the quiet did little to distract her from the pulsating headache that thrummed against her skull. Her stomach gave a jolt of needful want at the thought of a glass of whiskey back at the loft, and she massaged one of her temples to help ease the desperation.

Soon, she promised herself, but her need remained steady, ignoring her internal promise.

From across the lot, the sound of pelting salt continued to ricochet off the cement. Claire looked up at the sound, a grin of bemusement curving her lips as she rested her eyes on Maisy. Maisy was breathing heavily, still throwing salt in every direction, though weakly now, exerting herself against unseen enemies until sweat dripped down her face. The bridge of her glasses slipped down her nose. Henry circled her, trying and failing to communicate that the fight was over.

"Cease fire, Maisy Lo," Michael called. He tried to walk forward, but his ankle gave out. Claire grunted and did her best to keep him up, but his large frame almost crushed her own.

"I'm gonna need you to help me out here, or at least lose a couple pounds," she wheezed as she acted as his crutch. Ignoring her, he limped over to Maisy and gently pressed her raised arm down, still wound up and ready for the attack.

Henry looked over to Michael in gratitude. "Thanks, boss. I think she would keel over if you hadn't stopped by soon."

Michael nodded and addressed Maisy again. "They are gone," he said.

Claire rolled her head to the side and peered through the dark. Maisy's surroundings and hands were coated in salt, and not an apparition in sight. Maisy took a small step backward and tilted her head upward. Tears lined her cheeks, fresh droplets trickling from her chin onto the pavement.

"What in God's name just happened?" she asked maniacally, her voice cracking.

"God had no part in what happened here tonight," Michael said, and Maisy's face paled to a fainter shade of white. Noticing this, Michael added, "But what you've done has helped in ways you may never understand." He paused. "You saved Claire's life." Claire could feel the heat of his breath on her ear, and she suppressed a shiver, a line of goosebumps trailing down her cheek.

Maisy looked between Michael and Claire. Her pupils were completely dilated. Her lips refused to quiver in fear, yet

Claire knew her body had gone into living rigor mortis, a last-ditch attempt to keep the incontrollable terror of the night at bay.

Claire recognized that expression; it was the same one she held the night of her twelfth birthday, the day the dead made her presence known and claimed her life as their own.

Still holding onto Michael to keep him steady, Claire reached out and gripped Maisy's shoulder. Maisy flinched but didn't move away. "It's a long story," Claire said kindly, "I doubt you'd believe half of it."

Maisy sniffed, rubbing her nose on her sleeve. "I just spent the last ten minutes throwing salt into thin air while giant glowing lights and flaming swords appeared out of fucking nowhere. A man slammed into me and disappeared the moment after we made contact," Claire heard Henry take a sharp intake of breath. "Unless you're both performance artists executing the most shit-inducing play for an invisible audience, I reckon this requires a long story." Still, Claire hesitated. Maisy's eyes, swollen from tears, narrowed. "You owe me a long story."

Michael turned to Claire, an eyebrow raised in question.

Claire let out a long, slow breath. The adrenaline spike from the fight was fading fast, and her headache was inching at an ever-increasing pace toward a record-shattering migraine. Beyond anything she wanted to do—what she *needed* to do—was take a blazing shower to burn off the residue of the deceased, a drink—or five—and then drift into a dreamless sleep.

Claire looked at Maisy and instead saw herself: unruly red hair, crying soundless tears by a forgotten birthday cake, scared shitless and confused and alone on her personal island of hell.

Maisy deserved an explanation.

Sleep would have to wait.

But a drink won't, Claire thought. Her stomach lurched again, crooning for the burn.

Claire bowed her head. "Alright, but we're going to need a ride. And silence." She rubbed her temples. "Absolute silence."

I don't think I ever met a real-life psychic before. This is wild." Maisy sipped jasmine tea from one of Claire's few clean mugs, color returning to her face. Her hands were red and cracked from the salt. The one quilt Claire had brought from her mother's home in Arizona was draped over Maisy's shoulders, making her look like a patchwork burrito. With that thought, Claire took a long draw from her glass before responding, savoring the burn in her throat.

"Medium, actually," Claire corrected. "I can't see the future or anything; I haven't met anyone who can truly do that in the same way they portray in movies. The closest would be Madame Courtney, and he's as vague as ever," Claire corrected. Maisy nodded confusedly, warming her hands on the ceramic.

"What I'm hearing is that you see dead people. So,

you're the female version of Bruce Willis," Maisy joked.

Claire laughed. "You mean Haley Joel Osment?"

Maisy shrugged, the blanket falling off her shoulders. "Whatever; I never saw the movie, anyway." Claire sat across from her, hugging one of her knees to her chest, the other holding onto the glass like a lifeline. By the window, Michael was examining the orb, whispering quietly. He had explained that he was adding additional protective measures to the capsule. When Claire raised her eyebrows at him, he told her the "ancient magic" was too challenging for any mortal to understand. She internally rolled her eyes and considered pressing him further, but noting the pain he was in and the slight tinge of red his nose turned each time his wounds were mentioned, she decided questions could wait.

"Are there any ghosts in here with us now?" Maisy suddenly asked, wide eyes darting around the room. Claire glanced at Henry, who sat beside Maisy. He gave a wide grin and pointed to himself comically.

"Aside from Henry?" Claire shook her head. "No, I try not to let any in my apartment most of the time. They're not all as friendly as him, though few are also as annoying and stage-five clingy, either," she added with a saccharine smile in his direction. Henry stuck his tongue out at her. Claire tried not to avert her eyes from his dark, engorged tongue; if she were going to deal with more death in the coming weeks, she'd better get used to it. Besides, he was her friend.

"Well," Maisy chirped, pulling the blanket back over her shoulders, "tell Henry thank you again for saving me. I think I might have seen him as he pushed me out of the way."

She paused, then, face heating, added, "He's kinda

cute, isn't he?"

Henry seemed close to imploding.

Claire rolled her eyes. "You obviously didn't get a good enough look at him."

Henry glared at her, crossing his arms irritably. "Tell her she's damn right. I'd save that gal anytime. Try to capture my charismatic charm while you're at it." Claire rolled her eyes.

"He says no problem. He's happy to help."

Maisy beamed. "So, I know we just finished fighting for our lives and everything, but what's next?"

Claire opened her mouth to respond but closed it to consider the question. She realized that she had no idea. They had spent the last couple of weeks so hyper-focused on the capture of Sagittarius that she hadn't allowed herself to think about what would happen next. If she was being honest, she preferred not to consider any "next" beyond another drink.

"That's a good question," Claire relented and addressed Michael for the first time that hour. "Michael?"

Task completed, Michael pocketed the orb and limped around the room's edges, both hands tucked into his coat. Claire marveled at the speed he was healing; she would have given most of what she owned to be able to do that, though that wasn't saying much, given the state of her apartment.

He leaned his back against the wall. Claire stared, brain slightly fuzzy, as he ran one of his calloused hands through his disheveled hair. She watched the movement with a flare of hunger that surprised her. He caught her eye, and, reflexes dulled by alcohol and the events of the evening, she held his gaze. After a moment, she could no longer handle the intensity of his swirling blue flames staring into hers. She jerked her eyes over to Henry, who was grinning at an unsuspecting Maisy.

Michael made a slight sound in his throat before answering. "The Caretakers need not feed daily, though that does not mean they won't stalk and prepare for their attacks. Those few that escape will not stop until they can break the chains that hold them to the Pit, and as time goes on, they will become more desperate. Desperation breeds impulsivity, even amongst the ancients."

Michael seemed to be averting his gaze from Claire, who nodded at his words, attempting to stay focused. Maisy, on the other hand, gazed at Michael, enraptured by his explanations and the intensity with which he spoke of such grave matters. Not to mention, he just saved all their lives in an epic battle with an astrological murderous monster. And with his strong build and captivating eyes, he was, frankly, easy to take in.

Henry, seemingly annoyed by the lack of attention, spoke. "Great, so we know the demons will keep doing demonic things. So, we ask again, what next?"

Michael bowed his head toward Henry. "This past month held an advantage for Sagittarius. Throughout the year, depending on the position of the sky's celestial bodies, each Caretaker will have its day, their strengths and abilities made more powerful. As I've mentioned, seven of the Caretakers have shirked their duties and entered this realm, so we'll need to recapture them before they gain too much power. For Capricorn, its power grows to its fullest strength in three weeks' time."

"Just in time for the holidays; love it," Claire muttered.

"Capricorn does not attack as a consequence of mortal celebrations," Michael began to correct, but Claire cut him off.

"I was being sarcastic." Claire leaned back into her chair, sinking under the weight of inebriation and exhaustion. "You don't ever say things you don't mean?" she teased.

Michael stepped forward and crouched in front of her, his face level with her own. Claire felt a slow wave of surprise stir in her abdomen and lower. "I don't say anything I don't mean, Claire."

They were silent for a moment, Michael holding Claire's gaze. Even Henry was mute for once, watching the intensity between them. Maisy held her breath and pretended to find the quilt's edge very interesting. Henry broke the silence.

"Don't you have some undead army at your disposal? Maybe some lesser guardians can help us out. Despite what you saw tonight, I don't really know what I'm doing." Henry rested his arm on Maisy's shoulder as he awaited Michael's response.

"There are those I can turn to for help, if need be," Michael said, and Henry clapped his hands together.

"Great, let's call them up, send a flaming letter or whatever it is you do," Henry began, but Michael shook his head.

"They are best used as a last resort; not everyone from The Beyond is as . . . empathetic to the plight of man as me. They will need some convincing, but that will be for another time."

Michael strode to the window, his large frame a looming silhouette against the glare of the streetlights below.

Claire pinched the bridge of her nose, her thoughts sluggish and muddled. She tried to mentally catalog everything they would need to do in the coming weeks: search for the caretakers, research, fight, Send. It could take time to capture them all, if they could survive.

Maybe if she hadn't gone to the pier, Pisces would have chosen someone else to take, someone who could have become the Gateway instead of herself. The last few days would never have happened; she'd have moved on with her usual, albeit dull life.

Claire thought back to the moment of nostalgia and grief that had sent her to that pier that night. Claire could still remember her mother and father's conversation in aggressively hushed whispers that night. She had listened at the bottom of her bedroom door, her cheek squished into the carpet, the fibers scratching her nose as she tried furiously to listen and keep a sneeze at bay.

"Where are you going to go? Everything she needs is here," Deb had said, her voice uncharacteristically grounded, far from the wispy, ethereal tone she used with customers in her practice. Claire could make out the sounds of clips clicking into place and heavy footsteps attempting to be light. Their voices grew more muffled as they moved further towards the front door. Claire strained harder to hear, imprints of the carpet digging into her face.

Julian said something, but all she could hear was

Deb's response, her voice growing louder despite her attempt not to disturb her supposedly sleeping little girl. *And what am I supposed to tell her? If you* loved *her, you'd stay.*

Claire supposed it didn't matter that she couldn't hear Julian's retaliation because the slam of the front door, the crunch of the gravel, and the silence of an absentee father were answer enough.

Claire could no longer fathom why she even tried to pay tribute to the man. She errantly remembered something she'd learned during one of her psychology courses in college; a single choice led to a cascading domino effect of consequences, each tumbling one after the other. It made her wonder what other dominoes were about to fall.

Claire snapped out of her thoughts when she heard Maisy stifle a yawn. Stretching her shoulders and popping her back, Maisy rose from the sofa, folding the blanket and placing it neatly on the couch. "Well, that's enough for one night. I need to go home and get some rest. Let me give you my number so you can contact me the next time you need a salt delivery."

Claire was impressed she could crack a joke after their night. "I don't actually have a phone at the moment. Dropped it off the pier."

"Jeez, I don't know how you've survived without one!" Maisy shook her head. "I think I have an old burner phone somewhere amongst the cables and wires in my room. I'll take a look and bring it to the library; you can visit me there."

Claire felt an overwhelming sense of gratitude and fought back tears she didn't know she still had. Maisy, seeming to sense Claire's emotional seesaw, folded her arms around Claire's shoulders in a tight embrace. Apart from the brief embrace she'd given Michael a few weeks back, the last time she remembered being held this tight was the morning before Carlos had caught her in the evidence locker. She could still feel the curve of his body wrapped around hers as they awoke together, the blankets tangled over their legs, his arm under her head.

This was a different kind of hug: filled with camaraderie, a promise of friendship.

She loosened and returned the embrace before Maisy let go. Claire watched the three bid each other goodbye: Maisy, head cocked and smiling, Michael, oddly kind as he thanked her for her bravery, and Henry, hovering close to Maisy and pestering Michael to relay his own farewells.

Claire had lost a family member years ago, and that fallen domino had led to this ragtag family before her. Gratitude felt foreign in her heart, but it was there all the same.

Maisy left, and, shaking her head to clear it, Claire addressed the others: Michael—still at the window—and Henry—still staring at the door Maisy had shut. "I'm going to have to kick the two of you out, too. If I don't want to fall asleep during tomorrow's seances, I need to get at least three hours of solid shuteye."

Henry gave her a crooked smile. "I think I was promised a reading and a place to stay for the night. Or did you forget?" Claire, indeed, had forgotten but hid the oversight.

"The reading will have to be postponed to a later date

when I can actually function. You can stay in the living room; do not make me line salt along my bedroom wall."

Henry saluted. "I give you my word."

"Is that sarcasm?" Michael asked genuinely.

"It better not be." Claire shot a warning glance at Henry, who returned a mischievous smile. He stretched his legs to the end of the couch, taking up the entirety of the cushions, ready to settle in for the night.

"I guess if Henry is sticking around for the night, you're welcome to hang out here, too," Claire offered to Michael. She tried not to imagine him sleeping in the living room, several yards and one door away from her bed. *Room enough for two,* she thought against her better judgment. Deep down—though not as deep as she liked—she hoped he would say yes. His presence was calming. He made her feel secure. Safe. And to have him close, just a room away while she undressed and went to bed for the night . . .

She felt her body hum.

He paused as though considering the offer. His gaze wandered around the room, though she knew, at one point, it had paused on her exposed legs.

She held her breath. But then he let out a small sigh and shook his head. "I can't. Thank you for the offer, but I must press forward. Keep my focus."

He opened the window and stepped onto the balcony, head angled upward, staring at the night sky. Claire walked forward and stood on the other side of the window.

"Do I make it difficult for you to focus?" she asked.

Michael rested both hands on the balcony edge and didn't respond. She exited the window and joined him, glad to feel the heat emanating from his body in the cool night air.

"Michael, why is this happening? Why are they here?" Claire asked. This question hung in the air, floating above the city lights that flickered beneath them.

"They may be seen as leaders in the Beyond," Michael said in a low voice, "authority among the souls of the dead. But even they are chained to their posts, slaves to their duties. And every prisoner—monster or no—dreams of being set free." He paused, a hard look in his eye, before he turned back to her. "You conducted yourself with honor and bravery today."

Claire raised an eyebrow in surprise, and, keeping her head high, she gave a wry grin. "Yeah, well, I *was* scared shitless."

Michael shook his head. "Don't confuse courage with a lack of fear. Those who are afraid but commit are braver than those who feel no fear." He placed a hand on her shoulder and gently squeezed. It sent a tendril of warmth through her. Claire opened and closed her mouth, hoping to find inspiring words of gratitude, kindness, *anything* to say.

"I'm glad you're safe," he continued, his voice soft. Michael bent down, his lips hovering just above her own. She could smell the campfire smoke on his lapel, feel his breath like embers on her face. He was so close, yet not close enough.

"Thanks," she breathed. "I'm glad you're okay, too. Couldn't have done much of anything without you there. I'm glad I have you. *We* have you, I mean," Claire added, gesturing behind her to where Henry lay, his eyes closed. Claire was sure he heard every word.

Driven by a brief urge of impulsiveness and a need to feel him, Claire reached up to place her palm on his cheek. Their eyes met. The moment seemed to swell. But before she could allow her fingers to graze the edge of his jaw, the *whoosh* of a brief flame sent a rush of heat onto the porch, caressing her cheek, and Michael was gone.

"That was hard to watch. Back in my day, the fairer sex had a bit more tact and a lot less drool," Henry said. Claire snatched a nearby book and threw it at his head. He chortled as it sailed through and hit the wall, landing harmlessly on the carpet.

"Better than watching you pine over a girl who can't hear you, dumbass," Claire retorted.

He shrugged. "We'll make it work; I've got moves that'll make your toes curl."

Claire rolled her eyes. "And gag, I reckon. I'm going to bed. Goodnight, asshole."

"So long, doll face."

Claire strode into her bedroom and slammed the door behind her, reapplying the line of salt. Groaning, wondering if Henry would hear her scream into her pillow, she switched her sweat-stained clothes for a clean tank top and shorts before climbing under the sheets. The bed was cold and firm, but as the minutes ticked by, it gradually warmed and softened under her weight. Fatigue pressed heavily against her eyes, and her lids fell shut.

"Don't scream, Clarissa Reed. We just want a little chat." A whisper in her room.

Claire jerked up, her head swimming from the sudden lurch. Pressing the switch on her bedside lamp, she swung her legs from the bed and peered around the room.

"We won't bite; we promise. Take off the sheet so we can speak face to face." The voice emanated from the mirror she had propped on top of her dresser, the reflective surface still covered from Gemini's grand introduction a few weeks prior.

Halfheartedly, Claire walked over to the mirror, her bare feet padding silently along the floor, and pulled off the thin fabric sheet. She examined her reflection: the cut on her forehead was starting to scab around the dried blood; some of the freckles that dotted her face were marred by a light shade of purple and green; a raccoon mask had begun to form around her eyes. She frowned at the reflection.

Her face smiled back at her. But the smile was too wide for her cheeks, she had too many teeth, and the corners of her lips were turned up much too high, stretched like skin-colored taffy.

Her eyes were dark as a void, inspecting her up and down, clearly hungry for its tangible twin. "My, my, Clarissa Reed. Our siblings have been quite busy with you, haven't they? We've known mortals being used as implements on which We sharpen Our blades, but it seems they've gone the extra mile with you."

"You should see the other guy," Claire grumbled, and Gemini laughed.

"We see you're warming up to Us. Yes, it's about time we started sharing jokes like old friends."

Claire gritted her teeth, and Gemini mocked her, copying her jaw with an exaggerated sawing motion.

"We're not friends," Claire growled, keeping her

voice low.

Gemini tutted, wagging a finger in mock indignation. "We are everyone's friends. Ergo, We are yours, even if you think you are not Ours." Gemini curled Claire's fingers in the mirror, examining her nails. "We're still waiting for a thank you. That's often customary after someone helps you out."

Claire blinked. "Helped when? All you ever do is constantly talk in the cab, the interrogation room, the lecture hall. I think you just like hearing the sound of your own voice. And then you tried to drown me, if you don't remember!"

Another jarring smile.

"We rather think you should thank Us for all those delightful conversations, too, especially when you were under arrest."

"You did nothing in the Interrogation room. You bounced around in the background as a distraction while Núñez flayed me over the coals." Gemini paused from picking Claire's cuticles and looked at Claire under her lashes.

"How do you suppose Libra knew where to find you?"

Claire paused. "You sent Libra?"

Gemini nodded abruptly, causing her hair to whip forward and backward wildly, as though she was trying to break her forehead through the glass.

"You're very welcome, Clarissa Reed," it said in a sing-song voice. "It wouldn't have done Us any good to have you bound and locked away. We have yet to find the others, and We need you at peak performance."

"Why?" Claire asked. "Why are you helping us? Why would Libra help you?"

Gemini shrugged. "We have our reasons, don't you fret. And our dear Libra is cut from the same cloth as Ourselves; We understand each other. That's all you need to know for now."

Claire seethed; *what was it with these things needing to be so cryptic all the goddamn time?* She opened her mouth to argue but changed her mind, confident that if she pressed Gemini, it would continue to play coy, saying much while sharing nothing.

Claire moved on. "Why are you here?" Gemini rested a palm against the mirror's frame, leaning onto it.

"Can't a friend just come to say hello?"

When Claire did not deign to respond, Gemini continued. "We just wanted to congratulate you on your win. It's a job well done."

"I doubt you're only here to applaud me."

"Perhaps," Gemini said. "Maybe We are. Or maybe We're here to tell you that someone close to you is lying. Perhaps it's Us, perhaps not. We could also have chosen to visit because you have some Cardinals you must face, and eventually, your journey during the solstice will need to be at the Gateway itself and into The Beyond. We want to offer Our humble services." Gemini gave a deep bow, her mirrored nose disappearing under the bottom frame.

A cold trickle of sweat beaded down her spine.

Into the Beyond.

Into the realm of the dead.

"I'm not going there," Claire blurted without thinking. Gemini laughed.

"Not going to be much of a choice if you want the

final Sending ritual to be complete. How else do you expect Our brothers and sisters to be bound and chained once more if not in their sector of the Beyond? Had Michael not mentioned that?" Gemini tsked, shaking its head, Claire's red hair swinging in the mirror.

No, he hadn't, Claire thought, dread creeping like bile up her throat. If this were true, she would need all the help she could get. She didn't know what "Cardinal" meant, but from how Gemini spoke, it sounded more dangerous than their previous opponent. Gemini was a powerful being; it would be highly resourceful and beneficial to have it on their side.

But she didn't trust the Caretaker with the many faces and the disingenuous smile. Gemini acted as though it was all a game, collecting the tokens of their efforts and playing people like pieces on a twisted chessboard. It would take merely a single sour look, a change in the wind, or a single twig snapping for Gemini to change its mind.

And she couldn't go against Michael's back like that.

Claire shook her head. "Thank you, but hard pass."

The smile disappeared from Gemini's face, dropping like a cement slab on a stone floor. "We would think carefully about our offer, Clarissa Reed. You don't know what you are up against."

"Then we'll figure it out."

Anger—brazen and hot—flashed behind its eyes, and for a moment, Claire saw a face different from her own, distinct from the face Gemini had chosen to borrow. The lights flicked on in her bedroom, and the light bulb in her lamp fizzled and burst into a stream of glass shards. She gasped and looked toward her door to see if Henry had heard; no one came in.

"Clarissa Reed, We do not think you understand what you are turning down," Gemini hissed, its voice reverberating as though two were speaking simultaneously. Suddenly, the flickering stopped, and her reflection molded back into her frightened face.

All was quiet and still.

Must've given up and left, Claire thought, but somehow, something felt off, unfinished.

A tap sounded at the little window in her room. Bracing herself, Claire slowly stepped forward, her footsteps creaking on the wooden floor. As she crept closer to the curtains, she could hear heavy, rasping breaths heaving from beyond the window.

"Clarissa Reed, you need to see what you are missing, what powers you are facing, what We can do." Gemini's voice spoke hoarsely through the window.

Claire held her breath, then gripped the curtains and thrust them open.

Outside floated the ghost of the mother who had passed, the woman who had been begging for her child. She wore the same hospital gown, her legs still pale and weak, sweat caked under her hairline from the force of labor that took her life.

But her face, her smile, she was the Cheshire cat with too many teeth, Gemini's voice pouring from her lips.

"If I can do this to the dead," Gemini began. The woman took her fingers and fish-hooked the corners of her lips.

"Then imagine—" Gemini yanked, her cheek split in two, her lower lip hanging loose and folded over her chin.

"—what We can do—" She lifted her thumbs and thrust them into her eyes, the oozing, vitreous humor mixing pink with blood dripping like gravy down her face.

"—to the living." Gemini let out a wail of triumph and, thrusting her hand into her mouth, gripped her tongue and ripped it from her body.

Claire screamed, an awful, extended cry of horror and disgust as the woman's apparition collapsed to the street and burst into a cloud of fog.

She threw the curtains shut and ran to the trash can under her desk, retching watery bile. Henry yelled from the other room: "Doll! Claire! Are you okay? What's wrong?"

Claire couldn't answer; her body shook and continued to try expelling what she had seen, to no avail.

"Well, Clarissa Reed. If you think that was unsavory, just think what the others can do to you and your friends." Claire looked up from the trash can and saw that Gemini had taken her features in the mirror again, picking at her cuticles.

"Answer me, Claire!" Henry yelled again.

Gemini huffed. "You better answer the boy. Perhaps We will find it in our heart to provide our offer once more in the future … if you end up having one." A final Cheshire smile, and then her face melted back into one more familiar, more mortal, more human.

Claire panted over the trashcan, slowing her heart before calling out to Henry. "Just a nightmare; I'm going back to sleep."

"Like hell was that a nightmare; what the fuck was

going on?"

Claire groaned. "I told you; it was a nightmare." *Not a lie*, she thought to herself. "Please, I just want to go back to sleep."

There was a pause before Henry acquiesced. "Fine. But if that happens again, I'm finding a way in, salt be damned," he growled. Claire gave a weak laugh and fell silent.

Draping the sheet back over the mirror, Claire clambered back into bed, leaving the bedside light on. Anything to keep away the dark and whatever lurked in the crawling, undulating shadows.

Claire lay in bed, her mind swirling with fear, questions, concerns, and theories. She replayed Gemini's taunts, the supposed liar among her friends. The image of Libra pointing toward Henry bloomed in her mind's eye, but she pushed it away. Gemini may have possessed her face, but her mind was her own; she would protect it.

But after what she saw, could she protect herself?

Instead, she thought of the other beasts that still hunted at night. Who would they encounter next? Capricorn? Pisces? Perhaps others she had yet to meet: Virgo, Cancer, Taurus … What power did they wield? Was it anything like what Gemini showed that night? Where were they now? How much more dangerous would these be? And when would they make themselves known?

Clutching the edge of the blanket, she pulled it up to her chin, savoring its warmth. Fear danced on the edges of her mind, but she quelled the surge. There was no use losing sleep about what may happen in the coming days, weeks, or months. She and her family would deal with it.

One fight at a time.

ACKNOWLEDGMENTS

I find that writing my acknowledgments is both the easiest and hardest addition to my books because I can quickly think of a million different placements for my gratitude: my husband, my family, my publisher, my hyperfixation, the sunny San Diego weather, the four different drinks from which I always have on hand, not my cats who vomited on my keyboard at 3 am, etc.

Yet, unlike the Caretakers of the Beyond, I do not have all the time in the world to write everything down, so let's stick to the highlights, shall we?

First and foremost, my husband. In 2023, when I started suffering from stress-induced blackouts from my career, I sat him down and told him I wanted to be a destitute homebody. Not really, but I told him I wanted to write full time, which, to many people, may have equated to the same thing. Instead of listing all the scary reasons why everything could go wrong, he helped me realize everything that could go right. I love him very much and could not have done this without him.

Next, to the agent who told me my writing was worth publishing. I submitted my first 10 pages to Writer's Digest as part of the program where an assigned agent would tell me what worked well, what to change, and what would make potential agents want to quit their jobs. Less than 24 hours later, she wrote to me asking for the full manuscript. Unfortunately, I only had three chapters written at the time. So, I said, "Sure, give me a week." And that frantic motivation is what finished *Sagittarius*. While she did not end up representing me due to the genre difference, she helped me realize that maybe I had something worth pursuing.

To my brothers, my older who took the time to develop artwork for my future giveaways (get ready for those!) and my younger who consistently took the time in our Snapchat streak (going on 400) to ask about my book and develop a Reddit community on a whim. It's a privilege to have siblings who support your quarter-life crisis and turn it into a blessing.

To my mother and father, who both supported me in their own ways. Both could have easily told me the pie in the sky doesn't exist and that I should focus on the baked goods closer to home, like a steady teaching career, but instead, they nodded and said, "Okay, you do you," and I will forever appreciate their support.

To all my friends and colleagues who have been propping me up since the beginning, you all mean the world to me.

To my fantastic Fox and Dagger Publisher, Mallory. This woman singlehandedly edited, copyedited, formatted, created a cover, and developed social media material for this book in a way I would have never even known how to start. She is a faithful indie supporter, a wonderful writer, and fantastic— thankfully patient—person I am so lucky to have met.

And finally, to all my readers. There are hundreds of thousands of books and media and distractions out there in the world, and yet you still chose to pick up my book and enter the world of the Urban Oracle. I thank you more than you can know.

ABOUT THE AUTHOR

Sierra Zounes is a novelist by day and a poet by whim—as long as she's not too exhausted. She is the San Diego Chapter teacher for the Community Literature Initiative and teacher/coordinator for the San Marcos Writing Project Teen Writers Camp through California State University of San Marcos.

She has been practicing martial arts for the last 23 years, and she enjoys writing bizarre stories and spoken word poetry, though she mainly reads dark fiction, fantasy, and horror. She likes to camp with her husband, but unfortunately leaves their cats, Toad and Cucumber, at home while they travel, which is fine, since she loves her cats dearly, and they merely tolerate her back.

In addition to the first book in her *Urban Oracle* Series, Sierra has published a poetry book: *Teacher Haikus for the Educator's Non-Existent Free Time,* and her poetry comic book with World Stage Press is coming in summer 2025.

For updates and news in Sierra's world, visit
www.zouneswrites.com.